**J. ALISON COLE**

**E**VERNIGHT PUBLISHING ®

www.evernightpublishing.com

**Copyright© 2025**

**J. Alison Cole**

ISBN: 978-0-3695-1260-4

Cover Artist: Jay Aheer

Editor: Stephanie Marrie

**J. ALISON COLE**

# DEDICATION

To my husband. I couldn't have done it without you.

You have my heart and my love for ever.

I enjoy you.

*Wink, wink.*

**J. ALISON COLE**

## J. Alison Cole

## Copyright © 2025

## Chapter One

A mixture of bright whites and grays swirled in the haze over Erica's head. Her lashes fluttered. Wasn't the sky crystal clear when she left the house? Invisible weights shut her eyelids.

*Is today Tuesday or Wednesday?*

Tuesday, Wednesday, it didn't matter. Classes ended last Friday, so instead of counseling students, she could counsel herself for the next three months. And nothing freed her mind better than cycling. Something about a road and a bicycle tapped her inner Sigmund Freud. It worked on everything—well, almost everything. For the last two years, no matter how many miles she rode, she still struggled with the reason behind her failed marriage.

*It's Wednesday.*

An engine revved in the distance. Her eyes popped open. The haziness overhead thinned as she caught a glimpse of cerulean blue. Her veil of confusion lifted like the stage curtain on opening night of a disastrous version of *Guys and Dolls*. The sky she remembered from earlier returned—along with the rest of her comprehension. *New bull, out of control skid, swan dive over the handlebars.* A growing pain from sharp stones and coarse gravel jabbed into her shoulders to confirm that she was sprawled flat on her back in the middle of the country road.

"Ouch."

Erica slowly sat up, inspecting the damage on her arms. Both were bloody from wrist to elbow. Wincing, she plucked at the embedded pebbles stuck to her skin.

"Son of a biscuit." When people inevitably asked how she crashed, answering that part would be easy—the *why*, not so much. Yes, she was going way too fast. Of course she should've concentrated on the fresh layer of chipped gravel instead of gawking at the new stud bull in the pasture.

Living in Southern Pennsylvania meant having cows in a field. They were as common as trees and grass. But for whatever reason, this particular beast stood out amongst the herd, stately and snaring every ounce of her attention.

His velvet hide was the darkest shade of brown she had ever seen, his lumbering gait a magnificent display of unquestionable strength and power. The stellar example of selective breeding chose the very moment she was riding by to rear up and oblige his duties to the agreeable cow in front of him. His timing was beyond impeccable. Never in a million years would she have thought that bovine had such agility. Or that she'd lose control of her bike, skid on the stones, and go sailing through the air with that vivid image and obscure thought passing through her head.

*How did you wreck your bike, Mrs. Gebhart?*
*Well, I was watching cows do it.*

Several feet away, the overly curious herd had gathered along the fence line with the exalted ruler standing front and center. He snorted and turned away, sharing his disgust. How could she argue, watching like a pervert? Good grief. She didn't mean to watch. It just kind of happened.

Someone her age should know better. *Forty!* The number was still taking some getting used to. And how was thirty-nine okay, but forty somehow a decade away?

Footsteps crunched on the stones beside her. She raised her scraped forearm to block the bright morning light behind a tall figure. All she could make out was a pair of well-worn, faded blue jeans up to the knees. The rest was just a silhouette.

"That was one hell of a fall." The rich, baritone voice oozed over her like a blanket that just came out of the dryer.

"You think? What would you give it on a scale from one to ten?"

"At least a 9.5."

She lowered her arm when the man knelt in front of her. "I'm fi—"

He cut her off. "Just sit still." He cupped her chin with calloused fingers as he squatted deeper into an open-kneed stance. Their eyes finally met. Brilliant silver flecks shimmered inside a sea of bright blue, almost the exact shade of the sky above, holding her captive. His eyes all but glowed.

"Wow! Your eyes are so…pretty." Erica snickered. Did she really just say that aloud? *Crap!* "I meant blue."

"You've hit your head pretty good." He tilted her chin further to the side for a better inspection.

"My head? No, that's what the helmet is for. It's just my arms." Reaching for her head, she only found tangled strands of her shoulder-length auburn hair—and red sticky stuff. "Wait, where's my helmet?" Baffled, she glanced between him and the blood on her fingers.

The crease on the center of his forehead deepened, and he released her chin. A tingly warmth replaced his touch immediately. Well, that's weird. Was he wearing a glove? Curious, she checked his hand, which was now resting on a shapely thigh. His fingers, long and slender, dangled above the inside seam of his jeans, and with his knees spread like they were, the direction of the seams lured her gaze inward, like a 747 coming in for a landing.

*Don't look there.* Tearing herself away from that area, she charted his body the same way she mapped out her rides. *Above the zipper—a narrow waist leveling off to a flat stomach. Higher, spanning east to west, a broad chest and shoulders.* Something, not a chill or a shiver, rippled through her belly. Good grief, if she didn't know any better, she'd think it was desire. A rippling sensation surged through the rest of her body.

Her errant gaze returned to his face. He had one shapely brow lifted, making it clear that her unintentional but very liberal inspection hadn't gone unnoticed. *Good Lord, what's happening?*

Embarrassed for the first time in a long time, Erica turned away. It was by sheer coincidence that she spotted her missing helmet nestled in a clump of newly blossomed daylilies growing alongside the edge of the road.

"Oh, there's my helmet."

"Doesn't do you much good over there now, does it?" A hint of a smile tugged on the side of really nice lips, and he had just enough stubble on his face to accent the rugged attractiveness that seemed to be hiding behind that overly stern expression.

Erica's insides dipped and floundered as she fixated once more on his lips. She tried pointing to her helmet. But, as she swung her hand, a single drop of blood flew off her fingertip. It landed about four inches above his right knee. The symmetrical red dome perched like a shiny rhinestone on the taut denim material. Instinct took over, and her hand shot forward before it could soak in.

A precious few seconds passed before Erica realized two things: She was putting more blood on him and she was essentially rubbing the same well-developed thigh she'd just admired moments ago. Yanking her hand away, she glanced up again.

*Wow.* She could have done a half-gainer into the pool of blue in his eyes. Her insides fizzed again with a strange energy, and now she had to bite her tongue, hypothetically at least. The faint coppery taste in her mouth assured, physically, she already had.

She glanced at the bloody smears covering the inside of his pants. Red streaks ran sideways over his knee, dipping well below the seam and just inches from the crossroads below the zippers. "Holy smokes." Her head swung back and forth. "I'm so sorry. I didn't mean to..." *Fondle your...get that close to your...* "...smear...blood on you." Both of his brows lifted. "It's just..." *You make me nervous.* The revelation all but smacked her in the face. When was the last time anyone made her feel nervous? "I think that you've caught me off-guard." *Seriously, what is happening?*

"Well, *I* think you need to go to the hospital," he insisted.

"No, no, no. I don't want that." A wave of panic swept over her.

"What if you have a concussion?"

"Then I'll be concussed. Nothing is broken.

Everyone knows head wounds tend to bleed. My arms are just scratched up. I don't need to go to the hospital."

A trip to the ER felt extremely unnecessary. Word would spread like wildfire at the hospital, and Davis would be obligated to pull back the curtain, no doubt aided by his lovely, much younger assistant Bethany.

"No." Now her words sounded more like a plea, even to herself. "I'll sit there for hours, and they're only going to tell me to take it easy."

He tiled his head further to one side, the sun bouncing off the natural highlights of his wet hair. "Okay. How about I get you cleaned up first, and then we decide?"

"That works." The words came out like a sigh of relief, but that relief was short-lived because, in the next moment, chiseled arms snaked under and around her body. Now, somehow weightless, she floated and rose with him before settling against a firm, broad chest.

"Oh my gosh, you're carrying me?" It was a question as well as a statement. "Please, put me down. I'm too heavy."

He scoffed. "You're joking, right?" To prove his point, he hefted her just a little.

Surprised by the sudden movement, she stamped the front of his shirt with a mitten-shaped bloody handprint. "Oh, I'm getting blood on you."

He glanced at her. "Uh, you already have." Not that he needed to point out the obvious.

She drew another breath, ready to argue, when a spicy, earthy smell invaded her nostrils. Was it a type of shower gel or soap that only men use? Whatever it was, this blue truck guy smelled absolutely delectable.

Walking toward a Chevy pickup parked at an odd angle in the middle of the road, his steps synchronized in rhythm with the emergency flashers. At the passenger door, he used the hand that was under her knees to maneuver the handle open. Ducking inside the cab, he placed her sideways on the seat. The narrow space had them sandwiched together. His stubble rubbed against her cheek as he eased his arms away. The featherlike contact rendered the softest hum from the back of her throat.

He tensed and jerked upright, striking the back of his head against the frame. "Did you say something? Are you all right?"

*Are whiskers really that soft?* She had the most ridiculous urge to reach out and trace them. "I'm fine, really." *Touch them, quick, before he steps away. What? No, that would be crazy. Oh, gawd.* Why couldn't she stop smiling?

"Good." He stepped away.

Her smile spread even further when he ran a hardened knuckle over the very spot on his chin that grazed her face.

*Ah ha!* It wasn't just her.

Thoroughly intrigued, Erica turned to spy on him through the rear window. His long legs accommodated a commendable swagger, and Levi jeans worn to the perfect shade of comfort, complete with the telltale stamp from a wallet clearly imprinted on one of the back pockets. They hugged his muscular thighs but left just enough sag at his waist and rounded backside for her to appreciate how well he filled them out. She'd always thought certain men just looked good in jeans. He'd be a member of that club.

Next, he flexed his sculpted bicep as he bent to pick up the mangled mess that had been her bike. She spied the scant edge of a tattoo peeking from under the sleeve of his ash-gray t-shirt, but he was too far away for her to make it out. Sauntering to the side of the road, he scooped up her flyaway helmet. She hardly ever buckled it—something she'd need to remedy in the future so this didn't happen again.

He lifted her bike over the tailgate and wedged the helmet between a pedal and the hideously bent front tire. She spun to face forward and shut the door with two semi-clean fingers.

He climbed onto the driver's seat and shot her a sideways glance. "I'm Reese Mailing."

"That's better than 'Blue truck guy.'" *Why did I say that?* "Oh, sorry." *I sound like a ninny.* Shaking her head, she tried to recover. "I'm Erica Gebhart."

For a second, he gave her a speculative grin. "I know who you are." He turned the key, and the engine roared to life.

"I guess I said that because I've seen this truck before. You work with the Koontz brothers, right?"

He glanced at her through the maneuverings of a three-point turn, heading back in the direction from which he'd come. "That's right."

*Wow.* How did a man have such long lashes and pretty eyes? Seriously. His hair had started to dry and was lighter than she first imagined—more of a dirty blonde than a brunet. And even with the tiny crinkles near the corners of his eyes, he looked young. *He's younger. And I'm staring.*

This felt like the bull thing all over again. *Enough. Focus.* "It must be a prerequisite that everyone on the farm has to drive a truck. A week or so ago, there was a...silver Honda with a green door?" Reese gave her a slight nod. Her eyes darted to the cupped hands on her lap. *I'm rambling. That sounded absurd. Good grief, I never ramble.* "Not that I'm watching or anything. It's just that you all must go by a hundred times a day, and I live at the end of the road."

*Stop talking.*

He smiled. "I know where you live."

Reese turned the truck into the first driveway of three identical tenant houses that were part of the Koontz's farm properties.

On any other day, Erica barely glanced at the dwellings. Her only concern was whether any of the tenants had dogs that might chase her as she rode by. About a year ago, a young woman with a daughter in preschool lived in the middle house. The woman had a beagle puppy that chased her every time. But that family moved away. Now, to the best of her knowledge, only one of the tenant houses was occupied by Reese Mailing.

Erica studied the houses with renewed interest. All three had a fresh coat of pale yellow paint, crisp white trim, and new green shutters.

The truck stopped. Reese set the gear in park and flipped the ignition off. "Let's get you inside. I'll help. Wait!"

Erica made a swift exit from the truck, not wanting to see if he would carry her again. Her riding shorts only went down so far, and the spot behind her knees still tingled where his forearms made direct contact against her bare skin. She had serious doubts that it was some kind of allergic reaction to his shower gel but it had more to do with *him*.

Near the truck's front bumper, mid-stride, she glanced over her shoulder to see where he was, only her foot landed on the edge of an odd-shaped stone, causing her ankle to roll. She reached for the truck in an ungraceful attempt to catch herself.

But, instead of landing in a splattered mess over the rocks for the second time in one day, something vice-like seized her midsection from behind.

"Whoa, hang on now. I got you." Reese adjusted his grip around her torso, pinning her back against his chest. "Shit, I didn't think that you were lightheaded."

Completely enveloped by his massive form, the ripple started in her toes and worked its way up. "I'm not." *At least not from the fall.* "I stepped on a rock funny."

"Your heart is racing," he huffed. "Do you feel weird or anything?"

*Weird, yes.* But not in the way he meant. "The stones are bumpy. I wasn't looking where I was walking."

"So, you're going with clumsy?" Reese adjusted his grip, keeping his hands on her ribs.

"I'm fine. Trust me."

"Trust the lady with the head injury. Sure. And I mean that sarcastically, in case you couldn't tell." He slowly released her waist but maintained a light grip on her arm while muttering about proper medical attention. She may have found his mutterings amusing if her ankle wasn't stinging so bad. But if she showed even a hint of a limp, he'd probably sweep her off her feet and race straight to the hospital. By the grace of god, the side of the house was only a few steps away.

Inside the first door were a washer and dryer. A ratty-looking sweatshirt covered with smears and flecks of yellow paint was lying on the floor in a balled-up heap. Along the adjacent wall was a small wooden bench with three hearts and the quote *There's No Place Like Home* stenciled on the backrest. Above the bench were a row of hooks holding various ballcaps, some looking newer, and almost all having something to do with tractors or feed companies. Hats were just as common as cows and pickup trucks in this part of the country.

Reese opened the next door that led into an open kitchen. A modest-sized table with four plain chairs sat in the middle of the room. The basic white countertop was bare of clutter or bulky appliances, not even a coffee pot. And for some reason, she expected to see a woman standing at the sink wearing a red-checkered frilly apron. Why, she could not say. It was all so quaint.

Reese guided her in that direction. He turned on the faucet and pulled a clean towel from a side cupboard.

"Let the water get warm. It takes a minute. I'm going to get some things from the medicine cabinet." Reese hesitated. "You're not going to fall or anything, are you?"

"I'm good. I promise."

He gave her one last pensive glance before stepping away.

After Reese disappeared down the hallway, Erica's gaze roamed through an open archway into the living room. There was an oversized brown leather couch with a matching La-Z-Boy recliner, all very masculine and man cave furniture. Sitting on top of an old stereo speaker was a small flat-screen television. Next to that was a loaded bookshelf.

*A man that reads. Impressive.*

She combed further and caught a flash of shiny chrome partially hidden behind the couch—possibly the handlebars of a new bicycle, only smaller, maybe for a child.

Footsteps echoed in the hall.

Erica turned toward the sink and tested the water with her fingertips. She squirted some soap into her hand from a barn-shaped dispenser before placing them under the flow. A strained wheeze escaped through her clenched teeth, lathering the raw flesh of her hands and forearms. The sting gradually subsided.

Reese stepped closer, intent on supervising. His nearness made the tiny hairs on her neck stand up like a porcupine's quills. Once she finished, he turned the water off and gently patted her arms dry. She had to admit she was putty in his hands—warm, broad, generous hands. No man had ever made her feel like putty before. Ever.

*Putty.* The outlandish thought branded another smile on her face.

Reese flung the towel over his shoulder and lifted his gaze. When her eyes locked with his, he gulped and cleared his throat. "Umm…have a seat."

It was the first indication that maybe, just maybe, whatever was causing her head to swim or making her belly ripple in that feel-good way was happening to him, too. She found that strangely comforting. And bizarre. She didn't even know this person.

While he filled a bowl with water, Erica sat down and inspected her arms. Now that all the blood was gone, her injuries didn't look as gruesome as they had at first. Nothing too deep, just a few scratches like she'd tried to trim the toenails on one of the feral cats that hung out in her barn. She'd survive.

Reese set the bowl of warm water on the table and spun his chair to face hers. He scooted closer and readjusted his position, not once, but twice. Still not content, he let out a small huff and then grabbed the front edge of her chair—right between her knees and hauled the chair and her into the space directly between his legs. She barely had time to yip.

Her legs fit like a wedge against his inner thighs. The contact made her new putty body melt even more. Pretty soon, she'd just be a blob on the floor.

Nestled up against him as she was, now she had no choice but to stare. Not that she was complaining. He had plump lips—very shapely, downright luscious. And the way he smelled was more than shower gel. Erica's eyelids lowered, trying to decipher the unique aroma. Janine would call that a "man scent." Erica took another whiff.

"Ahem." Reese cleared his throat.

Her eyelids flew open to a poorly restrained grin on said luscious lips. "Umm, I'm—"

His eyes softened. "Just relax."

The need to explain burst free. "It's the way you smell." *Don't say man scent.*

"You think I smell? Because I just showered."

"Oh no. You don't smell bad." She giggled, but this particular giggle was a sound she'd never made before. It clearly hinged between enamored and demented. "I mean, I think you smell…" *Mouthwatering.* "…pleasant." *Pleasant, really?*

Reese lowered his gaze, somewhat confused. "Okay."

*Pleasant. Good grief. Just get it together. In through the nose, out through the mouth.*

He soaped up a washcloth and rose higher in his chair, virtually eliminating any measurable space between them.

The last time Erica sat this close to someone was when she had her eyes checked. Dr. McEnvoy leaned in and obliterated her personal space bubble with breath that smelled like potato salad. However, sitting this close to Reese wasn't at all unsettling, and his breath smelled like Colgate mint. *Even his breath smells good!*

*I should close my eyes. Yes. There, that's better. In through the nose, out through the mouth. Sit perfectly still… Is that… Yes, I can feel the warmth radiating from his skin. He's so close.* Her eyes opened a sliver. *Look at the tendons in his neck. Oh, look how they move when he stretches. And those scruffy whiskers go all the way down his jaw. Bet they're soft too. Who knew a man's neck could be so sexy?*

*Lick him!*

The voice in her head belonged to her sister. It *was* something Janine would say—and do. *No, don't. That's absurd.* Yeah, her sister would get a real kick out of this, a giddy Erica Gebhart. *Just breathe. No, don't breathe. Wait, I need to breathe. If I stop breathing, he'll have to give me mouth-to-mouth.* Her sister's boisterous laugh echoed in her mind.

And why was she so hot all of a sudden? Did he have his heat set to eighty? Instead of blood, it felt like lava flowing through her veins. Maybe this was a hot flash, but she wasn't that old yet. Was it possible that her libido awakened in such a state that she was thrust into menopause prematurely?

*No, that's ridiculous. Get your act together. I'm hot because of him, what with him being so close and all.*

She glanced upward to check his progress. Pressure and the hint of a shadow hovered as if someone had glued a lima bean to her eyebrow.

Reese leaned away. "It's a pretty good gash. You could probably use a stitch or two."

"It can't be that bad."

His steely blue gaze intensified. "Well, I'm not a doctor like your husband."

"Ex-husband!" Her immediate and adamant reply came out surprisingly fast. She even startled herself. *Calm down.* "I'd rather not go to the hospital."

"No one wants to go to the hospital, but a cut like this will leave a scar."

She admired his hardy features, inspecting him the same way he was her. He had a resilient jawline—the whiskers adding to the characterization that defined him as all man. And wait, was that a tiny scar above his brow? Yeah. Only his probably wasn't the result of watching cows mating.

"I'm not worried about scars," she murmured.

The spell she was under broke when Reese balked with disbelief. "Really?" His minty breath caressed the space between them. "If you say so." He sucked in a cleansing breath of his own and scooted his chair back to sort through a first aid kit. "You know, if something were to happen to you, I think a lot of people around here would be quite upset with me, and that's all I need."

"I don't understand."

"Hell, from what I hear, you're practically famous in this town."

"Famous? I don't think so."

Reese gave her a long, curious stare. "Everyone says you're this perfect pillar of the community and a celebrity of sorts. You've been on TV, and you wrote a book, right?"

"Oh." She took a confidence-building breath. "Trust me, I'm not perfect. As far as me being famous goes, that's just nonsense. The show was only a few episodes on PBS, and the book didn't get anywhere near the New York Times Bestseller list. All that happened years ago. How do you even know about that?"

"You have a good many admirers around here." Reese soaked a cotton ball with peroxide before dabbing it on the cut. "And I think it's safe to say that Steve is a pretty big fan."

"Steve Koontz?" She leaned away from his hand. "I know him and his wife Robin well. They're wonderful neighbors."

Reese reapplied the cotton ball to her cut. "He talks about you all the time."

Erica tried to imagine Steve Koontz as talkative. In front of her, he rarely said more than two words at a time. Of the three Koontz brothers, Steve was the middle brother, somewhere in his mid-forties. They were all married. Well, maybe not Paul. Keeping up with his flighty relationships was impossible. Paul was like Janine, always ready to get married, followed by always getting divorced.

However, out of the brothers, Steve was always the one to help with the property even before she and Davis divorced. It never occurred to Erica to be something different or out of character when he continued to help clear snow from the driveway or nail down the tin on the barn roof if it was flapping. Instead, she attributed any regard he may have for her as neighborly. Truth be told, farmers were a special breed in this area, and if anyone was to be admired, it was them.

Reese recaptured her attention. "Every time one of them sees you riding or out in the yard, I learn something new." He tore open a clean gauze and dried the cut. "I'm going to use some Neosporin." He squeezed a small amount of ointment onto the wound. "So…tell me about this book."

"It's ridiculous." She wanted to say it was a sad reminder of the shell of a person she once was, but that would sound overly bitter and be misleading. He couldn't possibly understand how she'd spent the last two years sorting through it herself.

"It's about dinner parties. *Ten Easy Steps for a Successful Dinner Party.* Not exactly life-changing material."

Reese's hands hovered above her brow. "Life can change in an instant. Now, hold still. I'm going to use Steri-Strips. I have to pull them tight." He placed two strips over the cut and covered them with a small gauze square. "You should leave these on for a couple of days." He finished and leaned back in his chair. His gaze seared a path over her body in the process. "You think you can walk to the truck without hurting yourself again?" The silver flecks in his eyes reminded her of a disco ball.

Her smile blossomed. "I can." They stared at one another for what felt like another full minute.

He looked away first and ran a hand through his hair. "Okay, I'll take you home."

In the truck, they rode in silence, except for a country song playing on the radio. It wasn't often that she listened to this genre of music. That's not to say that she didn't like country music. She was just more of a Norah Jones fan. The song playing had a lively tempo and was a declaration of being a redneck woman. Erica tapped on the edge of the door in rhythm with the catchy beat.

Reese turned into her driveway and parked next to her burgundy Jeep Wrangler. Getting out of the truck, she moved much slower than before. If she fell or tripped again, she wouldn't be able to talk her way out of going to the hospital.

"Just to be safe, is there someone you can call? I'd feel much better if you weren't here by yourself right now." Concern shadowed his voice.

"I'll call my sister. She's not doing anything today. She'll be more than happy to come by."

Accepting her plan with a hasty nod, Reese set off to retrieve her bicycle from the truck bed. He propped it next to the garage door.

His focus stayed fixated on the damaged bike, while hers rested solely on him. Reese was taller than Davis, maybe six foot two, an excellent height compared to her five foot seven. He was trim, nearly 200 pounds of salacious flesh. Another vivid description she could pilfer from Janine's lurid vocabulary. Most of his weight rested on one leg. His thumbs caught the top edge of his jeans just over the pockets. If she attempted to swallow right now, it would be audible.

Reese plucked at one of the spokes. "I'm not sure what we can do with this."

Her reckless appraisal swept the length of him again. *That's a shame.* She blinked, expecting the voice in her head to belong to her sister, but this time, the voice was her own. A strange thumping rippled low in her torso. What's going on with her body?

The answer came a second later.

*Kegels. They call them Kegels.*

Baffled, Erica's eyes darted away from him to her bicycle. The chain dangled around the gears like an old lady's necklace, and the front tire resembled the warped clock in a Salvador Dali painting. Her heart sank. The other bike she owned was older and needed repairs too. She couldn't afford to have someone fix either of them. Sure, there was money in the house account, but she'd never touch that money.

Her gaze drifted from the bike back to him, only to find his direct focus now poring over her. Deep in the pit of her belly, the thumping started again. The distinctive crease between Reese's brows deepened, and his dark lashes pinched to a sliver.

Abruptly, he turned and beelined for his truck. "I'll come by later this evening to check on you."

She stepped after him with a nervous shudder filtering into her body. "I'm sure you've got more important things to do."

Reese climbed into his truck. "I don't mind." He took a long breath before starting the engine. Then he looked directly at her. "It gives me a reason to see you again."

Words of another protest caught in her throat as Reese Mailing unleashed the sexiest, full smile she had ever seen.

*Thump, thump, thump.*

\*\*\*\*

Reese glanced in the rearview mirror. His mind

reeled over finally meeting the much-talked-about Erica Gebhart face-to-face.

*Damn.*

# J. ALISON COLE

## Chapter Two

"You called him 'ruggedly handsome' before." Janine shot back before flopping onto the sofa with a poop-eating grin smeared across her face.

Erica stared at her sister. Janine was one year younger and a shorter and slightly heavier version of herself, with just a few not-so-subtle differences. Janine's personality leaned toward flashy, thus her salon-aided, vibrant red hair. Her sense of style was a combination of new-age bohemian and Lady Gaga. Of course, no one dared overlook her perky boobies that always beckoned for extra attention with the added lift from thick padding and low buttons. Take all that away, and people could tell they were related.

"I believe the word I used was appealing." Erica sat in a chair next to one of the front windows and took a sip of her homemade raspberry iced tea.

Janine shook her head, arguing. "Nope, that's not what you said. You said he had that rough-and-tumble kind of appeal, which is like saying ruggedly handsome. Although…you thought Davis was handsome, so maybe I shouldn't trust your judgment of who qualifies as good-looking."

Erica regarded her sister with an extra slow blink. "For your information, Davis was—is handsome. As far as judgment goes, you can't expect me to take advice about men from a person that's been married three times and always on the prowl for number four."

"Ha, ha, ha. For your information, the first two didn't even count," Janine countered.

Leaning toward her sister, Erica smirked playfully. "Oh, they count."

Janine's head fell backward, and her eyes rolled toward the ceiling. "Let's be real. The first time I got married, I was too young. The second..." She giggled. "...too drunk. Heck, that one hardly lasted six months and may even have qualified for an annulment if it hadn't been for all that consummating going on." A peculiar look drifted over her face. "Rusty had a little wang, but I have to admit, he used it very well. I wonder what he's doing now."

"Euwh." Erica grimaced. "I don't want to hear about Rusty's—wang."

"And then my third, my sweet Edwardo Rodriguez. You know how hard it is for me to control myself around men with accents. Tell me, how was I supposed to ignore his bronzed skin and that sexy voice? He had this way of rolling his tongue, and I don't mean when he spoke." A naughty grin smeared over Janine's face.

Erica did her best to keep from laughing. "You're so gross. Please stop. Gross."

"I managed to keep that going for what, three to four years?" Janine said in a somewhat dignified manner.

"Your longest relationship to date, I believe."

"Well," Janine scoffed. "At least it didn't take me *eighteen* years to figure out I wouldn't be happy."

Erica shot her sister a dirty look.

"Oh, don't give me that. I know the reason your divorce has always upset you, and it has nothing to do with Davis—directly, anyway."

In a vain attempt to ignore Janine, Erica picked up a magazine. "I don't want to talk about this again. Oh, look, mac-n-cheese ravioli. That sounds so good." She flipped to the next page.

"Well, that's just great. The one person here with a degree in psychology doesn't want to talk about it. You, of all people, the perfect Erica Gebhart."

That was twice today that someone used that word to describe her. Did people actually believe that hogwash? She tossed the magazine aside. "Janine, I'm not perfect, nor have I *ever* pretended to be."

Janine snorted. "Uh, you don't have to pretend. You just are. And just so you know, you make it incredibly hard for us regular folks to keep up."

"That's ridiculous."

"It's all very intimidating, by the way. That's probably why ordinary men are afraid of you."

"What?" Erica cried. "Why would they be afraid of me? You're out of your mind."

"Oh, really. Look, I know that it's taken a lot of hard work to get where you are, but you have this way of making everything you do look so damn easy. I mean, Jesus Christ, look around this place." Janine fanned her arms around the living room. "I remember what this house looked like when you got it. I thought you were crazy, but you've turned it into the lovechild of a Gaines Fixer Upper and Martha Stewart's home in Bedford. It's like whatever you touch always works out, everything that is, except your marriage. That was *supposed* to be perfect, too. But…"

In her own wacky way, Janine wasn't far off the mark. Part of Erica's struggle was trying to accept that an aspect of her life actually failed—a first for her. From the beginning, her marriage to Davis appeared to be a match made in heaven. They were attractive, like-minded, and got along fabulously. He represented the last piece of a puzzle, only somehow, it never quite fit.

Erica's gaze drifted to the framed canvas print above the fireplace. The portrait was the quixotic example of her former pseudo-life. Davis, the dashingly handsome, successful husband, her the beautiful, loving wife and mother, alongside their adorable child, laughing and playing with a golden retriever puppy in a pile of autumn leaves. A picturesque family. But other than their daughter, the other two people may as well be strangers. Like the stock photo in the frame when you buy it from the store.

One day soon, that portrait would have to come down. Erica rubbed the protruding knot on her forehead. "By the way, Janine, you're an…A-hole."

"Tell me this. Did you say sugartits when you fell?"

Erica snorted. "Nope." *It was son-of-a-biscuit.*

"Really? Because I think you're the only person I know who doesn't like to swear. For God's sake, Erica, just say it, say *ass*. And I'm not an asshole, but we both know who is. Davis is the *King of Assholes*. I've always believed that."

For years, Davis and Janine only maintained the smallest margin of civility toward each other for her benefit. After the divorce, all bets were off.

A car door closed outside. Erica squinted through the wavy glass of the front window and saw her daughter heading up the front walk. "It's Lauren. Did you call her?" she grilled Janine.

"Of course, I called her. I knew you wouldn't, and she should know what's going on."

"I would've preferred that you hadn't bothered her. Lauren has a full plate, taking extra summer classes. She's too busy for…your shenanigans."

"My shenanigans? Hey, I'm not the one who got all juiced up over some guy."

Erica stepped onto the front porch and greeted her daughter with a warm embrace.

Lauren stepped back to survey her injuries. "Whoa, Mom, you got banged up pretty good."

Janine joined them on the porch and let out a resounding *Paha* before adding. "She wishes that she got banged."

Erica purposely ignored her sister. "I survived."

"What happened?" Lauren asked.

Janine interjected before Erica could respond. "The sexy new neighbor picked her up, and I mean that literally. He picked her up off the ground with really strong arms and carried her to his truck with his really long legs."

Lauren's eyes widened and her jaw dropped. "Oh my gosh, Mom. He carried you? Could you not walk?"

"I could walk just fine. Your aunt is...exaggerating." Erica deliberately stepped in front of Janine to escort Lauren to the far end of the porch. "Let's have a seat on the swing. Would you like some tea? It's a fresh batch with raspberries."

Lauren sat down. "No tea, but thanks, Mom. So, what does this neighbor look like? Did you see him, Aunt Janine? Is he cute?"

Janine plopped onto one of the large white wicker rockers next to the swing. "No, I haven't met him yet. I only *heard* about him."

Erica plucked at a few spent blossoms of purple and yellow pansies from a pot hanging next to them. *Cute* was not the word she would use to describe Reese. He was genuine in an "I don't care" kind of way that made you look twice just for sheer appreciation. *Rugged* was a much better word.

"I'm sure he was just being neighborly. He probably—" Erica stopped. *He probably picks up lots of women.* "Well, he was just being nice."

Janine shot her a sly smile. "Was he wearing a ring?"

Erica glared at her sister and pinched another

shriveled blossom from its stem, hoping to relay the message. "I don't know anything about him, and I didn't look, Janine."

"Is he young, old?" Lauren pushed the swing into motion.

"I'm positive that he's younger. He seemed very..." *Firm.* Reese didn't have a beer gut or middle-aged softness. Erica harnessed a smile, knowing how easily Janine could twist any and everything into some kind of phallic or sexual innuendo. Plus, if she'd said *firm* aloud, her sister's head might have popped off, just like the spent blossoms. "He seemed very polite."

Janine started rocking at the pace of a methhead. "All I know is your mother was practically *gushing* when she called me." Janine winked. "She called him handsome with dazzling sky-blue eyes."

*Did I say dazzling? I did.* "Good grief, Janine." Maybe she had said those things about Reese, but that was earlier in the day when her head was still swimming in man scent and neck whiskers. Erica could only assume that Janine's overabundance of excitement was because her encounter with Reese was the first time she'd...well...been in a man's arms in well over two years. *Strong, manly tattooed arms.* Her stomach muscles clenched involuntarily.

Erica turned toward her daughter. "All right! He's kind of tall, and yes, he was...very masculine with...several appealing qualities." Her eyes shifted to Janine. "I did hit my head, you know." She would've vindicated her actions further, but in the distance, a faint rumble of an approaching truck caught her ear. Once the truck was closer, she could distinguish who the truck belonged to.

Steve's truck had the recognizable sputter of a diesel engine. Paul's truck was a newer model with a smooth hum. Bob, the oldest Koontz's brother, drove a beat-up pickup that clanked with an assortment of loose tools that flopped in the back, making it rattle like things were falling apart. But the sound of the truck coming now differed from any of them. The steady roar she heard belonged to a blue Chevy. She'd bet her life on it.

Erica walked to the opposite end of the porch. From here, she could see a trail of dust drifting into the air above the country road. *Maybe he won't stop. But what if he does?* She turned and found Janine and Lauren standing two steps behind her. Apparently, they'd figured out who was coming too.

"Just behave okay, both of you—and stay here, please." From around the last bend, a blue truck came into view. Erica's nerves, usually made of steel, kinked like tinfoil. *Why does this man make me so…antsy?*

Reese veered into the driveway and parked between her Jeep and Janine's Lexus. Erica cruised down the front walkway to greet him. After all, that was the polite thing to do, and she needed to prove that she was capable of manners and could walk without tripping.

He stepped from the truck, and her stomach floated two inches higher.

*Oh, sweet sugartits.*

The tips of his hair were wet and curled from another shower. A grayish-blue T-shirt highlighted the sparkly part of his eyes, and darker denim jeans fit him in all the right places.

"Damn, sister," Janine whispered behind her ear.

Of course, her nosey sister and Lauren hadn't stayed on the porch. But she'd deal with them later. Right now, she was focused on the man ambling across her driveway.

Reese represented the male sex extremely well, rough edges and all. Her earlier giddiness and lightheadedness resurfaced between heartbeats.

Reese hit the edge of the flagstone sidewalk, and his understated hint of a smile flooded over her with a warm rush. Erica couldn't help nor hide the one that formed on her lips as he scanned her, all the way from the tops of her white Nikes to her lima bean-adorned brow.

"Hello." His husky voice landed deep into the center of her chest.

Janine stepped forward. "Well, hello! You must be the thoughtful neighbor I've heard so much about."

Reese gave Janine a brief glance and a polite nod.

Erica instinctively turned to introduce everyone properly. "I'm sorry, allow me. This is Janine Rodriguez, my sister, and this is my daughter Lauren. Ladies, this is Reese Mailing."

He gave each woman a quick handshake before returning his attention to her. "So, how are you feeling?"

"Oh, I'm fine." *At least I was five minutes ago.*

Janine interjected—again. "I found her piddling in the garage when I got here."

His piercing gaze all but scolded her. "I thought you were going to take it easy."

"Erica is so pigheaded that way," Janine said matter-of-factly.

"Actually, I was working on the mower," she offered as a defense to Janine and then Reese.

"She's been piddling with that thing since last weekend." Janine added a dramatic flip of her hand.

"If you want, I can take a look at that. See if I can fix it?"

"What, the pigheadedness or the mower?" Janine reached for Reese's arm, making discernable contact in the guise of selling the joke. She groped his bicep the same way one would test a ripened cantaloupe.

But his eyes never wavered from Erica's. "Yeah."

Straight white teeth greeted her in another full smile.

A smile like that had probably rendered more than one woman weak in the knees because it sure as heck was doing something to her.

A lengthy pause filled the next few moments before Erica regained her senses and returned to hostess mode. "Would you care for something to drink, Mr. Mailing?"

"Reese," he corrected. "And no, thank you."

"How old are you, Reese?" Lauren's question splattered over Erica's brain like an egg landing on the sidewalk.

*What is she doing?* Erica's chest tightened. Why couldn't she breathe?

His gaze bounced to Lauren and quickly returned. "I'm thirty-five."

"Thirty-five. Huh." Sweet Lauren, aka Janine's meddling partner in crime, didn't stop there. "Are you married or seeing anyone?"

*What does a panic attack feel like?*

"No?" His reply sounded more like a question.

*Could they be any more obvious?* Sadly, Erica already knew the answer—and it was *yes*.

Janine took a cozy step closer. "You know, Reese, I work for an entertainment company, and restaurants set up gratis dinners for reviews all over the place all the time. Erica and I were supposed to have dinner this weekend, but as it turns out, I can't go now. However, I still need the review."

*God, please open up the ground and swallow my sister. Please, please, please.*

Not even a pebble flipped over.

"And I think it would be a great way for her to thank you for all you did today if she took you instead."

Erica always had the ability to read people. It was

one of her gifts and why she was so good at her job. And right now, she wouldn't blame Reese if he took his thirty-five-year-old, nicely rounded backside and fled. She ventured a look.

Other than the tinge of a smile, whatever was lying beneath those vivid blue eyes was a mystery. Perhaps the man had gifts of his own.

Reese dipped his chin toward Janine and Lauren. "Ladies, nice to meet you." Then he gave Erica the slightest nod toward the garage. "How about I take a look at your mower?"

Instead of being put on the spot, he merely ignored Janine's bizarre suggestion and managed to dismiss the prying duo, for the most part, like a perfect gentleman. Erica didn't know whether to be relieved or disappointed. She directed Reese toward the garage before giving Janine a scathing glance over her shoulder.

He stopped at the open bay door of her two-car garage to look at her bike, still propped in the same spot from earlier that morning.

"I think my bike may be a lost cause."

He studied it for a moment. "Well, if you straighten the front sprockets, you could replace the tire. But, of course, you'd still have to fix the chain or get a new one, reset the gears, and then swap out the busted brake cable." His eyes flashed. "I think it's worth a try." This time, her stomach flipped like a pancake. "Show me the mower." They stepped into the garage.

Two days ago, she'd removed the hood and mower deck from her 420 John Deere lawn tractor. Various smaller parts and the tools she used lay neat and tidy on a work towel spread over the floor next to the front tire.

Erica wanted to study the directions and diagrams better before removing anything else.

Reese struck his manly pose—the one with his thumbs hooked on the top of his jeans. "You did this?"

"Don't be so impressed. It took me two whole days to get this far. I used the owner's manual, oh, and the Internet. The mower has been sitting idle for the last couple of years. But, from what I understand, I think it's the carburetor."

He knelt, much in the same fashion as he had that morning. The dark blue denim pulled tight at the thickest part of his thighs, outlining his hamstrings. She let out a silent breath of appreciation.

"Do you have a 3/8 inch socket wrench?" he asked, blissfully unaware of her shameful observation.

Erica moistened her bottom lip, hoping to stifle yet another surge of heat from rippling through her body and, no doubt, her cheeks. "I think so." She found the correct size and handed it to him.

Reese pulled an empty five-gallon bucket closer to the mower to use as a stool. "You planning on mowing all this ground yourself? I would've thought someone like you would just hire a company?"

*Someone like you?* Did he naturally assume that she was a rich celebrity too pampered to accomplish such a mundane chore as lawn care? Sure, on paper, she was an author, a former TV host, and the ex-wife of a doctor. But now, she was just Erica.

She smoothed down her ruffled feathers. "When we first bought the house, Davis and I did much of the upkeep ourselves. Granted, he usually did the mowing, but I did all the gardening and flowerbeds. It wasn't until our lives became too busy that he hired a landscape company. I have a bit more free time now. So I can do it myself. I want to do it myself."

Truthfully, her salary from school barely covered her day-to-day expenses, so paying for a lawn service was more of a luxury. And not in her minuscule budget.

At the divorce, she refused any kind of alimony. The only thing she wanted was the house, which she proposed to buy out Davis's half using the inheritance she received from her father. But the only way Davis agreed was if he could set up a "house fund" for maintenance and repairs. He could call it whatever he wanted, but two years later, every penny of the "house fund" remained untouched. And it would stay that way.

Fifteen years ago, when they came across the old stone two-story farmhouse nestled in the soft hills on a ten-acre parcel, the house was barely more than a shell. While Davis honed his career, Erica sidelined hers to go through room by room, sanding, staining, spackling, and painting, transforming the property into a home—a home for them. She always had the feeling that it was only a house to Davis, like he never understood the difference.

Not long after the renovations were complete, the "house" became more of a showpiece to share with family and friends, not to mention the perfect place to host numerous charitable functions for the committees she served on and even several posh medical events for the executives from the hospital.

The book release happened around the same time and, by some bizarre twist of fate, got mentioned on two national morning shows. The next thing she knew, the governor stopped by to visit, and someone pitched the idea of her hosting a show on PBS. She agreed to do three episodes, even though they begged for more. Once the shows aired, her notoriety took off with a life of its own, and the people in town never treated her the same. A lifetime ago.

Two years ago, out of the blue, Davis asked for a divorce. Her life was so consumed by committees and events that she never saw it coming. That's when she stepped away from her hectic social schedule, finished her degree, and got a job at the school. The pressure, most of it self-imposed, disappeared the day she bought her bicycle. It'd taken eighteen years to absorb twenty-plus pounds but only six months for it and then some to come off. In truth, she was in better shape now than when she first met Davis in college—mind and body. But she was far from perfect. Then again, who was?

Reese cranked on a few bolts and asked for a flathead screwdriver, but other than that, he said very little. He removed the fuel pump, the air filter, and a weird-looking cylinder that Erica couldn't identify from any schematics. Was that the carburetor?

He picked up a small flashlight and shined it into the gas tank. "Look here. Can you see it?"

Erica bent over and squinted into the shadows of the tank. "There's chunks of stuff floating." He leaned forward and shared the tiny beam of light. Invisible energy sparked from his near proximity.

A quick side glance skimmed his profile and the darkened stubble along his chin. Davis had always been clean-shaven. Maybe that explained her new fondness for whiskers.

"You were right. It's sediment and dirt from sitting for so long. All that gets sucked into the fuel pump clogging everything, including the carburetor."

Reese's manly scent was easily distinguishable over the vapors of gasoline wafting from the tank. Erica adjusted her stance and stepped away before Reese's fumes made her loopy. The last thing she wanted was a repeat of the morning's embarrassing smell fest.

Reese straightened and wiped his hands with a rag. He scribbled down part numbers on a scrap piece of paper on the workbench and put hash marks next to three. "You'll need these parts to be new. If you can't find the other two, I might be able to clean the old ones." He handed her the list.

"You think you can fix it?"

He pulled a ratchet from his rear pocket and wiped it clean. "I think so." He offered her the tool. "The pigheadedness might take a little longer."

Erica's easy laugh echoed off the garage walls. She took the ratchet and twisted it. The *clack-clack-clack* was almost as addictive as popping bubble wrap.

The "worry" crease between his brows formed, and the faint smile that played on his lips—vanished. "I can't have dinner with you this weekend."

The clacking of the wrench stopped instantly, drawing even more attention to his apologetic tone.

Reese rushed to explain. "It's my son. He's been staying with my parents in Michigan to finish out the school year, but this Saturday, he's coming here with me to stay."

That explained the new bike in his living room. "I understand completely, of course. My sister can be...." How did she even try to explain Janine? *She's an idiot.* "Well, she can be a handful." Her chin lowered, and much to her surprise, disappointment landed on her back like a cinder block.

He shifted from one foot to the other. "I put my phone number at the bottom of the list. Call me when you get everything you need for the mower." The crease on his forehead deepened.

She gave him a quick shake of her head. "Sure, and thank you again for helping me today." They left the garage and walked toward his truck.

At the driver's door, he turned abruptly. "I-I can do Friday." His voice clipped with noticeable apprehension.

"Oh, the mower isn't going anywhere. There's no

TALK OF THE TOWN

hurry..." Her voice trailed away.

One corner of his shapely lips tilted up. "I meant dinner. If you can make that work?"

Her brain sprung like a mousetrap. "Dinner on Friday shouldn't be a problem." *What am I saying?*

"Great. You can pick me up at, say…seven, and I'll assume it's semi-casual unless you tell me otherwise." He climbed into his truck and started the engine. His radiant blue eyes lassoed her gaze. "You have a good evening, Mrs. Gebhart."

She touched the open edge of the driver's door. "Erica," she corrected. The devil all but owned his smile.

# J. ALISON COLE

## Chapter Three

"I should've never agreed to let you and Lauren take me shopping. It's a thank-you dinner. That's all." Calling it a date just implied something Erica hadn't done in an awfully long time. "Call it anything else. Just please don't call it a date."

Sitting in a booth at the Olive Garden, Erica sat up straighter and took a sip of water.

Janine sat across from her with a smug look on her face. "Seriously, Erica. You're not fooling anyone. Besides, that's what it is. Two people sharing a meal, ogling one another—possibly more." Her eyebrows wiggled.

"And that's another thing. Don't talk like that in front of Lauren. Is it really just about sex for you, Janine?"

"I once read that a woman hits her sexual peak between the ages of thirty-seven and forty-five. You're peaking. God only knows how long it's been since you've seen the one-eyed snake. Besides, I think your daughter is old enough to figure out that her mother may one day actually have sex again. You are human."

Erica rolled her eyes.

"Oh, stop. I can tell you like him. I mean, I don't blame you. I'd jump his bones and hump him dry." Janine pressed her shoulders against the high back of the booth, lowered her eyelids, and began to gyrate in the seat. "He wouldn't have any juices left, but that's just me."

Erica quickly scanned their surroundings and prayed no one nearby saw or understood Janine's actions. "Good Lord Janine, we're in public. *Try* to behave. Or do you really suffer from some sexually depraved condition I've never heard of?" They chuckled together.

It never took much to get Janine going, and her stifling list of trigger words grew daily. Words like *come*, *stiff*, *wet*, or *hard* were the most obvious, but now even simple words like *rod*, *package*, or *finger* could generate a snicker.

Erica made the mistake of taking Janine to the local meat market once. The butcher never batted an eye when her sister enthusiastically asked how long his sausage was. Poor man.

Janine grabbed a breadstick and broke it in half. "Oh, lighten up. I just want you to be ready."

"Ready for what?"

"How people talk, especially in this town. They all think you're prim and proper, but I know you're no Mother Teresa."

"I don't care what anyone in this town thinks. I've never claimed to be Mother Teresa."

"You haven't, but you are a saint though. You endured sex with Davis at least once, anyway. I mean, Lauren came from somewhere. Oh, wait, please tell me you choose artificial insemination. Or better, you had to use an egg donor because his dick was so little, and his sperm count was empty. Yeah, that's it, isn't it? I promise I'll keep your secret, and Lauren never needs to know the truth."

Erica's lips pulled back in a fake grimace until her eyes scrunched closed. "Sorry. He's her father, and we made her the old-fashioned way."

"Now, who's disgusting? Gross." Janine quivered.

Erica leaned forward. "Not to upset you, but sex was never our problem."

Janine covered her ears. "La, la, la, la. Not listening."

"Really? Oh, come on."

"All right, all right." She waved. "Fine." One of her brows arched in speculation. "Do you think guys sit around and talk like this?"

"I'm sure they do."

"Yeah. Reese is probably back on one of them farms right now, telling the Koontz boys how he's going to plow your field and rake your mounds."

Erica chuckled begrudgingly. "Oh, that's lovely."

"They're the only farm puns I could come up with that fast."

Erica's chuckles subsided. "I'm not a prude, but I just don't think I could be that casual about it. I mean, is that what people do now? They just pounce on one another with no emotional attachments? As if such an intimate act has no meaning other than physicality."

"Yes, that's exactly what they do. You've heard of Tinder, right? Really, Erica, I don't know how you've survived this long. You must go through a lot of batteries." Janine pinched more bread and shoved it in her mouth.

"You're so disgusting. How were we raised in the same household?"

"I guess I don't have your high standards." Janine made a googly face at her.

Erica winked playfully. "Oh, you mean you actually have some?"

"What did I miss?" Lauren plopped onto the bench seat next to her.

"Hey, Sweetie, you didn't miss anything." *Humping, raking mounds, and batteries.* Erica knew better than to stare at Janine. "What do you have there?"

Lauren handed Erica a prestigious-looking black and gold shopping bag. "I thought you might need this for your date."

45

"Oh, how sweet."

Janine huffed. "Wait a minute, she can call it that, but I can't?"

"Yes, Lauren gets a pass." Erica removed the contents from the bag and unfolded the crinkly tissue paper to find a lacey beige demi-bra with matching lace panties. She slammed the tissue paper over the slinky undergarments. "Lauren!"

Lauren snatched the other half of the broken breadstick. "What? All your bras are those ugly sports bras. You should wear something like this, Mom. He seemed kind of, I don't know…like he could be into you. Right, Aunt Janine?"

Janine pretended to be indifferent. Then, as soon as Lauren looked away, she bounced in her seat.

Erica placed the undergarments back inside the bag. "Seriously, you guys are not helping. This isn't exactly comfortable for me."

"Mom, I didn't get you thongs. Trust me, you'll be comfortable."

She exchanged glances between the two women who represented her support system, a sex-crazed sister and a daughter who felt her mother needed lacy new underwear for her date.

*Not a date.*

Okay, it was kind of a date.

Two hours and three stores later, Erica placed a cream-colored sweater on the counter in front of the cashier.

Janine stepped in line behind her. "So you've bought black slacks, a pair of new blue jeans, and this sweater. I mean, it's not bad—for work, but the least you could do is get something sexy. Think sheer."

"Sheer pants? No, thank you." She grinned over her shoulder.

Lauren moseyed toward them. "Hey, Mom, there's one more store I want to check. It's kind of new, at the other end of the mall, next to that shoe store you like."

"I don't know, Hun. This will do it for most of my reserve fund money."

"I think you'll like it. And the walk to the other end of the mall would count as exercise."

"I see what you're doing. And this mall isn't that big. But we can check it out."

Erica had to agree with her daughter and her sister. She liked the store. While some outfits teetered on the extreme with unusual sequenced designs and tied-dyed features, the rest had a clean-cut elegance and refined style. Erica shuffled through a rack of dresses near the back of the store. One dress immediately caught her attention—a neatly pleated V-neck that narrowed and gathered at the waist of a full skirt. The supple cotton fabric was a light shade of aqua, with a layer of embroidered cream flowers across the bottom hem. The color alone complimented her summer complexion better than any other. It could be dressed up or down, depending on the occasion. It was perfect.

Erica checked the size and searched for the tag near the armpit of the dress. The hanger almost fell out of her hands when she read the price: 178 dollars. "Figures."

Janine plucked the garment from her to see the price. "It's an additional twenty percent off."

"It's still out of my budget. I can't spend *seventy-eight dollars*, much less *178* dollars on something I don't really need." She ran her fingers over the smooth material. "It's beautiful, though. Maybe next time."

"What, in another two years? Let me get it for you."

"Thanks, but no." She smiled at her sister and put

the dress back on the rack.

****

"I hope you know how much I appreciate this, Marcus."

"Heck, for a Friday morning, the traffic wasn't even that bad. And it's my spare bike, Erica. If you're up for it, we can ride again tomorrow, but I'll need it back for Sunday. I think I finally talked Phillip into going with me." Marcus Schuller, Erica's friend from school and sometimes riding partner, secured his bicycle to the rack on the back of his red Prius.

"No, you can take it with you now. I've got a lot going on this weekend. Do you have time for some tea before you have to meet Phillip? I made some before we left."

"Raspberry or strawberry?"

"Peach."

"Even better. God, this is why I love you."

Erica had to laugh. "Yeah, yeah, yeah. I'll be right back, lover boy." She entered the kitchen from the patio and poured two tall glasses of Peach tea. Her mind drifted to when she first met Marcus. It was her second day working at the high school.

Marcus taught ninth-grade science. All the young girls hoped to be in his class. He's young and gorgeous, after all. His build was on the slim side, not overly muscular. He had chiseled features and coal-black hair that somehow always fell into place, windswept or not. Instead of teaching, he could be on billboards modeling expensive European fashion in front of the Eiffel Tower.

He'd approached her seeking advice to get through some trouble he was having in his own relationship. At the time, she felt like the last person in the world qualified to help. He was big into cycling and asked her to join him. She thought he was joking but soon found out he wasn't when he showed up at her house with two bikes hooked to the back of his car.

The rumors in town sprouted right away about the hot young teacher and the new and newly divorced guidance counselor. Of course, the rumors were just that—rumors. Aside from Marcus being twelve years her junior, he was also gay. Not many people knew, and for now, he preferred to keep it that way. Sadly, small towns have small minds.

Erica pushed the screened door open with her hip and headed across the patio with two glasses of homemade peach tea. Marcus was stretched across the stone knee wall near the fire pit. He got up and took one glass from her.

"You are the best." He took a hefty swig. "So, got any plans for this weekend? Maybe a hot date that I don't know about?"

Surprised, her chin jerked in his direction. "Why, what did you hear?"

He grinned. "Holy crap, you do. Wow! Who is he?"

Her cheeks ballooned with a full breath. "Don't you worry about it."

"Well, you have to give me something."

"I just gave you tea. Hurry up and finish it. You don't want to be late picking up, Phillip."

"He'd want to know this too. Tell me. Who is he? How long have you known him? When do I get to meet him?"

"No one, you know. Not very long, and I don't have a clue whether or not that will ever happen."

Marcus's phone dinged with a text. He checked it. "You're so lucky. I'll call you when I get home."

"I've got some errands to run in town."

"Well then, later this evening."

"I won't be here."

He finished his tea in a single gulp. Then gave her a sly smile. "Ooohhh. Well, don't do anything I wouldn't do. And there's a lot I would do."

"Oh my gosh, you're as bad as Janine."

\*\*\*\*

After a shower and a change of clothes, Erica headed into town for the parts she needed for the mower. There was a large John Deere dealership outside of Pittsburgh, but she decided to try Jackson's Hardware first. They carried a wide array of stuff, and she'd rather support someone local versus a big chain that jacked the prices just for the name.

Technically, the name of the store was Jackson's Hardware and Pharmacy. It was an old, hole-in-the-wall, third-generation owned store. Decades of foot traffic had bowed the hardwood floors, and dust-covered merchandise packed the shelves from floor to ceiling. It had only been within the last five years that they had modernized the cash registers to the new UPC barcode readers and installed an updated computer in the pharmacy. Herb Jackson had a hard time making the changes. But, at ninety years old, who could blame him?

Decked out in a colorful pastel, blue, and green bow tie, Herb Jackson sat in the rear of the store with men of similar age. They'd gossip and reminisce for anyone who'd listen. Herb's son, Vernon Jackson, a spry man of seventy, ran the hardware section.

Erica handed Vernon the list. He adjusted the pair of thick glasses on his nose to read it. "I think I have all these mower parts, Mrs. Gebhart. It shouldn't be a problem."

"Wonderful, that would save me a trip to the dealership. Thank you, Vernon." He disappeared behind a floral print curtain into a back room.

Waiting at the counter, Erica struggled with her spidey senses. The geriatric group sitting in the corner seemed all too curious. She greeted them with a polite smile. "Good morning, Mr. Jackson, Mr. Taylor, and Mr. Wilson."

"Mower parts, huh? You got someone to work on that for ya?" Herb Jackson tapped on the arm of a rickety wooden chair that looked even older than him.

"Yes, actually, the neighbor down the road from me was kind enough to offer."

"That new fella in town, Mailing." Herb Jackson grinned at the two old geezers seated next to him. "I'll bet he offered."

A retired postman, Maurice Taylor often referred to people by house numbers. He sipped from his wobbly cup of coffee. "That's 327 on Roop, first unit. I heard he's a bit of a scoundrel." "Best watch yourself, Mrs. Gebhart."

Mr. Jackson shook a bony finger at his two cohorts. "He served as a marine, but I also heard he had some ties with the law." He leaned back in his chair. "Got himself into some kind of trouble, is what I heard."

"If by trouble, you mean the reason he left Michigan." Jed Wilson's thick, wiry eyebrows practically hooded his sad-looking eyes. "I heard he left so he wouldn't have to take care of all the kids he has. Seven is what I heard."

A chill trickled down Erica's spine like ice water. She didn't know anything about Reese Mailing other than he worked for the Koontz brothers, smelled good enough to lick, and was attractive in ways that made her tingle in places that hadn't tingled for quite some time.

"More than likely, all seven have different mothers. You know the type." Maurice Taylor gave the other old men in the corner an overzealous wink.

*Hmm.* The icy chill spread to her fingertips. According to these old men, Reese was a lawless thug, baby-making machine—a cad. *What if they're right?*

Herb Jackson puckered his lips and blew on his coffee. "Not to worry, our Mrs. Gebhart wouldn't be interested in the likes of someone like him. She's refined and far too sophisticated for a Don Juan like him.

*Our Mrs. Gebhart?* As if she belonged to them. *Refined and far too sophisticated?* They really thought she was Mother Teresa. She huffed.

"You heard of Don Juan before, haven't ya, Mrs. Gebhart?"

*Seven kids, really?* Erica shuttered, trying to flatten any tremor in her voice. "Don Juan, yes. I've heard the saying, Mr. Jackson." *Don Juan, no.*

"Don't see it myself. I guess it's something you ladies can sniff out. Always going after the potent ones."

*Potent. He used the word potent. He'd have to be to have seven kids. Or would he?*

Erica wondered if the expression on her face safely hid her rising panic. Janine always told her never to play poker. That type of deception wasn't in her.

Herb relaxed against the back of his rickety chair. "I saw it on the Nature channel. It's scientifically proven that most females go after the alpha male, the king of the herd, the one with the biggest—" Herb paused before glancing in her direction. "Set of antlers."

*Frickity, shiznit, William Shatner. I'm going to kill Janine.*

Whether Erica canceled or not, these old geezers would eventually find out that she agreed to have dinner with the younger potent, womanizing former marine, apparent thug, Don Juan, Reese Mailing.

Everyone in town also knew that Mr. Jackson and his friends loved spewing gossip. If they didn't have all the details, they just fabricated the missing pieces. Heck, most of the time, the end result wasn't even close to the truth.

The curtain from the backroom whipped open, and Vernon slapped a handful of dusty boxed parts onto the counter in front of her. "I had everything you needed."

Erica took a calming breath. "Perfect. Thank you, Vernon."

A second later, a voice came over the intercom. "Hardware, line one."

Erica gathered the boxes. "I'll take these up to the front to check out." She turned toward the Chatty Kathy club in the corner. "You gentlemen have a good afternoon."

The senior Mr. Jackson called after her. "You have a nice day as well, Mrs. Gebhart. Take care now."

Heading toward the front of the store, Erica reassembled her wits. *They're probably wrong. I'm—sure they're wrong.* Everyone had some kind of reputation, including her. *How could they possibly know anything about Reese?*

"Hello, Mrs. Jackson." Erica placed the dusty boxes on the counter.

"Well, hello, Mrs. Gebhart. Mower parts, huh? You got someone to work on this for ya?"

*Here we go again.*

Outside of Jackson's store, walking across the parking lot, Erica spotted a group of teenagers near the telephone pole beside the sidewalk. She recognized one of the boys from school. The other two, she didn't know.

The boy from school, Travis Baker, definitely had a reputation. He was a brilliant seventeen-year-old who had not only fallen through the cracks, but he'd been shoved, pushed, and forced into them. His father's name didn't appear on any of his official records, and after meeting his mother, it was easy to see why trouble always found him. One time, Erica called Travis's mother to the school to discuss his attendance. It was the middle of the afternoon, and the woman reeked of alcohol. She had clearly been drunk, high, or both. The woman became belligerent, and they ended up calling the police to restrain her. Shortly after that incident, Travis's conduct went from bad to worse.

He was a great kid with a hard road in front of him. So she started keeping him after school for detention, whether he actually earned it or not, and after some time, she finally established an excellent mentor relationship with him.

The boys standing with Travis looked older, but the two girls speaking with them looked much younger. One girl wore a short skirt and hooped earrings the size of salad plates. The second girl had on heavy, crude makeup and pink fluorescent streaks sprayed throughout her hair. Younger, naïve girls dressed the way they were, seeking the attention of older boys, were prime candidates of another ripe statistic of teenage pregnancy.

Travis lifted his chin as a discreet nod of hello. Erica was okay with that—until she noticed he was smoking a cigarette. Ironically, she hoped it was just a cigarette. Somewhat disappointed, she glanced away and, by doing so, caught sight of a police cruiser coming up the street.

Unfortunately, most of Kensington's law enforcement officers already knew Travis. They wouldn't think twice about hassling him for loitering and underage smoking.

Erica stopped in the parking lot and sat her bags down to rummage in her purse. "Travis, could you help me for a minute?"

Without hesitation, he loped away from his group at the corner. Once out of the earshot of his friends, he gave her a genuine heartfelt greeting. "Hey, Mrs. G."

"Spit that out." She tilted her head, indicating the patrol car coming up the street. He flicked the cigarette to the ground and stomped on it with his big black boot. "Could you carry my bags while I find my car keys?"

"Sure thing." He picked up the bags and followed her to the Jeep.

Erica took her time searching for her keys, watching as the police car slowed and then stopped to question the other youths.

"Those girls over there look a little young." Erica tried to keep the judgment from her voice.

"Tell them that." He shifted his gaze downward, somewhat embarrassed. "Don't worry, I kind of like this older lady, even though she treats me like a kid." Travis was a natural charmer.

"Maybe that's because you could be that older lady's kid."

"If I could have been so lucky." He snorted before giving her his best smile.

She cast him a sideways look while unlocking the car door. After a minute, the police officer drove away, and the group on the corner dispersed.

His eyes trailed after the patrol car. When it disappeared around the corner, Travis's attention returned, but he didn't meet her eyes directly.

Sadness squeezed her heart. Travis was capable of so much. Underneath his shredded pants and devil-may-care hardened exterior, she could almost make out the tenderness of a lost child. Erica stepped forward and hugged him, wondering how many he'd received in his lifetime.

After a timid returned embrace, Travis stepped

away and shoved his hands into his pockets. "Thanks."

"No, thank *you*, Travis." He walked away in the opposite direction of the patrol car. No doubt he'd meet up with those other boys sooner or later. Getting into the Jeep, she reanalyzed his behavior. He'd thanked her. Was it for being a friend or for seeing the cop? It could even have been for giving him a hug. She started the Jeep and decided that, most likely, it was all three.

## Chapter Four

Pulling into her driveway, Erica noticed a package on the front porch. She was expecting any deliveries, but she carried the box inside and opened the envelope attached. "You better wear it." Janine bought the dress for her.

At six-thirty, Erica exchanged glances between the clock and her reflection in the mirror. Her hands smoothed over the front of the dress. Adding the cream sweater solved several dilemmas. One, the evenings still tended to be cool, and two, it covered up the scratches and scabs on her forearms. The dress fit like a dream. She couldn't remember the last time she'd felt this radiant—or this eager.

The telephone rang. She darted into the kitchen for the cordless phone.

"Hello," her greeting sounded a tad peppier than her usual self-assured composure ever allowed.

"It's me." Janine declared from the other end. "My God, what are you still doing there?"

"It's only going to take three minutes to drive back to the road. I don't need to leave yet."

"Are you wearing the dress? How does it fit?"

Her fingers pinched the soft cotton fabric. "Yes, I am. *And* I will repay you. Thank you, by the way, it fits perfectly." Hopefully, Janine wouldn't ask about the new undies and bra. They fit too.

"Good, I almost came over. Hey, you got the other bag, right?"

"Another bag?" Erica balked. "I didn't see another bag."

"It's small. I put it inside the big box. God, I hope you didn't throw it away."

"No, I didn't throw anything away. The box is still on the center island. Let me look." She rooted under the wrapping and tissue paper. "I'm looking."

"I just wanted to make sure you have everything you need?"

"I'm sure I do, Janine. Why do you insist on making this a big deal?" She discovered a small brown bag in the back corner of the box. "Oh, here it is."

"Well, it could be big. I think I got the big ones. Check to make sure."

Erica unrolled the brown paper bag and removed another small square box. "What in the world is—?" She scoffed, trying to read the writing upside down. "MAX—Rib. What—?"

"I did get the big ones then. Good. They're condoms, Erica, prophylactics, ribbed for your pleasure. I always use the ribbed ones."

The box fumbled through her fingers. It bounced off the corner of the butcher block and shot across the floor. She huffed. "Oh my god, Janine!" Erica retrieved her sister's contribution from under the corner of the dishwasher. "Goodbye." She punched the end call button with a bit of extra force. It didn't have the same effect as slamming down a receiver, but it would have to suffice.

*Condoms? Really?* As if she wasn't edgy enough after listening to the ramblings of a group of old men discussing the vigorous prowess of Reese Mailing, now her own sister was prepping her for bone-jumping sex.

Granted, something about him suggested it would be fantastic. Erica closed her eyelids and conjured a dreamlike image of Reese as he knelt beside her in the middle of the road. But, as he stood, his shirt was gone, and the lilies behind him blurred and faded into the background. No longer outside, the surroundings changed to the inside of her barn—of all places. She could almost smell the sweet, clean straw mounded high in the loft.

Then—she was in the loft, lying on her back in the middle of the straw. Her skin glistened in the heat. What happened to her clothes? All she had on was her new lace panties—and Reese was hovering over her. The muscles in his arms are thick and bulging to support his weight. Tiny droplets of sweat dangled from his sun-lightened hair as his luscious lips lowered to hers.

Erica's eyelids flew open. A mixture of shame and excitement exploded in her lower regions.

*Lust.* It had to be nothing more than animalistic lust and physical loneliness. Where was the connection, the commitment, the love? Or she was just horny, and Janine was right. Maybe it had been too long since she'd been entwined in the thralls of passion with a man. At this point, any man.

During her marriage, she and Davis had fine-tuned their lovemaking to what she thought was the perfect blend of fulfillment and pleasure. With Davis's schedule, sex typically happened on Saturday nights. First, he'd unwind with a glass or two of wine, and then his eyes would twinkle. After eighteen years together, the routine was easy to predict.

Standing in the middle of the kitchen, Erica snickered. As long as she'd lived at this house, not once had she had sex in the barn. Heading toward the back door, her hand hovered above the hooks holding the keys to her Jeep. It was just dinner, for goodness sake. She had no real expectations of finding herself in some type of situation she couldn't handle. She grabbed a different set of keys. "Darn cronies and the Nature Channel."

\*\*\*\*

Reese answered the door after the second knock. Erica couldn't stop herself from doing a complete top-to-bottom admiring sweep. While the man looked good in faded, tattered blue jeans, he looked beyond GQ in black slacks and a savvy, untucked plum-colored shirt. When their eyes finally met, she realized he'd just done a similar inspection of her. The interest and appreciation on his face was all very…stimulating.

Using the tip of his middle finger, he pushed her hair away from her healing eyebrow. His smoky blue eyes seared into hers. "You look great."

"Thank you." Erica caught a whiff of his spicy man scent. It took every ounce of her willpower—not to lean closer and breathe him in. "You look quite dapper yourself." *Lord, I'm in trouble.*

An adorable grin she hadn't seen before made a brief appearance on his lips. "Dapper? Jesus, what does that mean?"

"If I thought you didn't really know, I'd tell you." She extended a set of keys toward him. "Would you mind driving? It's a stick, and I don't drive it that often. You can drive a clutch, right?"

"Yeah, I can drive a stick." Looking over her shoulder, he blindly took the keys. "Holy shit…Ah, I'm sorry." He apologized for his unguarded language. "Is that a Porsche?"

Together, they walked toward the car. "It's a 1985 Porsche 911. Before you jump to any conclusions, it was my father's."

He strolled to the front of the car. "Now this is classic."

Her putty insides turned to mush. "What, you don't like the Jeep?"

His chin twisted in her direction, and one of his eyebrows lifted. "The Jeep's fine, but this is more how I see you."

*He sees me?* "And what does that mean?"

A tiny chuckle huffed from his lips. "If I didn't

think you really knew, I'd tell you." He gave her a straight-faced wink and walked to the rear of the car, running his hand over the scoop. "What the hell did your father do for a living?"

"My father was a mechanic. A man owed him money, so they worked out a deal. He refurbished this from practically nothing. And three years ago, after my father passed away, this was part of my inheritance. Janine wanted the Trans Am. It looks just like the one from that old movie *Smokey and the Bandit*."

His fingers trailed along the roof to the driver's door as he studied her from his side of the car. "Looks like a pretty nice ride." He squinted. "I hope you know where we're headed."

Erica half-wondered if he was talking about the car, dinner, or something else. "I do." *Trouble indeed.* She scrambled onto the passenger seat and needed to gulp down her excitement.

Reese did a quick exam of the dash, mirrors, and levers. She'd never been materialistic when it came to things like hot cars, but dang, if he didn't look even sexier sitting behind the wheel. *How was that even possible?* Smiling to herself, it dawned on her that Davis had never driven this car, not even once.

"So." One of his gorgeous brows lifted higher. "Where are we headed?"

Her mind flooded with more than one answer to the simple question. *Don't say the barn.*

"Head to 68 West outside of Oakland."

The motor purred to life. Reese swung his arm behind her bucket seat to back out of the driveway. His plum shirt gaped open, exposing more of his chest and delectable neck. The dip below his Adam's apple was the perfect place to start. She'd move lower from there. *He probably tastes good, too.* Her tongue popped against the roof of her mouth.

"What?"

"Nothing. I didn't say anything."

His arm swung forward, and he switched gears, going slow over the gravel until they reached the regular pavement of the main road. "Let me ask you this. Who picked first, you or your sister?"

"I let Janine pick what she wanted. She said the Trans Am was more her style. She's always been loud and bold."

"Makes sense. The Porsche is sleek and stylish like you."

Erica blushed. Good Lord, when was the last time someone made her blush?

"So, your dad was a mechanic. Is that why you tried to fix the lawnmower yourself?"

A tiny huff of laughter escaped him. "Oh, my father never allowed us down at the garage. So, sadly, my education in auto mechanics is severely lacking. You saw that I didn't get very far."

"Yeah, but you had the gist of it figured out. Not many people would've even tried." He checked the rearview mirror, almost like he was debating his next words. "It was impressive. Was his garage around here?"

"No. I grew up in a small town just outside Baltimore, a place not much bigger than Kensington."

"Hm. So how did you end up here?"

"Uh, well, Davis has family in the region. I was a freshman going to a small college near Temple University. He was in med school at the time, and we met at a coffee shop between the two campuses—much to his mother's dismay."

His brows rose skeptically. "Hold on. Do you mean there's actually someone you don't get along with? Or was this before you became famous?"

"Oh, I had no problem with my ex-mother-in-law. But she made a point to tell me that she had never watched the show and somehow, her copy of my book had gone missing. Heck, I could've found the cure for cancer, and it wouldn't have made any difference. We were from different worlds, and because of that, I could only assume that she never really thought I was the right person for her son. And that *famous* thing you keep bringing up? Need I remind you that the pond we live in is very small?"

Reese adjusted his causal grip on the steering wheel. "You're still a pretty big fish. Anyone can see that."

They crossed the border into Maryland and merged onto a two-lane highway. Reese used the opportunity to experience the car's potential. It was nothing reckless or excessive, just a healthy rush. Once the adrenaline evened out, he spoke. "I saw you this morning—riding. Were you able to fix your bike?" His gaze remained forward.

If he saw her, then he saw Marcus. "No, actually, my friend had a spare for me to ride." It felt necessary that Reese understood that she and Marcus were just friends. "Marcus is a teacher at school and introduced me to riding. He asked for my help to get through a rough patch in his own relationship. Riding may not work for everyone, but I've found it to be very therapeutic. I can clear my mind and tackle problems, big or small. Plus, it keeps me in shape."

His fleeting glance blazed a trail that started at her ankles, hiked up her legs, across her waist, over her breasts, and then met her eyes before returning to the road. "Can't argue with that."

In the quiet that followed, the sexual tension in the car blossomed like a new rose. No one had ever checked her out in such a casual but sultry way.

She blushed again.

Reese cleared his throat and changed his grip on the steering wheel. A second later, he leaned forward in the black leather bucket seat and flexed his shoulders. Then his legs shifted apart wider.

The subtle movement was hard to ignore and alluring as hell. At least she wasn't the only one squirming.

## Chapter Five

So far, Erica's read on Reese was that he was a quiet, straight-to-the-point kind of man. What was nice was that he didn't seem nervous and wasn't trying to dazzle her with a macho ego or forced wittiness to control the situation. Very nice, indeed.

They exited from the highway and followed the voice prompts from the phone on which turns to make. After 5.7 miles, Erica pointed to the sign attached to two massive stone pillars. "There it is."

"You have arrived at your destination." She punched the app on her phone to end the route.

Reese turned onto the narrow drive and circled the lot, searching for an open parking space. "Have you eaten here before?" He found a spot not far from the main entrance.

"No. I haven't. A few similar places, but never this one in particular." It looked semi-fancy. God only knows what Janine had up her sleeve. "All we have to do is fill out a card when we're done. Believe it or not, my sister is a food critic. She really does this for a living." Erica wasn't sure if he saw this whole thing as a pathetic setup. Which, technically—it was.

They exited the car at the same time. He slipped the key into his front pocket and waited by the front of the car with his hand extended. Without hesitating, Erica planted her palm against his. Her breath hitched from the jolt of energy that shot into her body.

He gave her hand a firm squeeze, leading her to believe he felt it too.

Inside, the hostess greeted them with a pleasant smile. "Welcome to The River Palace. Do you have reservations?"

Erica spoke up. "Yes, it should be under Rodriguez or Gebhart."

The sophisticated older woman combed down the list with a finely manicured fingernail. "Yes, here it is. A Mr. Mailing and a Ms. Gebhart. Oh! You're on the veranda." The woman's eyes widened with esteem. "This way, please."

Erica offered Reese a generous smile. Leave it to Janine to be thorough with the arrangements. They followed the hostess through a maze of tables inside the dining area.

"Erica!" someone called. "Oh, my god. It is you."

Three tables away, a man rose from his seat. Erica recognized him immediately and cringed inside. "Walter?"

Like the snake that he was, Walter slithered around the tables to reach her. Ignoring the hand she put forward, he wrapped his arms around her in an incongruous embrace. After the hug, he placed an excessively friendly kiss on her cheek that came way too close to her lips and lasted far too long—in her opinion.

She withdrew from him the first chance she got and glanced at Reese. His eyes were narrowed on the brazen man, and to make matters worse, Walter had yet to acknowledge that she was actually with someone.

"You get more and more beautiful every time I see you."

"Thank you. Walter, this is Reese Mailing." Then she addressed Reese. "Reese, this is Dr. Walter Greenstein. He's a colleague of…Davis's. They work at Westmoreland Hospital together."

Reese extended his hand.

Walter's hesitation spoke volumes. Even with his own version of good looks, he was clearly intimidated. And rightly so. As far as she was concerned, Reese had it all, appeal, demeanor, not to mention the whole Don Juan vibe, minus the manwhore, out the yin-yang.

Walter took the hand Reese offered and gave it two quick shakes. "Aren't you a lucky son of a bitch?"

The corners of Reese's eyes tightened, but he didn't give Walter the satisfaction of a verbal reply, only a polite smile and a possessive hand that came to rest on the small of her back.

*Great, the only thing missing is a low growl.* She needed to move this along. "It was good to see you, Walter."

Walter, known for being crass and persistent, took a foolish step closer. "I'd love to give you a call sometime to catch up—if we could."

Erica had always thought of Walter as a bit sleazy and overly flirtatious, even before her divorce. He was the type of man just arrogant enough to ignore politeness. She ventured a look beyond him to the table he'd vacated. The blonde-haired woman sitting there was *not* the current Mrs. Greenstein. "I don't think so."

Reese's barely-there grin emerged to dismiss Walter with a curt nod. "Enjoy your dinner, Doc." The hand on her back immediately dropped to claim hers, and the same jolt as before needled the center of her palm as they caught up to the waiting hostess. She directed them through a set of French doors.

Stepping onto the veranda, the clinking glasses and the chatter of people vanished. Here, pristine black linens and candles graced small private tables while tiny flickering white lights hugged the rustic timbers of the structure's framework. On the terrace below, an older man wearing a tuxedo played a striking version of Ed Sheeran's *Perfect* on a baby grand piano. In the background, the Youghiogheny River bubbled softly over the nearby rocky slopes. The entire scene was serene, elegant, and *way* more romantic than it needed to be for a simple thank-you dinner.

*Janine picked this place on purpose—the hussy.*

Reese surprised her by holding the back of her chair until she was seated, then took his seat across from her. It might have been the warmth of the evening or the heated way he was looking at her, but the sweater needed to go. Once her arms were free, he reached over the table for her hands.

His long fingers trailed down her forearms, examining the cuts and scratches from the other day. Everywhere he touched left her skin tingling. Even now, she could still pinpoint the exact location where his hand rested on her lower back as if he had branded her.

"Looks a lot better." He released her hands and gave her a cheeky smile. "I don't know about you, but I sure could use a drink."

"It's not just you. That sounds like a great idea." Perhaps a drink would help stiffen up the parts of her putty body.

A pristine waiter appeared for their drink order and shared the elaborate specials of the evening. Once they were alone again, Reese leaned away from the table and draped his napkin over his lap. "I guess that happens a lot." He used his head to point to the tables inside.

It took a second to comprehend what he was referencing. "Who? Walter?"

"He seemed quite…friendly."

She laughed without thinking. Then, it occurred to her that Reese suspected there was more to it. "I wouldn't exactly call us friends. I only know him through the hospital. I would never be involved with someone like him."

"Why not?" A hint of curiosity lifted his tone.

"For one, he's a moron. Just in case you couldn't

tell."

His smile mellowed and his blue eyes intensified. "And two?"

"Two, I'm not the least bit attracted to him. But I think being a moron really sets the bar in his case." The waiter returned with their drinks. She raised her gin and tonic. Reese lifted his draft of Coors Light.

She quickly organized her thoughts. "A toast. To the bluest skies." Of course, he'd never understand her hidden meaning. "And the unexpected." His chin lowered a fraction, and the silver flecks in his eyes glowed. "Thank you, Reese, for finding me." She touched her glass to his.

His devilishly sexy smile appeared. "You're welcome."

He took a swig, and she emptied half of her glass.

****

The waiter returned for their order. "What may I get you this evening?"

Erica set her menu aside. "I'll have the stuffed rainbow trout."

"Excellent choice. It's served with couscous and braised carrots with fennel. And for you, sir?"

Reese closed his menu. "I'd like a T-bone, rare, with a baked potato and Coleslaw."

It didn't take a genius to figure out he was a meat-and-potatoes kind of guy. The waiter gathered the menus, and they were alone again.

If the art of conversation was a monarchy, Erica was the Queen. She'd always been able to listen to others and speak effectively. Discussing the restaurant and the music laid the foundation for the easy small talk. However, for such a quiet man, Reese had a knack for offering his answers with questions of his own.

After a short time, the food arrived, and she was

halfway through her second drink, feeling quite comfortable with the ruggedly handsome man sitting across from her. It was time to move beyond the small talk.

Erica took a sip from her water glass. "So tell me about your son. How old is he?"

A slight grin skirted over his features before turning into a mild grimace. "He's seven and a half and talks pretty much nonstop." Reese chuckled. "In all honesty, he's already been through a lot. That's one of the reasons I didn't want to rip him out of school to move here sooner." He broke eye contact. "I've never been away from him this long before, so tomorrow is a big day for both of us." He cut into his steak, not offering anything more.

"So, how did *you* end up here in Kensington?" Erica nibbled the tip of a tender carrot.

Reese sighed. "My daughter."

The faint voices of three old men echoed in Erica's head, and her throat turned into the Sahara. She reached for her drink and took two hefty gulps. Then, to hide her non-poker face, she glanced down and gathered a forkful of trout. "Oh, and how old is she?"

"She's thirteen and lives here with her mother. I have some fences to mend." After a short pause, he added, "With my daughter, not my ex-wife."

"But your son was living in Michigan?"

He sped up his chewing and gulped. "Different mothers."

Mr. Jackson's shriveled grin manifested in her mind. "And...do you have...any other...children?" *For the love of God, don't say, "Why yes, I have five more."*

His eyes narrowed before shaking his head from side to side. Then he continued eating.

"Two then," she said, comforting herself—*stupid*

*old men.*

Reese studied her. "Were you expecting me to say more?"

So much for hiding her poker face. "No, no." *Quick. Change the subject.* "I understand you were in the military?"

He set his fork down and reached for his beer. "Wow. It's definitely true what they say about small towns." His gaze skirted around the table. "Yes, I was in the Marines years ago."

This time, she took a smaller sip of her cocktail. "Not that I asked, mind you, but you're not the only one who hears things." Hiding her smile was impossible.

"It was those old men that sat in the back of the hardware store, wasn't it? What else did they say?"

*Ties to the law, a harem of women, and large antlers.* "I'm afraid they're the center gear works for the gossip mill in town. They usually get more wrong than they do right. I'm sure it's nothing worth repeating." A pang of guilt squeezed at her throat.

He cut a wedge of potato. "Well, what about you? Tell me about your daughter." He stuck the bite into his mouth and gave her a lazy smile.

"What would you like to know?" She couldn't stop admiring his lips as he chewed.

He gulped and ran his tongue over his bottom lip. "How old is she?"

Erica cleared her throat with a light cough. "Okay, um, Lauren just celebrated her twentieth birthday three weeks ago."

His brows lifted higher. "Were you like twelve when you had her?"

*When I was twelve, you were only seven. Oh, that's gross.* Erica banished the thought. "No, and you do realize that's a very twisted compliment."

He surprised her by laughing outright, and his playful smile engulfed her completely. "I didn't mean it in a bad way. It's just you don't look old enough to have a daughter that age."

"Our birthdays are two weeks apart. I had just turned twenty when I had her." He blinked once. It was probably the abacus in his mind clicking off the years. *That's right, I'm forty.* "If you must know, it's hard for me to believe that I have a twenty-year-old daughter. In my head, I feel like I'm twenty-eight, and it's been that way since. If that makes any sense." *When I was twenty-eight, he was twenty-three. That's a little better.*

"I understand perfectly." He pointed to her plate with his fork. "How's the trout?"

"Delicious. How is your steak?" Her smile was just as playful.

"Succulent."

*Succulent.* A new word for the list. Janine would say, "You should succulent him."

Erica grabbed her drink before plunging back into the safety of their conversation. "Do you like living here in Kensington?"

His gaze roamed to the sinuous river before returning to hers. "Well, I can say, with all certainty, that I really like my neighbors."

Reese had the potential to charm the pants right off of her, or in this case, her new lacy panties. Oh, the possibilities.

Once their dinner dishes were cleared, a different waiter appeared, carrying a tray of desserts. To complete the restaurant survey for Janine, they needed to sample at least one dessert.

Reese ordered a slice of cheesecake and coffee.

"No dessert for you?"

"I'll just have a bite of yours if that's okay?" He

glanced up, startled. "Or not." Maybe he didn't like sharing his food. Some people were like that.

"No, no, no. It's fine." When he laughed, it was mostly at himself.

"I can't eat a whole piece. I just want a taste."

"Don't be dainty on my account." He tried to egg her on.

"I may be a lot of things, but dainty isn't one of them." She could take a good ribbing as well as the next guy.

"I guess that's true. You pretty much devoured that fish."

She giggled that odd way again. The one that sounded possibly enamored or demented. It was so weird that it had come from her. It made her think of Beavis and Butt-head.

*Never make that sound again.*

His gaze lifted and held onto hers with an easy smile. "I will accommodate you, madame." The smolder that followed threatened her thigh muscles with a Charlie horse.

A waiter appeared and placed a black and gold-rimmed cup and saucer in front of Erica. He filled the tiny cup with a rich brew from a small French press. Then he served Reese a single slice of cheesecake drizzled with chocolate and three perfectly placed raspberries. "Is there anything else I can get for you?"

"No, thank you. I think we're all good." Reese stabbed a berry and carved the front wedge of cheesecake onto the fork. Then he held it across the table, about an inch away from her lips. "Here you go." The challenge was in his voice and his smile.

She eyed the massive wad on his fork. "Oh, that's too big." As soon as the words left her mouth, her mind honed in on the potential innuendos attached to those words.

Reese crooked his brow and moved the fork closer. He seemed to be enjoying this. "I'm sure you can handle it."

Erica tried to soften a throaty laugh as her insides quivered from his remark. She eyeballed the fork and leaned forward to let him shovel the bite into her mouth. His steamy gaze latched onto her lips. And just like that, the scenario of sampling a piece of cheesecake turned more provocative and suggestive than she could have planned.

Not that she did, but as she started to chew, she couldn't help but think about where the evening may end. It felt natural, inevitable.

After the fork slid out, Reese released the breath he'd been holding and scooped a bite for himself. He finished his bite before hers. "Damn. You're pretty good at that."

Erica took a sip of hot coffee. "At what, eating cheesecake?"

"No. You keep surprising me." He dragged the napkin over his mouth. "I guess I should be surprised, though. You're not at all what I expected."

Several reasons immediately flooded her mind: She was five years older, she didn't listen to country music. She didn't know how to fix a lawnmower. "What did you expect?" Something told her that it wasn't any of those things.

He shrugged lightly. "Erica, you're exceptionally beautiful and by far the classiest woman I've ever met. You're nothing like the women I normally spend time with. I'm just a regular guy."

"You're anything but regular." Why did her response sound so breathy? "Reese, I'm just me."

He veered forward and propped his elbows onto

the table. "Sure, that's how you would see it, but regular people don't drive around in collectible cars, write books, and have friends that land them on television."

"First off, the show was only three episodes on PBS. It just kind of happened, but I don't regret it. And it's *book*, not *books*. As for the car, I didn't have it until three years ago. The person I am today is perfectly ordinary. I even mow my own grass. Or I will, once the mower is running." Erica tried to play down the differences he was so intent on pointing out.

They sat in silence for what felt like a full minute before Reese's gaze floated to their surroundings. "It's more than that. The places I go don't look like this. The music is different and louder with the type of women who are all too eager to show off their tattoos." A warning flashed in his eyes—suggesting the type of place she'd never be caught dead in. "A different world, as you put it."

She knew the kind of places he was talking about. The next town over from Kensington had one seedy bar. Martini's looked like a rundown shack from the outside, and the inside wasn't much better. Right after Janine's second divorce, they stopped there because of the link it shared with one of her favorite movies, *It's a Wonderful Life*. The clientele was loud, drunk, and obnoxious. Janine called it a "righteous shithole." But they stayed until closing and had to call Davis to pick them up. It wasn't the worst night out she'd ever experienced, but she had no plans to visit Martini's again anytime soon. Unless, of course, Janine went through another divorce. God forbid.

She didn't get the sense that Reese was trying to keep her at arm's length so much as he was trying to let her know where he was coming from. He was being honest, unpretentious, and unapologetic, more admirable traits. However, society had a way of categorizing people, dictating who belonged where and deciding what they were capable of. Who gave society so much power?

"How was everything?" The first waiter sat a billfold on the table containing the checklist they had to complete. "I hope you enjoyed your visit with us."

"Everything was fabulous. Thank you."

After the waiter stepped away, Reese raised his bottle for one last toast. "May we always be grateful for the past, find joy in the present, and remain excited for the future."

"I'll drink to that."

They finished the survey in under a minute. As they walked through the restaurant, her mind kept rolling over what he said.

She firmly established that Reese was setting barriers. And the man had existing walls. It could be that he wasn't looking for anything serious, and this was his way of letting her know. He called her classy and said she wasn't the type of woman he usually spent time with. *Do Don Juans only have one type?* Or maybe he thought she was a snob or, worse, a prude. Was she? Sure, after hearing the rumors about Reese, she'd balked—for a second. But, it didn't seem fair to judge him without bothering to get to know him, and the same was true for her.

Reese twisted the key, unlocking the passenger door of the Porsche. The hinge squealed, conveying the actual age of the car as it swung open. He stepped aside, giving her the space by the door.

Erica squared off in front of him. "Yes, it's true that I was once heavily involved in the community and got to know a lot of people, some in prominent positions." She composed herself with another full breath. "Basically, people formed options of me based on what they heard and, in some cases, what they thought they knew. For some bizarre reason, the people in town treat me like a celebrity. But, I'm just a person. I hang up on telemarketers. I don't always separate my recyclables. And if I'm thirsty late at night, I'll take a swig of milk right out of the carton—why dirty a glass?"

The adorable grin snagged his lips. "Please say none of that's true."

After her ovaries pinged, she continued, "My point is, *I* don't live my life based on the preconceived notions or expectations of others. No one should have to live that way—and I have the tattoo to prove it."

His brows lifted, and his adorable grin unleashed another brilliant smile.

Having said her piece, she calmly settled onto the plush leather seat, keeping her gaze forward as he closed the door. If anything, she'd shocked him. He probably thought, *How could someone like her have a tattoo?* It took forever before he moved to his side of the car and another ten seconds beyond that for him to get in.

The seat groaned when he swiveled to face her. "I want to see it." Interest riddled his voice. "Your ink."

Erica's heart thudded. His scruffy whiskers made her fingers twitch. And now, the tendons along his throat were more pronounced by the twisted angle of his head. How had she never noticed how sexy a man's neck could be? Shame that hickeys aren't a thing anymore.

"I can't show it to you." *Without undressing.*

One side of Reese's mouth rose. He understood that meant that the tattoo was somewhere private. "I don't think you'd lie, so I guess I'll have to take you at your word." The steaminess in his eyes added, *For now.*

Reese shifted around and started the Porsche. He tuned the radio to a country station, and they headed home.

**\*\*\*\***

In the driveway of the small yellow tenant house, the engine went silent, and Reese climbed out. Erica met him at the front of the car.

"Would you like to come inside?" He captured her eyes with the question.

*Come. Cum—inside. Dang it, Janine.* That question was loaded seven ways to Sunday. But she didn't need Janine here to corroborate that she and Reese were adults clearly attracted to one another. Nothing was more apparent, and she had no doubts that he could make her do just that. According to the cronies in town, Reese Mailing had lots of experience in that department. And according to Janine, this was what people did nowadays.

Another unnerving option popped into her mind. Perhaps she was misconstruing his simple invitation because of her own urges. *Great.* One thing was for sure. He was bound to figure out her exact thoughts no matter what she said at this point.

"I think I should probably head home." Yup. She took the coward's way out but praised the level of her subconsciousness that found the ability to pluck those words from her surreptitiously sex-craved delirium. *And I left the condoms at home.* "You said you have a big day tomorrow." *He probably has a drawer full. Oooh.*

He glanced toward the house before letting his gaze trail back to hers. "Okay."

*Now he'll think I'm a tease and a prude for sure. Great.*

"I guess this is the part of the evening when I tell you that I had a really nice time," he paused for the length of two heartbeats. "And then—you kiss me goodnight."

An unexpected half-giggle popped free. Thankfully not, the Beavis and Butt-head laugh. But how slick was Reese? *Slick.* He was actually going to put this on her.

Reese's rugged features tightened with a knowing smile. "I had a really nice time tonight." He veered forward an infinitesimal amount into the space between them, filling it with his broad shoulders and intoxicating appeal.

Every fiber in Erica's body fed on the undeniable attraction she had for him. Her eyes dropped to his lips. She'd been studying them for most of the night in anticipation of this very moment, wondering if it would happen and secretly hoping it would. They had shared a delightful evening. A simple kiss *was* appropriate. Tentatively, she stepped closer, placing her hands on his chest. The thump of his heart was steady compared to the thrashing storm hammering against her ribcage. His hands landed on her hips and glided to a comfortable spot on her waist.

Erica raised her chin and pressed her lips against his silky, smooth smile. Her body tingled when the hot tip of his tongue barely grazed the edge of her bottom lip. It almost felt like a dare to go further. Oh, she would accommodate him. Her lips parted, and her tongue searched for his.

His response was instant.

Reese dove into the kiss. His tongue latched onto hers, swirling and coiling, hungry and delicious. The kiss synchronized into one sweeping wave after another. Then his hands slid tantalizingly lower, grasping her bottom. A gust of passion whooshed through her body when his firm midsection levered against hers. The urge to be closer warmed and pooled inside, the very way nature intended.

His hands returned to her waist, and he veered away from the kiss enough to speak against her lips. "Are you sure you don't want to come inside?"

"I—Ummm…" Breathless and mesmerized, she gulped in some much-needed air. Right now, she wasn't sure if she could remain standing. *Oh, lordy.* The kiss left her knees weak and curled her toes. She felt like one big blob of quivering putty.

Reese leaned away a little more, creating space between them without letting go. Then he cupped her chin and gazed into her eyes. The man could see her soul if he wanted.

"Goodnight, Erica." One last tender kiss landed on her lips before he smiled and stepped away.

## Chapter Six

The wrench slipped, and Erica's knuckles scraped against the metal sprockets of the front tire—again. If she couldn't fix her bike, she wouldn't be able to ride, and if she couldn't ride, she didn't know what she'd do with all this pent-up energy. It was still dark when she entered the garage, but now the sun was cresting the skyline, spewing an orange hew to the new morning.

Miraculously, she straightened the frame of the front arms and reset the gears and chain to their appropriate position. The last thing she had to do was swap out the front tire, but a kink in the metal kept her from getting a good grip on the nut.

Erica squeezed the pliers, prying harder, repeating the mantra, "Righty tighty, lefty loosey." The nut shifted, and a sense of triumph swelled within her chest. She readjusted the tool until the nut twisted free.

The worn front tire from her old bike would work. It had to. She checked the air pressure and resecured the brake cables using black electrical tape and a few nylon ties.

"Ta-da." Erica stepped back to admire her handy work. *Not bad.* A quick test around the driveway on her Frankenstein bike filled her with a sense of accomplishment and relief. She'd be on the road within the hour, right after she grabbed a shower.

In the main bathroom upstairs, she stripped out of her comfy sweats and came to a standstill, eyeing her reflection in the mirror above the sink in nothing but her lacy beige panties. Her eyes trailed up and down the image that greeted her. If Reese hadn't let go when he did, she would have gone inside with him. Knowing that is what kept her up most of the night.

Erica fingered her breasts. Her nipples hardened into pert pink gumdrops. Her hands slid lower, pushing the lace panties over her hips and down her legs. What would Reese's hands feel like on her naked body? What would he feel like inside of her? She couldn't deny wanting to know.

At first, the five-year age gap felt like a big deal, but it disappeared the second his lips met hers. Erica lowered her eyelids as she remembered the kiss. Anyone who kissed that well had to be spectacular at doing other things. No doubt, the man probably honed his skills with countless willing participants over the years. A troublesome detail she preferred not to dwell on.

Her eyes opened, her figure blurred by the steam from the shower. She had a lot to sort through on her ride today.

Erica kept her shower quick. Then she dried off and shimmied into her spandex riding gear.

Janine hated all cycling apparel, especially on men. She said it showed their bulges and made her think of fruit bowls and rubber. Rubber was, like, third on the list.

Erica neatened the bathroom and gathered her dirty clothes from the hamper. She'd start a load of laundry and, hopefully, make it out of the house before Janine called for details of the date.

With a spring in her step, Erica headed down the back set of spiral stairs to the kitchen. Near the bottom, she nudged the door open with an elbow. But as light from the kitchen seeped in, a shadowy figure moved.

Erica gasped. "Davis! What are you doing here?

Her ex-husband switched his stance, leaning against the butcher block island near the center of the room. "The door was unlocked, and I heard you in the shower. I thought I'd wait for you to finish." The coffee pot chugged and hissed the last bit of water from its reservoir. He pushed away from the island and retrieved a cup from the cupboard. "I made some fresh coffee. Would you like some?"

Erica took a calming breath. "No." It was rare for Davis to stop by unannounced, and when he did, it was seldom about her. Generally, his visits were about some files packed away in the attic or an old piece of furniture stored in the barn. *Why is he here now?* "You might have called first. It's early." She set the laundry basket on the island. Unlike most divorced couples, they maintained a friendly relationship and not just for the sake of their daughter.

"I knew you'd be up. And if you must know, it was a last-minute decision." He blew on the coffee before taking a sip.

Davis always looked so confident and comfortable. This morning was no different. Most of the time, he wore dress slacks or khakis, something you'd expect to see a respectable doctor wearing, but every once in a while, he'd wear jeans like the ones he had on today. She'd always had a fondness for him dressed like this—for several reasons. The first being that it drove his articulate mother insane, and second, he was in that elite club of men who look good wearing them. Janine could think what she wanted, but Davis had 'it.' The man was sexy in his own right. Not that it mattered to her anymore.

He took another sip, eyeing her over the rim of the cup. "I heard you had a spill earlier in the week. I thought I should check you out." He sat the cup on the counter by the sink.

"I'm fine, really."

He waved her closer. "Come over here under the light. Let me see."

His superior tone wasn't meant to be condescending. It was more a matter of him being direct. Erica understood this about him, which was one of the reasons they'd always gotten along so well. She crossed the room and stood beside the sink in front of the window.

Davis positioned her shoulders and tilted her head so more of the morning sun landed on her face. "Did you clean it well?" He nudged gently at the cut above her brow with the side of his thumb.

"Yes."

"Headaches?" His sage green eyes twinkled.

"Just a tiny one, the first day."

Davis stood taller and sniffed. He slid his hands down her arms and stopped near her elbows. He inspected the red scratches on her forearms before running his thumbs over her palms. Right before letting go, he gave her hands a tiny squeeze.

"You should have called me, Erica," he reprimanded. "You probably could have used a stitch or two on your head. But, it's closed up nice, so it may not leave much of a scar."

"If it does, maybe it will get lost in my wrinkles," Erica joked.

Davis huffed. "You don't have any wrinkles, but speaking of your age, when are you going to stop this? The roads are dangerous." He did a quick visual inspection of her body. "You've obviously hit your target weight." He reached for his coffee cup, which just happened to be sitting on the counter behind her. "You look good, Erica." His eyes twinkled again. "You look real good."

It hit her all at once. It may be a bit early in the day, and he was drinking coffee instead of wine, but it was Saturday, after all. She scampered away from the sink, positioning herself on the far side of the island. The laundry basket made an excellent added barrier. "It's more than physical exercise, Davis. It's like therapy for me. You know that."

"Yeah, I know," he replied, perfectly composed.

"I was getting ready to start some laundry before I went for my ride. Is there something else you wanted?"

Sauntering away from the sink, he stopped at the island directly across from her. He fixated on the basket.

Erica angled her eyes down without moving her head. And there, perfectly displayed on the tippy-top of the dirty laundry, were the lacey bra and panties she'd worn the night before.

Davis reached into the basket and picked up the delicate see-through fabric. He raised it higher so the sexy panties dangled from his fingers for a torturous three or four seconds. She snatched them from his hand and shoved them deep into the basket.

"So, it's true," he said accusingly before biting into his bottom lip.

"What's true? That I wear underwear?"

"Really, Erica?" He shook his head, uncharacteristically befuddled. "You know, last night, I got the most interesting phone call from that douche Walter Greenstein."

*Ohhhhhh—Walter.* As it was, she knew Davis only tolerated him strictly out of professional courtesy.

"He told me that he saw you having dinner." Davis crossed his arms and inhaled a full breath through his nose. "I didn't think anything about it at first. I know you and Janine eat out all the time. Only Walter said you were with some homegrown stud." He batted his eyes sarcastically. "Still, I figured it was Marcus, your friend from school. But he said the guy you were with 'looked like more than a friend.'" He paused, waiting for her to explain.

Davis had been living with Bethany for the last year. And he'd never been the jealous type. So where in the world was this reaction coming from? Regardless, she didn't owe him any kind of explanation.

Her prolonged silence prompted him to continue. "I thought about it for a while and decided to call Lauren. She told me about your accident, but that's all she said. I guess she doesn't know about your *little outing* either."

"You shouldn't put her in the middle of things like this. It isn't fair to her, and just so you know, I can have dinner with whomever I want. It's not your concern anymore."

His jaw practically hit the floor, insulted by her reply. After a long breath, he slowly maneuvered around the island to stand in front of her. "Do you want to know what else Walter said?" The tension in his voice ebbed, and his chest deflated. "He wanted to know what I did to *fuck it all up.*"

Erica scoffed at the absurd notion. "You know that's not the case, Davis. No one is to blame here. No one. It just..." *Failed.* "...wasn't meant to be."

"No, I think he's right. I should've never—" His slender hand landed on her cheek. "Why does our divorce suddenly feel so wrong?" His body eased closer, and his head tilted and lowered.

His lips were a mere inch away when she blurted the first thing that came to mind. "Does Bethany know you're here?"

Davis's advance came to an abrupt stop, and his hand fell away from her face. The green in his eyes darkened faster than an angry chameleon. He straightened. "You really want to do this *now*?"

*Absolutely.* Erica squared her shoulders and stiffened her spine. It had been a long time, a little more than two years to be exact, that she'd played this game with Davis. During their marriage, they didn't have arguments—but mostly point and counterpoint discussions.

"I will take that to mean no. She has no idea that you're here at *my* house. Look, if the two of you had some kind of a fight, you need to work that out with her."

He recrossed his arms, taking a more assertive stance. "I'm exactly where I should be. Do I know him?"

Erica ignored his question. "And what would your mother have to say about that? I doubt she'd agree to you being here."

His eyes flashed to the basket. "Christ, Erica! Are you sleeping with him?"

*Oh, I wanted to.* She scoffed again because of the near-miss prospect. Until last night, she hadn't been on a date, much less slept with anyone. But she didn't want to answer or share how last night almost changed both of those things.

Her chin rose higher. "Did you know your mother sent me a Christmas card last year? She wrote, 'Celebrating these joyous times.' Call me cynical, but I don't think she was referring to the holidays."

"Think of your reputation, Erica, or are you just doing this to hurt me or get even somehow?"

Now it was her turn to be shocked. How dare he? How dare he show up, looking all-handsome, rifle through her undergarments, and accuse her of actually living her life just to get even with him?

"Hurt you? If I wanted to hurt you, I would've slept with Walter."

A surplus of emotions flooded his face. *Crap.* Caring for someone is much different from being in love with them, and his reaction tugged at the core of the feelings she would always have for him. *Yes,* her reply was misleading, but as far as she was concerned, this discussion was now over.

"You didn't want anything else, did you, Davis?" Not waiting for an answer, she picked up her socks and shoes and headed for the front porch. She'd just finished tying her second shoe when Davis stepped onto the porch behind her. She stood and faced him.

"Erica, I don't want to see you get hurt. I hope you know what you're doing." Davis stepped closer and placed something on the railing. As he pulled his hand away, she saw the small square box Janine so thoughtfully included for her date.

*Ooooohh, sugartits.*

The man standing before her was intelligent, sensible, and distinguished to a fault. His dark hair had just started to pepper with gray, adding to his already chiseled good looks. His perfectly starched white shirt almost took away from the casualness of his jeans, but he could get away with that. She and Davis had once made a great pair.

He'd need one more push. "Tell Bethany I said hello. And give your mother my love." Erica hopped down the steps and walked down the flagstone path. Then she jumped onto her reinvented bicycle and took off. After leaving the driveway, she glanced over her shoulder toward the house. Davis was leaning against the front pillar—brooding. He wouldn't hang around long.

She switched gears and pedaled harder. "Dang it. I didn't get to start the laundry."

\*\*\*\*

After two hours and a legion of miles, a cool gust of wind smacked Erica in the face. Along the skyline ahead, gathering clouds from the West shrouded what was left of the early-morning sun. At the next intersection, she turned east, beginning her journey home.

Twenty minutes later, the swift-moving storm front was a curtain of steel gray filling the sky. Now, her ride turned into a race.

Erica entered the outskirts of town. Orange cones lined the road where a steel plate and several patches of blacktop were being repaired. She checked over her shoulder and slowed down to navigate around them. Her bicycle jostled over the rough section and rattled in protest. A loud ping followed. Clearing the last metal plate, her foot spun dangerously fast, and the chain popped and knotted in, out, through, and around the rear set of gears. The back tire locked up completely, and she careened to a stop. At least it wasn't a repeat of her fall from the other day.

She'd barely caught her breath when a crack of thunder shook the ground under her feet. Then, one large drip landed on her forearm, followed by another on her shoulder. The angry heavens opened with a deluge of rain, like buckets of water being dumped over her head.

Since Frank's back wheel refused to spin, she dragged him along. Six miles away from home may well have been sixty in this weather. A few cars zoomed by, splashing runoff from the street over her legs as if she wasn't wet enough. Headlights flickered between the falling rain until one set swerved off to the side behind her. Erica turned, blinking against the drops and the lights shining in her eyes.

A moment later, Reese jogged toward her. Laughter danced in his eyes while the rain instantly darkened the shoulders of his camo tee shirt.

"Do me a favor. Let's try to keep the roadside rescues to one a week." He took Frank to the rear of the truck.

Erica unstrapped her helmet and carved the wet strands of hair away from her forehead. "Does this mean

I owe you another dinner?" she shouted over the rain.

He grinned. "I think so. Hop in."

Erica opened the door, ready to flop onto the seat, but she had to wait for the small boy sitting there to shift to the center. Reese climbed in behind the steering wheel, shaking the rain from his hands. His gaze locked with hers as if trying to gauge her reaction to seeing his biracial son.

The small boy had light honey-brown skin and a head full of lush ebony curls. But the sparkly set of eyes staring at her was a sea of blue, just like his father's.

Once she had enough room, Erica hopped onto the seat and closed the door. She gave Reese's son a warm smile. "Hello. What's your name?"

The boy scooted closer to Reese. "You're wet."

She laughed. "Your name is 'You're wet?'"

He let out a timid giggle. "No." He looked at his father and shook his head. "My name is Sawyer. I meant––you are wet." He scooted closer toward his father.

Erica lifted her palms. "No, no, my name is Erica." She smiled at both of them. "And yes, I'm drenched."

Reese hit the blinker and reentered the flow of traffic. Lightning crackled the sky in two, and the hot white flash filled the inside of the cab. Sawyer jumped and grabbed her hand from the seat. Both gave Erica a start. But, after the thunder's rumble faded, he released her hand.

"You can hold my hand if you want, Sawyer," she offered.

He looked down, semi-embarrassed. "Aren't you afraid of thunderstorms?"

"Nah. They're just clouds bouncing around like big ole marshmallows in the sky."

"But you're a girl."

Reese snickered from his side of the truck. He shot her a sideways glance over Sawyer's head. "I didn't teach him that. I promise."

"Are you saying I'm supposed to be scared of storms because of that?"

"Yeah."

"Now, why would I be scared? I'm in a truck with two really handsome men to keep me safe." The crinkly edges around Reese's eyes tightened. She hadn't meant to express it so openly, but it was true.

Reese hit his blinker again. "If it's okay with you, I've got to make a quick stop." His eyes shifted between her, Sawyer, and the oncoming traffic. "It'll only take a minute. Someone has allergies, and I need to pick up a few prescriptions." His teasing focus zeroed in on the small boy sitting between them.

Reese pulled into the parking lot of Jackson's Hardware and found a spot not too far away from the door. "I'll leave it running." He nodded at Erica and then questioned Sawyer. "Do you want to come with me?"

Sawyer shrugged. "No, I'll wait here."

The small boy seemed content to sit with her. "We'll be fine." She did her best to reassure Reese.

Reese stepped from the truck into the driving rain and darted into the store. Sawyer slid to the front edge of the seat to watch his father enter the store.

He nestled back into the seat and began to fidget. "I don't like getting wet."

Erica shook her head in amusement. "Not ever? How do you get clean?"

He lifted his feet onto the console. "I take showers but I don't like baths."

Children his age still had the gift of honesty. Not that she needed to have this particular tidbit of information about his hygiene. But the old saying *Out of the mouths of babes* came from somewhere for a reason. "I see."

"My dad started laughing when he saw you. Are you his new girlfriend?"

Erica coughed.

*Reese must have a lot of new girlfriends.* She cleared her throat again. "Um, your father and I are neighbors. I just met him the other day.

"I think he likes you." Sawyer twisted the nob settings on the radio. The channels mostly crackled and hissed from the disturbance of weather. "I have a sister."

"I heard."

"I don't know her very well. Do you think she'll like me?"

"Well, I just met you, and I like you."

He shook his head. "Dad said I can get a hamster, and I already know what to name it." To share his enthusiasm, he turned toward her. "If it's a boy, I'm going to name him Sunny, and if it's a girl, I'll call her Ginger."

"Those sound like great names."

"Yeah, I know."

The driver's door opened, and Reese jumped in. He threw a skinny white bag on the dash above the steering wheel. Erica hadn't seen him exit the store. He gave Sawyer two light taps on his knee. "Everybody all right?"

She and Sawyer answered together. "Yep."

"Okay, let's go home."

In less than ten minutes, Reese backed into her driveway and parked. Erica leaped out of the truck and opened the garage door. Reese grabbed her bike from the bed of the truck and darted beneath the door as it was still going up.

Sawyer had turned in his seat to watch them

through the rear window. He was less than twelve feet away, but his face lit up when she waved.

"You make friends fast." Reese propped the bike against his side and ran a hand through his wet hair. His intense blue eyes came to rest on her. "So are you good—with this?" His gaze dropped, and his hands landed on his hips.

"I am in your debt, sir. Thank you again."

"No, I mean, are you okay with…Sawyer?" His eyes darted toward the truck.

It dawned on her what he was really asking. He wanted to know if she had a problem with his son being biracial. "Why wouldn't I be?"

"You know why." There was no mistaking the sharp edge in his voice.

Kensington was a small community. But they had minorities and a blend of people of different beliefs and ethnic backgrounds. Most everyone in town was indifferent, like her. But sadly enough, there were a few who were not. She wouldn't put it past some of those wretched people to use this to somehow exacerbate Reese's already seedy reputation. Sadly, racism exists, so, of course, he would want to protect his son.

Erica tried to ease his worries. "Is it because he doesn't like to take baths? He said he prefers to shower, but hey, as long as he's clean, I'm okay with him."

Reese stared at her for a moment, apparently trying to decipher her ridiculous answer. He sighed. "He told you that?" They both glanced at the little boy in the truck.

"He also implied that he's nervous about getting to know his sister." Last night at dinner, Reese seemed reluctant to say much about his daughter, or his son for that matter. He was definitely a private person.

Reese huffed and rolled his eyes toward the

rafters. "Well, yeah. Kara is thirteen and not overly fond of me, so his concerns with her may be justified. Her most recent stepfather hasn't exactly influenced her with an open mind, but that's on me and something I'm hoping to fix."

He did say he was here to rebuild his relationship with his daughter. The task of introducing a new sibling could be challenging under normal circumstances. Add that into an already tumultuous atmosphere of a thirteen-year-old girl while keeping in mind that she came from a possibly unaccepting or even slightly dysfunctional family, and there were sure to be casualties. Hopefully, it wouldn't be Sawyer.

Erica placed a hand on his arm. "The fact that you are here and willing to try says a lot. Reese, that counts for something. You can't change what's behind you. Start building from here. Focus on that." She took the bike and propped it against the inside wall of the garage.

"What the hell did you do to that anyway?"

"The bike? I fixed it, can't you tell?"

Reese let out an honest, heartfelt laugh. It was like having a glimpse of the man with his guard down.

His easy smile remained. "Don't touch the mower. Promise?"

She lifted her right hand. "I promise."

The corners of his eyes scrunched. "If you're going to be around tomorrow, maybe we'll come by, and I can put the new parts on for you."

"Sure, I should be around, and hey, Sawyer said you were getting him a hamster. Lauren had one not that long ago, and I believe the animal habitat she used is stored away in the barn. It's barely used. You're welcome to it if you want. "

He shot another look toward the cab of the truck. "Christ, I didn't think I was in the store that long. What else did you guys talk about?"

*New girlfriend.* No way was she going to share that morsel. "Huh, that's pretty much it."

He pushed a wet piece of hair away from her forehead. His thumb ran over the healing cut above her brow. Erica's heart thumped when his gaze lowered to her lips. The memory of the kiss from the night before ignited her senses with anticipation.

"That'd be great." He glanced toward Sawyer. "I guess I'd best be going." After a quick swallow, his hand fell away, along with her hopes for a kiss.

"Thanks again, Reese."

"Erica." He said goodbye, and then he was gone.

## Chapter Seven

Erica made a mad dash for the house. She entered the rear door into the kitchen, kicked off her shoes, and peeled her waterlogged socks away like a second skin. The telephone rang, and without even looking, she had a good idea of who was on the other end.

"Hello."

"Oh my gosh, where have you been? I tried your cell phone, but you probably didn't take it with you again. I swear to God, Erica, why do you keep doing that?"

"Who is this?" Erica feigned confusion.

"Ha ha ha, very funny," Janine scoffed from the other end.

"I'm sorry, I just walked in the door."

"Wait—you're just now getting home! Oh my god, you must be sore. Was it good? Is it big? Did you use the whole box?"

An unexpected blush swarmed over Erica. "Geez, Janine. I was riding." A trail of wet footprints followed her into the laundry room. She grabbed a clean towel from the shelf above the dryer and dried her face.

"Good for you." Janine chuckled sleazily.

Erica buried her heated cheeks in the towel. "My bike, Janine. And you are so bad."

"Humph. I'd still like to hear all about it because you know I always share stuff with you."

"And I pray every day that you'll stop doing that."

"Come on now. I do it for you." Janine's manner relaxed. "You see, I know that your sex life has had to live vicariously through me. If not, it would have shriveled up and died."

Erica squeezed the wet ends of her hair with the towel, smiling over her sister's unbridled enthusiasm. "Janine, I'd like to think my sex life is my own. And, well, one other person's. Not that you and Davis seem to think so."

"Davis?"

*Crap on a stick.* Erica's eyes pinched shut. Mentioning Davis was a colossal mistake, but the cat was out of the bag now. "He stopped by this morning." The other end of the phone stayed silent. "Hello?"

"Just pick me up, and we'll go to Nicco's."

At the mention of food, Erica's stomach rumbled. She'd skipped breakfast, and the ride left her famished. "I'll pick you up about one."

"Erica?"

"Yeah?" She held her breath, unsure what Janine might say.

"I'll let you off the hook with Davis as long as you tell me everything that happened with Reese."

Erica grunted. "Oh, shut up." She ended the call and headed upstairs.

****

Janine flung the passenger door open and clambered onto the seat. The excessive glare followed, as expected. "What the hell did that bastard Davis want?"

Erica prepared her defense on the ride over. "Now, just calm down. He heard from Lauren that I fell, so he offered to check me out."

Janine's face contorted. "Oh, gross! You didn't let him, did you?

"Not in the way you're referring to. Need I remind you that he and I *have* tried to remain friends?" *For the most part.* "Look, I don't want to damper the afternoon by talking about him. I'm starving." Erica, in her cunning way, redirected the conversation.

Janine patted at the rain on her jacket using a small, soggy tissue. "Fine," she snapped. "But he's still an asshole."

"Yes, Janine. Davis is the reigning king of a-holes."

**\*\*\*\***

As far as places to eat, Kensington had a total of three restaurants, not including the sandwiches they slapped together at the gas station. Nicco's restaurant was located in the town's only shopping center. The small strip mall included a nail salon, a tax preparation facility, a karate studio, a seven-lane bowling alley, and a state-run liquor store.

The restaurant's newest owner Tom Smith didn't bother to change the sign. Instead, he covered the words "Italian Cuisine" with four strips of duct tape, and every so often, if the tape peeled, he'd replace it with new.

However, despite the flawed sign, the food was an excellent assortment of Caribbean, French, and Pennsylvania Dutch dishes. The weird combination somehow served the community well.

Around town, most people knew Janine as Erica's sister, but at Nicco's, it was the other way around. When they opened a little over a year ago, Janine gave them an unexpected but well-deserved favorable review. Tom's thick, suave accent was icing on the cake for Janine. So now, when either of them came to the restaurant, they were treated like royalty.

Wendy, the head waitress, greeted them at the door. She claimed to be a relative of Tom's and had an accent just as thick and heavy as his.

"Hello, Ms. Rodriguez and Ms. Gebhart. How good to see you again."

Wendy's "s's" sounded more like "z's," no matter how hard she tried to iron out her enunciation.

Janine's smile beamed. "Hello, Wendy. I'm hoping that you have a table for us."

"For you, Ms. Janine, always. One moment, please."

Erica did a quick search for any open tables. The restaurant still had a crowd leftover from the lunch rush, and she didn't see any.

Wendy stepped away, and Erica braced herself for Janine's ongoing bizarre theory that the restaurant was filtering illegal immigrants into the country like spies. *Spies, really?* Her main argument was that they all had American-sounding names, so the community would accept them better.

Erica had to admit the name "Wendy" didn't fit the hostess. The brute of a woman looked more like a "Helga" or "Olga." It also didn't help that Wendy was built like a linebacker for the Steelers. Subsequently, that noted observation prompted another argument from Janine that maybe Wendy was only impersonating a woman—a theory that Janine tested by trapping the poor lady in the bathroom, pretending to need a tampon. When Wendy graciously pulled one from her pocket, she left Janine dumbfounded.

*Spies. What was there to spy on in Kensington?*

Wendy appeared beside Janine. "This way, please." She escorted them to a table near the large front windows.

They must've somehow squeezed in another table.

About ten feet away, a tall, slim, older man was filling a workstation. Erica spotted him around the same time as Janine.

Janine poked her in the arm. "Look, he's new."

Erica acknowledged the man with a friendly greeting. "Hello."

He offered a nervous smile but didn't reply.

Janine waved to get his full attention. "Hello. Are you a scientist or an engineer in your country?" The man gave her a blank stare, clearly confused.

Erica tried to stifle her sister. "Janine."

Wendy appeared with two glasses of iced water and set them on the table. Then she barked some crisp words at the man that neither Erica nor Janine understood. It could have been Hungarian, Norwegian, or Vulcan, for all she knew.

The man took a second to compose himself and then stumbled through what appeared to be a rehearsed greeting. "Gooood. After-noon." He lowered his head, picked up a tray, and fled.

Wendy apologized. "So sorry. My cousin Rodger is helping Tom for a few weeks. He's so shy of the beauty you both possess."

"Where's he from?" Janine inquired, sounding more like the amateur detective.

Wendy replied without missing a beat. "Connecticut." Janine's jaw snapped shut. "Would you like the usual, Ms. Erica?"

Erica suppressed a chuckle. It wasn't often that someone got the best of Janine. "Yes, please. Thank you, Wendy." Erica's usual was a spinach salad with blue cheese crumbles, cantaloupe, and blackened grilled shrimp.

"And for you, Ms. Janine?"

Unlike Erica's selection, which was actually listed on the menu, Janine made up food dishes to test Tom's skills as a chef. "Yes, let's seeeee. I think I'll get salmon, poached in some kind of dill sauce, potato dumplings like he made me that one time, and zucchini, if you have it, cut into ribbons, maybe sautéed with cherry tomatoes. That'll do it."

"Of course." Wendy bowed and left their table.

Erica waited until Wendy was gone. "Zucchini ribbons?" She rolled her eyes at her sister.

Janine relaxed in her chair. "You just watch. That crazy little bastard will make it for me. But, hey, did you see his whiskers?"

"Rodger's?"

"No, Wendy's."

Erica laughed in earnest. God help her, but she always laughed.

"I guess I might have to cancel my trip to Chicago."

"Why, what's up?" Erica's curiosity was genuinely piqued.

"Apparently, Davis's tiny dick." Janine sounded even more annoyed than she had been on the phone. "Tell me for real, what the hell did he want? Why is he sniffing around now?" She leaned forward over the table. "He didn't try anything, did he?"

Erica already made one mistake by mentioning Davis at all. Telling Janine that he tried to kiss her would be catastrophic. "I think his ego got pricked." How else could she explain it?

"Well, you got the prick part right."

She pointedly ignored Janine's comment. "He got a call last night from Walter Greenstein, who happened to be at the restaurant and saw me with Reese. It was a marvelous place, by the way, truly beautiful. And the food was delicious. So, thank you. We gave it top scores across the board."

Janine leaned back in her chair. "I remember sexy Walt. He must be hung like a horse because he seems like a real dick. And contrary to popular belief, when they act as arrogant as he does, it usually means they can back it up."

"I wouldn't know anything about his…*that*. Anyway, Davis has never had to deal with me possibly seeing anyone. And it didn't help matters that he saw the sexy underwear *and* found the box of condoms. *Thank you*." This time, she added the proper amount of sarcasm to her *thank you*.

"How the hell did he see your underwear?"

Erica huffed and surveyed the nearby tables to be sure no one was listening. "That's not important. But, between the underwear and the condoms, he thinks I'm sleeping with Reese."

Janine released a naughty smile. "So, did you?"

Erica placed her napkin on her lap. Inside, she turned into a sixteen-year-old girl talking about her first time. Only her first time, she was eighteen, and it was with Davis. "He invited me in, but I went home instead."

"You didn't go inside? Uh!" Janine uttered with exasperation and slammed her hand on the table.

A few heads turned at the loud noise. Erica waited until they lost interest before replying. "We—we kissed. That's all." Her cheeks flushed as she recalled the spectacular, lip-smashing, panty-wetting kiss. But listening to herself now, she kind of felt like a prude.

Janine peered down her nose. "I…I'm speechless. You're good at so many things. I just don't know how you can be so bad at this. Why didn't you just do it? You should've leaped all over that thing."

Erica leaned back in her seat. Unraveling Davis's behavior on her morning ride only took a mile to figure out. The rest of the miles were spent daydreaming of Reese and trying to understand why she didn't leap all over that thing.

Was it her age? Was she not hip enough to have a one-night stand? Or did she want more?

Men looked at her because she'd been blessed

with her grandmother's elegant features. But when Reese looked at her, it felt different. Sure, he offered a hot night of sex. But then what? How does she give her body to someone with no strings, no ties, and no emotion involved? Love versus lust. And what would it mean to him? Anything? Being with someone that way should mean something, and was it really so wrong to want to know the man first?

"We've been on one date, Janine. But I'll admit, I thought about it. Okay!" Her core muscles quivered. "He has something."

"What?" Janine lowered her voice. "Did he say that, or did you see some kind of rash?"

Erica snorted. "No. I don't mean like that. I feel drawn to him. I don't know how to explain it other than it's like he emits some kind of chemical. He, he's so…" Her words trailed away as his image came to mind. "He makes me want to—"

"Bend over, grab your ankles, and hold on for dear life?"

Erica snickered and waited for Janine's smart-aleck grin to disappear. Her sister could be so disgusting at times. But in this case, she was right. "Well…yeah."

Janine's eyes widened, and her jaw nearly smacked the table. "No fucking way. So much for Ms. Prim and Proper, huh? But hey, I know what this is. Guys like him have the Vee gene."

"The Vee gene?" Her skepticism rang clear.

"Yup, they call it the Vee gene because it forces women's legs open like a giant V."

An elderly couple walking past the table glared in horror, clearly having heard Janine's ill-timed explanation. Erica covered her face.

Janine disregarded her concerns. "They're old. They didn't hear me."

"I'm pretty sure they did." Erica shook her head and let her gaze wander outside through the window. "Vee gene." She snickered. "God, and not to mention he's only thirty-five."

"You're only forty? So what, Erica? I haven't seen you light up like this, well, ever. He did that. Hell, if you make each other happy, isn't that all that matters? Live a little, have some fun. Tomorrow isn't promised." Janine propped her elbows together on the table. "Right now, those five years can be interpreted as stamina. I'm sure he could make you all kinds of happy." Her wrists drifted apart, forming a V. "If you know what I mean?"

Erica's incessant gasp turned into an energetic chuckle. "I think Mom and Dad adopted you."

"Yeah, right. Hey, when are you going to see Stud Muffin again?"

"Maybe tomorrow. He might come by to put the mower back together."

"Is that all?" Janine shrilled.

"Yes, Janine. He'll have his son with him. And unlike you, I can restrain myself." Her playful tone was meant to sound superior.

Wendy appeared with their food. "Should you ladies need anything else, just ask William." She pointed to a man helping someone a few tables away. His English didn't sound all that great, either.

Maybe Janine was on to something after all.

****

The rain had stopped, but the pavement was still wet. Walking across the lot, Erica fished inside her purse for her keys. "So, how were your zucchini ribbons?"

"Perfect. I told you to try some. Zucchini is easy to overcook, but this was nice and firm. *He, he, he.* Did you get it? The zucchini was firm."

"Yeah. I got that."

"I don't like it *soft."* Janine giggled some more. "Next time, I'll see if he can do something with Brussels sprouts. Maybe shaved." Janine lifted her upper lip playfully.

"I happen to like Brussels sprouts. Don't ruin them for me."

They were almost to the Jeep when two police cars came flying into the parking lot near the other end of the shopping center. They screeched to a halt.

"Whoa." Janine's mouth stretched into a long O. "Someone's in trouble."

Red and blue lights sprayed the entire area as officers scurried from their vehicles and stormed toward the building. Through the pandemonium and excessive shouting, two officers started dragging someone toward their car. Recognition hit Erica like a bullet.

*Travis Baker.*

"Bring the car up." Erica shoved the keys toward Janine and hurried toward the chaos. One officer hoisted Travis's arms behind his back and then slammed his face onto the hood of a squad car. Erica ran the rest of the way.

"Hey!" she shouted with the authority of an angry mother. The officers closest to her responded like little boys ready to be scolded. She ignored them and shouldered her way through the wall of black uniforms to confront the one holding Travis.

"What's going on?" she demanded. The man's elbow pressed harder on the back of Travis's head.

"This doesn't concern you, Mrs. Gebhart." The lumbering officer shifted his weight and clicked the handcuffs closed with a satisfied sneer.

Travis squirmed from his awkward bent-over position across the hood. "Get your junk off me, Dude. I didn't do anything, Mrs. G. I just got here."

"Okay, I believe you, Travis."

Because of her involvement in the community several years back, she had some recollection of most of the small town's police staff. "Officer Wendham, is it? Let's figure out what's going on. And for God's sake, he's not resisting. There's no need to be so rough." She turned toward the other three officers standing around her. "Where is Chief Snyder?"

"Chief Snyder's inside the liquor store." Officer Barney Pascone was Kensington's own version of Barney Fife. Out of the four officers right next to her, he'd probably tell her anything she wanted to know.

Travis winced when his arms got tugged higher.

Inside, Erica was seething. "Officer Wendham, can you at least let him stand upright?" She'd never been this close to losing her trademark refinement.

The officer yanked Travis by the collar into a standing position—the ratty t-shirt and jacket he had on gathered and bunched next to his ears.

Erica took a necessary calming breath. "Now, Officer Pascone, could you explain this to me? Please."

The man visibly perked up, having been singled out amongst his peers. "Sure thing, Mrs. Gebhart." He cleared his throat in preparation. "Well, we received a call from Junior." He caught himself. "I mean, Mr. Stevenson, the owner of the liquor store. He notified us about a bunch of hoodlums inside. He said a few were milling around the candy counter when one of them knocked something from a shelf near the back. The two in the front did the grab and dash out the door. We arrived on the scene just after it all went down."

Erica turned toward Travis. He swiveled his neck, trying to loosen his disheveled clothes. She touched the glowing red mark on his cheek and straightened the front of his shirt for him. "Tell me what you saw."

"I don't know. I didn't do anything, but these peckers wouldn't listen. I swear, Mrs. G., I came around the corner and saw Kyle and Randy with those two chicks from the other day. About that time, I heard sirens, and they took off running. The next thing I know, I'm getting it up the ass from this dickhead."

"Travis," she cautioned, not wanting him to antagonize the situation further.

Wendham snickered. "We saw a couple of them running as we pulled up. This dumbass was just standing there."

Erica's brows arched higher. "That should tell you something, shouldn't it? Did you bother to ask him anything before you slammed him against your car?"

"We know this punk," Wendham barked.

Erica took a menacing step toward the pugnacious officer and lowered her voice. "Well, you, of all people, should know how appearances can be deceiving."

Marcus had seen Officer Wendham several times at one of the more flamboyant social clubs for men, even though he was married to a woman and had two children. If Erica's instincts were right, and they usually were, his wife was probably clueless about his extracurricular activities.

"Does your wife go with you to the clubs in Pittsburgh, Officer Wendham?"

Wendham's face paled, confirming her suspicions. And now, he knew—that she knew.

Chief Snyder and another officer exited the liquor store and came across the parking lot. With a flip of his wrist, he directed Pascone to remove the cuffs from Travis. "We just watched the video surveillance. It appears Mr. Baker wasn't with this group and never entered the store. He was crossing the street as the others ran out. He's not part of this."

Travis rubbed his wrists and began taunting his innocence. "That's what I told you, motherfuckers."

Erica's swift glance stifled his foolish celebration. "Is he free to go?"

"For now, yes, ma'am," Chief Snyder answered with relief.

"Go get in my car, Travis. I'll take you home." After he was far enough away, she gave each man a formidable glare. "I believe you have some hoodlums to catch. Good day, gentlemen."

Erica used the time walking toward the Jeep to gather her emotions. It angered her to think about what may have happened to Travis had she not been there. Even though he was innocent, he probably would have acted out enough to get into trouble another way.

She opened the door of the Jeep and climbed behind the wheel. Janine remained eerily quiet in the passenger seat, and from the rearview mirror, she waited for Travis to make eye contact. Once he did, he gave her a timid smile.

"Are you hungry, Travis?"

"I... I don't have any money."

The police lights from across the lot stopped flashing, and all but a few of the squad cars drove away. The incident was over with a simple flip of a switch.

"That's not what I asked you."

He watched the police leave. "I don't know."

Erica started the Jeep and drove to the town's only fast-food restaurant. She ordered Travis the large combo of a burger with fries. He practically inhaled the food before she even got out of the drive-thru.

Travis's house wasn't too far away. He lived on the other side of the tracks, both metaphorically and physically. One might even say that this part of town was buried under the old train wreckage, behind the heap of seedy activities and run-down dwellings.

Eric turned left onto Prospect Ave. The irony was immeasurable. Rows of low-income homes lined either side of the road. Broken shutters dangled from the weathered facades, and nearly every structure had at least one window covered with plywood. A waterlogged sofa crowded the front porch of one house, padding from the ripped cushions scattered over the front lawn like clumps of dirty snow.

An old work van on three wheels and a cinder block rusted away on the corner lot next to two gutted washing machines. She made a right turn onto Optimism Court. Trash cans lined both sides of the streets, with more trash floating around them than in them.

Erica pulled over at the third house on the right where Travis lived. Watching him in the mirror, her heart pinged with sadness. Shame smothered him like a blanket, but he eventually got out. She met him next to the front walk. "Are you okay, Travis?"

He stole a fleeting glimpse at his house. His features pulled tight. "Yeah, thanks for the burger, Mrs. G."

"You're welcome, Travis."

He gave her a spontaneous nod and started up the cracked, weed-ridden sidewalk. He'd only taken a few steps when he stopped and turned. Tears welled thick in his eyes. "Why does this keep happening to me?"

Erica stepped toward him. "I don't know."

"You believed me, didn't you?"

"Of course I did, Travis. I believe in you too. You have the potential to be anything you want. Don't ever let anyone tell you differently." His body trembled from emotions too big for his young mind. Erica closed the distance between them just as he fell to pieces. She placed motherly arms around him, struggling to suppress her own benevolent feelings. His sobs nearly broke her heart.

After a minute, he seemed to remember himself by sucking in a shaky breath and sniffing the moment away. "See ya, Mrs. G." He stepped away, shoved his hands into his pockets, and loped the remaining distance to his house. The door of his private hell opened and closed quickly. A muffled shout competed with the loud television playing from the darkness inside.

"Goodnight, Travis," she whispered. Getting back into the car, she found Janine wiping her eyes.

"Is that the kid you were telling me about?"

"Yes. He's got a rough road ahead." *Hopefully, he'll choose the right one.*

# J. ALISON COLE

## Chapter Eight

The air in the upper barn was thick and stuffy, but the beams still carried the sweet smell of straw even though a bale hadn't been present in the loft since she'd lived here. Not even for nonexistent barn sex.

The hamster cage had to be here, somewhere. Erica moved two more boxes marked *Beautification Committee*. Why did she still have these? She slid those boxes aside and caught a flash of neon green peeking from underneath the folded flap of the box on the floor.

*At last.*

From outside, the sound of stones crackling against tires carried through the gabled shutters at the end of the barn. Erica grabbed the box in a frantic heap and darted for the stairs. Halfway down, she slowed. It didn't sound like Reese's truck. She stepped out of the barn just in time to see Steve heading for her front door.

"Steve." She waved to get his attention. "What can I do for you?" She sat the box down on the end knee wall of the patio.

Steve Koontz adjusted the brim of a well-worn John Deere mesh ball cap. "Erica." His blonde lashes fluttered, and his cheeks were as red as the rose bushes blooming along the side of the house. Okay, so maybe she'd always sensed he had a little crush, but ignoring it somehow made it easier on both of them.

His lips twitched with a warm smile. "I ran into Reese this morning, and he asked if I'd put your mower back together. He had something come up." His smile faded. "You know, you could have asked me to fix your mower." He actually sounded hurt.

"Gosh, Steve. I know you're a busy man, and

113

well, Reese happened to stop by while I was working on it and just offered."

"I've told you before, if you needed anything—anything at all, to let me know." The weathered wrinkles around his eyes deepened.

"I'll remember that for next time, promise. Come on. It's in the garage."

Thirty-five minutes later, Steve Koontz turned the key to the mower. Two clouds of black smoke belched from the exhaust. He made a quick adjustment with a screwdriver, and the engine settled into a steady hum.

Steve spoke over the running motor. "Now, don't set the blades any lower. It will only kill the grass. Leave it here, where I put it." He turned the key off and shoved the dirty, oil-stained rag into his rear pocket.

Erica handed him a tall glass of raspberry lemonade. "Here, I brought you something to drink. You've earned it."

He drank the entire glass without stopping and then swiped the back of his hand across his lips. "Augh, that was delicious, thank you." The brim of his hat received a tug. "You know, if you're not planning on mowing everything, I could probably rent those seven acres along the back fence for something. I made the same offer to Davis a ways back." He glanced away. "Before the divorce. Just something to think about." He shifted his hat again. Apparently, mentioning the divorce made him uncomfortable.

"Sounds good to me. I'd rather you put the ground to good use. Do I need to sign something?"

He couldn't disguise his surprise. "Sure, but shouldn't you discuss this with him first?"

Erica took no offense. Steve was an old-fashioned, traditional man in every sense of the word. The thought of her—a woman, making a decision without the input of a man, aka—her husband, or in this case, even her ex-husband, would seem foreign to him. Plus, he probably thought Davis still owned the house.

"It will be fine, trust me," she reassured him.

Another tug had his hat sitting on his ears. "I...I can give you some time to think about it. Talk it over if you need."

"No need. Bring the papers by any time. I can sign them for you." She laid a hand on his shoulder, using her best networking smile, hoping to dismiss his apprehension. "And thank you for putting this back together."

Steve's cheeks brightened from her tactful but innocuous contact. "Sure thing. I'll let Reese know I got your motor running." His expression blanked. "On the mower. Mower motor, that is." His eyes shot to the concrete floor of the garage, and he adjusted his hat. One of these times, the brim was going to come off. "I gotta go."

Steve backed out of the driveway, and she reentered the garage. *Reese couldn't come. Maybe he didn't want to.* That was hard to imagine, especially after the way he'd kissed her. *Was he brushing her off because they were too different? Or was she really so horny that she'd misread everything?* Her rock-solid instincts begged otherwise while begging for him in general. She'd never been so reckless. But Janine was right. When was the last time she felt that way? *Never.* Should she be worried or excited?

Erica placed the owner's manual on the workbench and climbed onto the seat. She cranked the key, and the machine rumbled beneath her. Next, she checked the levers, pedals, and gauges. Then, with a firm grip on the steering wheel, she set off and mowed the grass.

An hour and a half later, Erica stood at the kitchen window admiring her handy work. Other than a few skippers and one small patch she missed completely, she approved. She sipped her tea slowly. It would've been nice if mowing freed her mind the same way riding did. Because now, she had a lot more questions.

## Chapter Nine

"Stay where I can see you, Sawyer." Reese stopped his son from sneaking around the corner into the next aisle.

"You said I could look at the toys," Sawyer whined.

"I said after I find what I'm looking for."

The boy sighed. "Aw, man."

"Hey. Patience." Reese cocked his head and made googly eyes. He'd never been able to be overly stern with his son. Sawyer laughed. The boy was just too cute. "Just give me another minute."

"Fine," Sawyer said, less pouty.

Reese turned back toward the book rack. The one thing about Jackson's Hardware and Pharmacy was they had a little bit of everything. Knowing how people in this town treated Erica, surely they'd have a copy of her book. But the books didn't appear to be in any specific order. How did they expect people to find anything? *National Geographic* and *Health* magazines were layered with *Motor Week* and *Classic Trucks*. *Better Homes and Gardening* was stacked between *Guns & Ammo* and *Birds and Hunting*.

The novels, sitting on the front of the self, all paperback, depicted Vikings, vampires, and southern belles with torn bodices. He picked up one that had a pirate holding the mast of a ship amid a storm and a woman curled around his leg.

Did women really like this kind of stuff?

"I never would've guessed those are the kind of books you read."

Reese turned toward the voice behind him. Erica stood about four feet away with a large bag of chicken feed hanging against her hip.

A surge of something he hadn't felt in a very long time washed over him. He put the book back onto the self and huffed. "You caught me."

She set the bag on the floor next to her feet, got up, and then pushed a few strands of hair behind her ears. "I'm only teasing. Of course." Her hands landed on her hips in an easy stance.

Her flowy linen shirt and khaki shorts might look casual on anyone else, but on her, it was somehow casual and classy.

It was hard to take his eyes off her. "Me too. And if you must know, I was looking for your book." *Damn, she's beautiful. And her mouth is amazing.*

"Oh," she said with a sudden look of guilt.

"I'm surprised they don't have it here."

"Well actually, they do. They have a special display near the front of the store." She looked semi-mortified telling him this.

"Ah, I see."

A smile stretched over her gorgeous mouth. "But I only do book signings on the first Monday of the month. You'll have to wait 'til then."

"So I shall." Reese checked over his shoulder to see if Sawyer was still at the end of the aisle.

She tucked a strand of hair behind her ear and followed his gaze. "Anyway, how are you? I hope everything is okay."

Now it was his turn to feel guilty. "Oh, yeah. I'm sorry I wasn't able to come by over the weekend. I had a..." *Don't even try to explain.* "A bit of a family emergency. But everybody is okay. I just had to take care of some stuff."

"Steve said as much."

"Ms. Erica." Sawyer charged by him and

slammed into her.

"Whoa, take it easy, buddy. You'll knock her over."

"It's fine. Hello, Sawyer. How are you?"

"I'm good. I just left Ms. Robin's. She's going to watch me when Dad's at work. I asked him if you could watch me, but he said no. Did you know Ms. Robin has a little boy my age? His name is Joey. I'll probably have more fun with him anyway. Hey, guess what? I got a new bike, and Daddy told me that it's a lot nicer than yours. I can go real fast and do wheelies."

Erica took a big breath. "I do, in fact, know Ms. Robin and Joey, and I'm sure you will have way more fun with him. Your new bike sounds fantastic, and yes, I can safely say it's nicer than mine. Your wheels probably turn."

"Hey, Dad, can we look at the toys now?"

"Hold on, Sawyer, let's help Ms. Erica with this bag of feed."

She bent over and had it anchored back on her hip before he had a chance to help. "That's all right, I got it. Hey, Sawyer, did you get your hamster yet?"

"No, not yet."

"Good, I've got something for you. I'll bring it by this weekend."

From the back of the store, the group of old men shouted from their huddle. They'd been watching the whole time. "Goodbye, Mrs. Gebhart."

Erica glanced in that direction first. She gave those men a sweet smile and a nod. "Gentlemen." Then her eyes shifted toward him and her gaze dropped to his lips. "Reese."

His groin tightened. *Holy shit.* "Erica."

**J. ALISON COLE**

## Chapter Ten

Erica rounded the bend where the three tenant houses sat in a straight line next to the road. A flash of blue confirmed Sawyer riding his bicycle into the backyard.

She'd barely turned onto the driveway before Reese came out of the side door and flashed his dazzling smile. Her pulse quickened at the mere sight of him—and what he was wearing. Today, he wore a simple, gray cotton button-up. The torn-out sleeves showcased impeccable biceps, and his faded jeans were nearly white—what was left of them anyway. The frayed material exposed his thighs and the bottom edges of the pockets. *Not only a member of the "Look good in jeans club"—he'd be the president.*

Even in rags, the man stirred her juices. She stepped out of the Jeep and walked to the front of the vehicle.

"Hi, Ms. Erica." Sawyer reappeared and rode a circle around her before coming to a skidding halt.

"A bike that works. Can I borrow it?"

Sawyer scoffed. "Nah, you're too big. Hey, watch me do a wheelie."

"Okay." She watched until he rode out of sight behind the corner of the house. Then, her attention shifted back to Reese. He'd been watching her, and she liked it.

He took a meaningful step closer. "So, how does the mower work?"

Erica relaxed against the front of the Jeep. "I used it a couple of days ago. I think that I did quite well."

"I have no doubt." Reese glanced over his shoulder, doing a quick search for Sawyer. Stepping closer, his hands landed on either side of her against the hood, virtually pinning her to the grill.

The blue in his eyes looked like sapphires today as he inched closer. Her body warmed as his weight eased against her. Then his minty breath brushed along the top edge of her mouth. She fingered the delicate hairs along the base of his neck, nearly paralyzed with anticipation and longing. After two light passes, his lips claimed hers.

A tiny whimper escaped the back of her throat. The man tasted like heaven. He replied with a needy groan.

His thumbs skimmed over the bottom of her aching breasts. She arched against him, and the kiss intensified, their tongues venturing deeper, each wanting more of the other.

When their mouths parted, Reese panted. Then he cupped her chin and ran a thumb across her bottom lip. "I guess I wasn't the only one that needed to get that out of their system."

Her body ached for him, and it felt like the most natural thing in the world to swirl her hips against the distinct hardness pressing her midsection.

Reese lowered his eyelids, enjoying the feeling as much as she did. He gave her a faint, deviant smile right before he glanced over his shoulder.

They weren't alone. Sawyer was nearby. *So much for restraint.*

He blew out a determined breath and levered his body away from hers, rubbing his face. Then he reached down and brazenly adjusted things.

Erica followed his every move. Who would've ever thought that watching a man shift a substantial erection could be so stimulating? She couldn't deny the satisfaction of knowing she did this to him. Her gaze lingered on the elongated bulge. "Well, well, well." Desire burned in his glowing eyes. At least she wasn't alone.

Reese gave the pucker on the front of his jeans one last tug. "Just so you know, this isn't the first time you made that happen." He leaned against the hood of the Jeep beside her and took another calming breath. His head drifted back, and his shirt gaped open from a missing button. A light spattering of chest hair caught her eye.

Before she could stop herself, she ran a finger over his bare skin at the lowest secured button. "You're missing a button." His skin was warm.

"It's an old shirt."

She pulled her hand away. "It looks good on you." His smile turned bashful. *How adorable and intriguing.*

Sawyer reappeared from the side of the house, jostling her memory for the real reason she came by. "Let me get this cage for you."

"Hey, Sawyer. Ms. Erica brought something for you."

Sawyer's eyes widened with disbelief when she lifted the box from the rear of the Jeep. He carried it to the small front porch and went into a frenzy, organizing the pieces by size and shape.

"Thanks, Ms. Erica. Dad, can we go to the store and get my hamster now?"

"Not right now. We're getting ready to eat, remember?" Reese flexed his shoulders before his gaze swept toward her. "I was going to throw some hot dogs on the grill. Would you like to join us?"

*Wieners.* "Uh, no, but thank you."

Leave it to Janine to ruin something as simple as hot dogs, not because they were made with the hooves and snouts and all the other gross leftover parts—no, her dear sister once said there was no way to eat a hot dog in front of a hot guy and not imagine it as his dick. Reese was definitely a hot guy, and Erica was already thinking about his wiener.

A brow shot up on Reese's forehead. "What? You don't eat hot dogs."

"Of course, I like wieners." *I said wieners.* "But I have—plans." *Yup,* plans on beating the heck out of her sister. "Maybe next time I'll...stay for a hot dog." *Lord, I've got to get out of here.* She patted Sawyer on the shoulder. "Have fun, Sawyer."

Sawyer was halfway through the box, too consumed to look up. "Thank you, Ms. Erica. I'll let you know when I get my hamster."

"Sounds good."

Reese walked her to the Jeep and opened the driver's door. "That was really thoughtful. Thank you again, Erica." He propped one arm along the roof and the other on the door—boxing her in the narrow space.

It somehow felt cozy and more private, away from little eyes. "You're welcome." The urge to touch the whiskers on his chin bubbled to the surface. This time, she didn't hold back. Her fingertips raked over his jaw. The scruff was somehow bristly yet soft. What would it feel like against her flesh—or the softer skin between her thighs?

From his heated gaze, she could tell he wondered the same.

Then his chin twisted in her hand as he bent to kiss the center of her palm. The slightest wind could've knocked her over.

The blistering sexual tension was disrupted by a vehicle swerving around the far bend in the road. It was moving quickly and recklessly, spewing dust into the air.

Reese stepped away from the Jeep and moved Sawyer's discarded bike from the middle of the driveway to the yard.

At first, he seemed okay, but a scowl soon pinched the center of his forehead. He cleared his throat. "It's my daughter." His voice grew hoarse. "And my ex."

"I can get going," she offered.

"No, just stay for a minute. It's probably nothing." The crease over his brow deepened. "I hope." The vehicle rounded the last curve, spitting stones into the yard of the house next door.

The skin on Erica's arms prickled. *Huh. A silver Honda with a green door.* The car lunged into the driveway, and before it came to a complete stop, the passenger door flew open. A young girl jumped out, yelling and screaming at the driver.

Erica barely heard the profanities. Recognition hit in the form of bright fluorescent pink streaks going through the girl's hair.

She was one of the girls from Jackson's parking lot. And that meant Reese's daughter was one of the hoodlums involved in the trouble at the liquor store.

"I hate you! I hate you!" the girl screamed before slamming the car door closed. "I'm not living with her anymore." Sidestepping Reese, the girl headed for the side door of his house.

The green door on the driver's side of the Honda opened, and a petite woman with the air of California climbed out. She was a Malibu Barbie incarnate, tight and tanned, wearing a midriff cutoff t-shirt and Daisy Dukes. The only thing that didn't fit the pin-up poster image was the cigarette clamped between pinched lips.

Suddenly, forty felt much, much older.

"What the hell's going on, Steph?" Reese demanded.

Steph approached, giving Erica the stink eye. She answered Reese without bothering to look at him. "You wanted her. She's your problem now." Her lips pursed around the cigarette, drawing a puff. "Who the hell are you?"

Reese touched Erica's elbow. "This is Erica Gebhart. Erica, this is Stephanie Collins, Kara's mother."

The woman's dull expression changed on a dime. "Oh my God, you're Erica Gebhart. I've heard of you. Heck, everyone around here has heard of you." She stepped forward, offering her hand. "How in God's name do you know him?" Stephanie's expression lit up again. "Aren't you good friends with Dr. Phil or something? And you've been on television with that lady, the one kind of like Martha Stewart? Oh, I can't think of her name. I told Kara you lived somewhere around here. How cool is this?"

"I've never met Dr. Phil, and I think you mean Rachel...Ray. I don't know her personally. She only mentioned my book. I work at the high school as a counselor."

Reese shifted impatiently. "Stephanie, maybe you could wait inside. We'll get Kara settled once and for all."

Stephanie glared at Reese. "Sure." Then she gave Erica one last smile. "It was nice to meet you." Walking toward the side door, she called for Sawyer using baby talk. "Hey, how's my sweetie?" He stared at her but said nothing.

Stephanie ignored the slight and disappeared into the house. A series of loud shouts followed.

Reese's eyes darkened like clouds before a harsh storm. "My daughter got into some trouble last weekend. We sat her down and had a serious talk." He turned away and kicked at a couple of loose stones in the driveway.

Erica could almost see the thick slab of concrete coming up between them. "Having a teenager can be rough." She wanted to make him feel better. But truthfully, she couldn't relate. Lauren never loitered on street corners or knocked off liquor stores. Her daughter had been a happy and well-balanced teen—a true blessing.

He spun back around, a sneer marring his otherwise perfect lips. "Nice try." A crash came from inside the house. His broad hands snaked through his dark blonde hair, wholly distraught. "I don't know what I was thinking. Look, I moved here to make things right. And I need to do that." A bitterness entered his voice. "It's...it's not something you can be a part of. I'm sorry." He turned and walked away.

*What just happened?*

# J. ALISON COLE

## Chapter Eleven

Reese marched toward the front porch, fighting the urge to turn around and explain himself. *No, just let her go. She probably can't get out of here fast enough.* His jaw tightened when the Jeep started. And he damn near broke a tooth at the sound of her backing out of the driveway.

Sawyer was squatting behind the railing, trying to make himself small. Guilt poured over Reese. He'd done a shitty job of shielding his son from the drama and turmoil that seemed to find him no matter where he lived.

He flopped onto the top step and gestured for Sawyer to join him. The boy's lanky frame crawled closer. "I'm sorry, Sawyer." Reese offered him a shoulder-to-shoulder cuddle and ran a hand over his son's dark curls.

Innocent, bright blue eyes met his. "It's okay, Dad. I know you're trying."

It almost hurt to laugh. "Thank you." More shouts resonated from inside the house. Reese took a long, calming breath, hoping to harness his inner frustrations. "Hey buddy, it's probably best to stay out here for a few minutes. Until I get things inside straightened out."

"Don't worry. I'm not going in *there*." Sawyer picked at the fraying edge of the cardboard box. "Hey, Dad?"

"Yeah?"

"Can we still have hot dogs?"

"You bet."

\*\*\*\*

Reese entered the side door into the kitchen. The table was two feet from where it belonged, and one of the chairs was teetering against the refrigerator.

"You're nothing but a little whore," Stephanie huffed through the cloud of smoke from her cigarette.

Reese charged forward, plucking the cigarette from Stephanie's lips. "I told you before not to smoke in here." He tossed the cigarette in the sink and doused it with water. "Take a seat, both of you."

From across the room, Kara argued back at her mother. "Like mother, like daughter then. Did you know Mom's cheating on Curtis? *Again*." The contempt in her voice was perfectly calculated. "And she has the nerve to call *me* a whore. How many does that make, Mom?"

"I said, sit down." It took most of Reese's control to keep the volume of his voice at an even kilt. He was so tired of the yelling.

Stephanie sat down. "I'm done with her, Reese."

"Fine," Kara spat. "I hate living with you. Talk about a fucked-up family. What kind of woman has four kids by four different men? At least with *him*, it's only two."

"That he knows of anyway." Stephanie smirked.

Ignoring Stephanie's jab, he braced Kara by her shoulders and steered her toward the table. She plopped onto the chair.

He knelt in front of her. "Kara, you're thirteen years old. You don't need to talk that way."

"What's the matter, *Dad*?" She pronounced "Dad" with extra clarity to point out his absence in her upbringing. "Are you afraid I'll be a bad influence on your precious son?"

Reese took the hit. What choice did he have? "I'm here now, Kara. And I'm just saying that little girls who talk like that don't stay little for long."

"Mom talks like that."

"And look how that turned out." Putting

Stephanie down wasn't his intent, even though saying it aloud felt good.

"You son of a bitch. Like you've never messed up," Stephanie snarled.

"I've messed up plenty and made more than my share of mistakes." His gaze reconnected with Kara's. "The trick is, you have to learn from them. At the end of the day, ask yourself what kind of person you want to be."

"Oh, my god, you think you're better than me now." Stephanie tossed her hair over her shoulder. "I need a smoke."

Reese stood, placing his hands on his hips. "Yeah, but you can't do it here. Just go, Stephanie. I think you've already said all you needed to say."

Stephanie's glare swept over Kara before landing on him. "Good luck. I'll get the rest of her shit together."

"Perfect," he said with a hint of sarcasm. "I'll walk you out." He wanted her out of his house. *And out of his life.* But sharing a daughter made that impossible. Watching her taillights disappear couldn't happen fast enough for him.

Reese reentered the house and found Kara in the living room, flipping through television channels. He snatched the remote and turned the TV off. She let out an exhausted huff.

"I meant what I said before. Living here, you follow my rules. You *won't* guilt me into letting you do whatever you want. We need to give each other a chance. Do you understand?"

Her eyes rolled before mumbling, "Yeah."

"I mean it." He hoped that he sounded convincing. This would be new for her, heck it was new for him, and as far as he was concerned, she was right, and they were all fucked up in some way.

And that's what had him worried the most.

****

The hot dogs burnt, and the oven-baked French fries were limp and soggy. The air fryer was still in storage with the rest of his stuff.

Ironically, he hoped dinner was the only thing he messed up.

In one week, he'd gone from a leisure dad to a full-time father of two on his own, in a small rented house, working as a farmhand. It was all happening out of order.

But it was happening, whether he was ready or not.

The tenant house only had two bedrooms, so, for now, Reese took the couch. He peeked over the back of the sofa, checking the clock above the sink in the kitchen. It was just after nine o'clock at night. Sawyer had fallen asleep an hour ago, but a thin strip of light was still visible under Kara's bedroom door. Every so often, her girly laughter mingled with the soft music she had playing.

Taking her phone away might've been a better punishment, but knowing that Kara had a way to get a hold of him was more for his own state of mind. Therefore, his first official act of parenting his thirteen-year-old daughter was to put her on house arrest for two weeks. No mall, no movies, no friends over. And no more roaming all over town. That was just asking for trouble.

Apparently, Stephanie let her get away with a lot. She even tried to laugh off the liquor store incident as kids being kids. But actions had consequences. It was better that Kara learn that lesson sooner rather than later. Out of the little group in the store, his daughter got off lucky. She told him she had no idea what they were planning, and the video somewhat confirmed it. When they ran, she appeared confused but took off running just the same.

Reese sighed. This was *not* how he envisioned rebuilding his relationship with his daughter. And Erica was right. Getting back the time he lost was impossible. All he could do was move forward from here.

Reese twisted his chin, trying to relieve the pressure of a mounting headache. His gaze landed on his cell phone, teetering near the edge of the coffee table. He acted like such an asshole. The least he could do was apologize to Erica.

His eyes closed. Thinking of her somehow soothed his frazzled nerves. When she showed up today, he'd only meant to kiss her lightly, but that plan was shot to shit the moment their lips met. "Damn." He hissed.

*And the way she moaned.*

He conjured the memory of the first time he saw her. He'd only been in town for two days. Paul Koontz had just hired him, and they went for a bite to eat at that Italian restaurant in the shopping center. When Erica walked in, heads turned with admiration and respect, men and women alike. He'd never witnessed someone enter a room and create a stir like that. Small-town celebrity or not, he instantly knew she was someone special.

The following day, in the truck with Steve, they spotted her riding along the highway. Steve, the man whose conversations rarely exceeded a handful of words, chirped non-stop for a solid twenty minutes, sharing borderline stalkerish details of what he knew about her. Learning that she was divorced is what surprised him the most. *Who would divorce her, or better yet, why?*

But he'd never forget that day in the restaurant with Paul. Erica was wearing a navy blue wraparound dress, the clingy kind. It hugged her slim waist and accentuated her perfectly sized breasts—not small or overly big, just a good, firm handful. She glided through the restaurant in killer spiked heels that showcased her calves and slender legs—poised, confident, and sexy as hell. Her chestnut brown hair was loose and wavy around her face, and every so often, she'd tuck a few strands behind her ear that made the light jump off her gold earrings when she laughed. He knew they were gold because she laughed a lot that day, and he couldn't take his eyes off her, just like every other straight, hot-blooded man in the room over the age of fifteen.

Not that he was a wildebeest or a fug-ugly Neanderthal, but it seemed reasonable to question why someone like her would want anything to do with a man like him, especially after today.

Reese opened his eyes as a hollowed breath emptied his lungs. *Fuck it.* He snatched his phone from the table and scrolled for Erica's number before he could change his mind.

"Hello." Her voice cracked with sleepiness.

*Shit.* "Erica. Did I wake you? I know it's late. I'm sorry."

"No, I'm waiting for the news to come on. I was actually hoping you'd call."

"Really?" A pang of silence carried the moment.

"Yeah."

He sighed. "I…wanted to apologize."

"For what?"

*For the clusterfuck that is my life.* "For the commotion you had to see. I didn't think it was going to play out like that. Otherwise, I never would've asked you to stay." His eyes pinched shut.

*Calling was a mistake.* Now that she had a glimpse of the bullshit he was dealing with, she'd distance herself away with all the grace and dignity he didn't deserve. *Dammit.*

"Reese, I was wondering if Wednesday might be a good day for you guys?"

"A good day for what?"

"I owe you dinner, plus it will give me a chance to meet your daughter. The right way."

He laughed cynically. "Erica, you don't need to do this."

"Wednesday, 6:30 PM, my house?"

After two long breaths, Reese swallowed his earlier frustrations. "All right. Wednesday, 6:30 PM."

"Goodnight, Reese."

"Goodnight, Erica."

# J. ALISON COLE

## Chapter Twelve

"Erica, you told me two days ago that you'd call me back."

"I'm sorry, Marcus, but the last two days have flown by. Yesterday, I had to take Janine to the airport, and then I had some things to pick up from the grocery store."

"Would this be for your special dinner?"

She had the receiver pinched between her shoulder and chin while heading toward the sink to wash out her coffee mug from the morning. "It's just...a dinner."

"If I didn't know any better, I'd say you sound a little anxious." Marcus snickered into the phone. "You're usually the Rock of Gibraltar. In the two years I've never known you, I've never seen you anxious about anything."

She didn't know how to respond except to be perturbed. She grabbed the dishrag from the side of the sink and took out her frustrations on a spot on the counter. "What is it that you needed, Marcus?"

"Okay, okay, look, the reason I called. The bike sale I told you about ends today. You need a new bike, and they have a payment plan."

"It's a great deal, but I know what shopping with you can be like. We'll be gone all day."

"It's ten o'clock in the morning. I promise I'll have you back home by two. I'm only thinking of you, Erica."

"Two o'clock?"

"Yes. I'm already on my way."

\*\*\*\*

At ten past four, Erica pushed her new bicycle

through the front door. She propped it next to the sofa in the sunroom and stormed into the kitchen to finish prepping her dinner. Thankfully, the chicken had been marinating since morning, and macaroni and cheese didn't take long to prepare. The salad was even quicker.

Once the mac-n-cheese went into the oven, she headed to the patio to set the table. Having dinner outside would be less formal than in the dining room, and the evening weather was perfect for what she had planned once they finished eating.

Four years ago, they'd painted a large white square on one end of the barn. Davis set up a projector in one of the smaller outbuildings and several outdoor speakers in a few of the flower beds, thus creating *Movie Night at the Gebhart's*. It quickly became a revered neighborhood event of summer. Plus, it made entertaining fun and easy. Who didn't love watching a movie outside on the side of a giant building?

At six o'clock, Erica placed a pan of store-bought pinwheel appetizers in the oven. Then she lit the grill. While that was heating, she checked the drinks in the small outdoor refrigerator: a jug of iced tea, various sodas, and the same beer Reese had ordered at the restaurant.

The chicken landed on the grates with a sizzle, and when the lid lowered, she had ten minutes to spare.

She popped the cork from a bottle of Pinot Noir and poured herself a glass. Over the years she'd learned enough about wine to know that it would pair perfectly with the meal. It was also one of her favorites. The sun glowed through the rich, dark liquid like a giant ruby. She swirled the liquid in the glass before enjoying the first sip. *Dry, silky tannins with earthy notes of cherry and raspberry.*

She made her way across the patio and

straightened a paisley cushion on one of the wicker chairs circling the fire pit before sitting down.

The back of her head lay against the comfy cushion. She couldn't have asked for a more perfect evening. Overhead, an azure sky sculpted the horizon before stretching toward the heavens. On the recently "mowed" lawn, a pair of robins danced around one another. A few feathers floated over the grass. Was this some kind of mating ritual? She'd seen a rooster mount the chickens before. It appeared aggressive, almost vicious. *Huh.* It also seemed that she watched animals having sex more than she thought. The robins flew away.

She tipped the glass again, savoring the wine and this moment of clarity. All felt right in the world for the first time in a long time. Her world, at least. All the pieces of the puzzle were there. She could almost see Reese in that final image.

The rumble of an engine echoed somewhere across the fields. The wine in her belly warmed. Reese and his children would be here soon.

After the longest minute of her life, Sawyer jumped from the truck first. He ran across the patio and slammed her with a bear hug. "Guess what? I got my hamster. You should see it. It's a boy, and he runs on the wheel all night long."

"I can't wait to meet your hamster." His enthusiasm had the same infectious results as before.

Reese strode up beside his son, looking utterly delectable—and his man scent was more intoxicating than a whole bottle of wine. He leaned in and gave her a friendly kiss on the cheek, perfectly restrained, no doubt for the benefit of the children. After their last kiss, she could totally appreciate the need for propriety. No kid needed to witness their father making out.

"Did he mention that it runs all night?" Reese

added a note of fun sarcasm. "How can I ever thank you?"

*I can think of a few ways.* The naughty thought made her pause and giggle. "I guess I should have warned you it might squeak some. I have some WD-40 in the shed if you need it."

"Thanks, but I have some, and I told Kara she could have a fish," he said mockingly.

Kara joined them. She looked like she wanted to be there as much as someone about to have a root canal.

"Hi Kara, I'm Erica."

"Hey." A bored breath followed her dismal greeting.

"Behind the counter, there's a small fridge with some drinks: iced tea, water, and sodas. Help yourselves." Erica glanced at Reese. "I also have wine and beer. I need to grab the appetizers. I'll be right back. Make yourselves comfortable."

Erica filled a platter with the swirly ham and cheese pinwheels and returned to the patio. Thanks to her unexpected shopping trip with Marcus, she didn't get to put together her signature Grilled Potato, Onion, and Bacon Skewers. Getting them to look right required time she didn't have. Her other go-to appetizer was Garlicky Marinated grilled mushrooms. But mushrooms could be tricky when it comes to kids. The pinwheels were her backup. Chapter Six of her book, *Always Have a Backup*.

Reese brought her glass of wine over from the fire pit. "Do you need any help?"

"That'd be great." She handed him the tongs. "Here. Could you check on the chicken for me? I'll get you a beer."

"Sure, and thanks." Reese took the pinchers and flipped a few pieces, dodging the rogue flames that shot up. He adjusted one of the knobs.

"Still have your eyebrows." Erica handed him a beer.

"I think so. You tell me."

She stared into his eyes, not bothering to check his eyebrows. "Everything...looks...good."

"Thanks for the beer." After a long swig, he doused her with one of his sexy smiles. "I turned the flame back a little."

A wave of heat swept over her body. She couldn't tell if it was coming off the grill or him. "Could have fooled me."

"What?"

"Nothing." Sawyer's boisterous laugh drew her attention away from Reese. "Hey, guess what, Sawyer?"

Sawyer picked up an appetizer. "What?" He took a small nibble first, approving of the taste, before shoving the whole thing into his mouth.

"I have three laying chickens, and yesterday, four eggs hatched. Do you want to see the new chicks?"

"Yeah." A full mouth muffled his response. He crammed a second appetizer in before smearing his hands over his khaki shorts.

Kara was slumped low in a chair by the firepit with her nose crammed into her phone.

"Kara, would you like to see them too?" Erica asked.

Reese closed the lid of the grill and answered for his daughter. "Sure, she would. Come on."

Kara scoffed and shoved her phone into her rear pocket. "Whatever."

Sawyer followed Erica inside the small chicken coup. The older chickens clucked and squawked to get out of the way as the tiny chicks corralled themselves into one corner. Erica carefully handed Sawyer two of the baby chicks. He raced outside and offered one to Kara.

She took it hesitantly. "It's so tiny and so soft."

Reese was smiling with his daughter. He stood semi-propped against the side of the coup with one ankle casually crossed over the other. Erica used the unguarded moment to drink in the sight of him. A charcoal-colored Henley fit snugly over his shoulders and torso. His jeans were button-fly, not that she intentionally studied that area of his anatomy at great lengths. It was evident by the faded marks left by the underlying buttons, and she knew jeans—and yeah, she saw the marks when she looked at his crotch.

Her hormones must be raging.

*Hormones, whore moans. He'd make anyone moan.*

Reese looked up and caught her ogling. His stance shifted, and for a brief moment, he appeared *bothered.* Hot and bothered, but in a good way—a really good way.

But this wasn't the time or the place. Erica shifted her focus back to Kara and Sawyer.

Sawyer held up his hand. "Look, Dad, mine pooped on me."

Kara squealed. "Yuck. Take it, take it, take it. I don't want it crapping on me." Sawyer smeared his hand over a bale of straw and rescued the chick from his half-sister.

Erica released the chicks back into the pen and secured the latch on the door. "I think dinner is close to being done by now. Let's get washed up."

"Can we use the little sink outside?" Sawyer asked with renewed enthusiasm.

"Sure. It works."

He took off running, but Kara yanked on the back of Sawyer's shirt when he threatened to beat her to the small sink.

Erica stepped beside Reese. "I see things have

settled down some. They seem to be getting along."

A small laugh came through Reese's clamped lips. "For now, at least. One thing Kara is used to having little brothers. She has three from Stephanie." His gaze trailed toward his children. "Any words of advice?"

"Looks to me like you have everything under control."

Reese snickered. "Far from it. I can assure you.

**J. ALISON COLE**

## Chapter Thirteen

Reese picked up his napkin and draped it across his lap. It was cloth, not flimsy paper like the ones he bought from the grocery store that came packaged in a thick cube. Erica sat the platter of chicken on the center of the patio table with the rest of the food. If he was being honest, the entire spread looked like something from the cover of a magazine. As a whole, nothing was fancy. Yet somehow, she made it not so ordinary. The woman sitting across from him was capable of living up to the hype without even trying.

The salad was a simple spring mix with blueberries, crumbles of feta, glazed pecans, and a light dressing already on it. Erica had cut the yellow pear-shaped tomatoes in half, and the small red things turned out to be beets instead of tomatoes. Beet salads were a thing. Why had he never tried this before? He'd helped her grill the chicken, but his never tasted like this. And this mac-n-cheese definitely didn't come out of a box.

During the meal, Erica bantered playfully with Sawyer and somehow maneuvered Kara into a full-fledged conversation about her upcoming first year of high school. It was the most he'd heard his daughter talk in any particular setting without yelling, screaming, or storming off. It gave him a sliver of hope that he could get back the happy little girl he left behind so many years ago.

"Did everyone get enough to eat?" Erica's warm smile bounced from the kids to him.

Reese wiped his mouth and dropped his napkin back onto his lap. "I'm stuffed. I can't eat another bite. It was delicious."

"Okay, then." Erica scanned the three of them again. "After we set the dishes inside, you'll need to pick a movie to watch over there." She pointed to the barn. "Tonight's choices, *Babe* or the original *Ghostbusters*?"

"We're going to watch a movie outside?" Kara said skeptically.

"Coooollll," Sawyer cooed.

*She's thought of everything.*

"I've never seen either of those movies. Aren't they, like, super old?" Kara flipped her hand into the air.

Sawyer added his two cents. "I've never heard of those movies."

"They're classics. Maybe your Dad can decide." Erica turned to him.

*Damn. Who wouldn't be impressed?* "How about we flip a coin?"

"Wait. I don't want to watch a movie if it's stupid." Kara rolled her eyes at him.

Reese fished a quarter from his pocket and held it toward her. Heads, it's *Babe*. tails, it's *Ghostbusters*. Call it." He flipped the coin.

"Wait!" Kara squealed with laughter.

Reese snatched the coin from the air and flopped on the backside of his other hand. "Do you want Sawyer to call it?" Sawyer grinned eagerly.

"No, I'll call it. Heads…No, wait, tails. Tails."

"Are you sure?" Reese peeked at the coin. Kara shook her head with her final decision. He revealed the winner. "It's tails."

"I love *Ghostbusters*." Erica moseyed across the patio for the tray to carry the dishes.

But, when she leaned over the counter to get it, all the blood in Reese's body went straight to his dick. Her tight-fitting jeans hugged her ass perfectly, and with the setting sun behind her, the modest white shirt she wore gave him a clear outline of all her slender curves.

He'd already had to fight off one ill-timed erection down by the chicken pen. She had the best *come-fuck-me eyes* he'd ever seen. It was strange to think that having a brick in his pants was the least of his problems right now.

Reese looked away and took three healthy gulps on his beer. The attraction between himself and Erica was undeniable, which wasn't the problem. The problem was what would happen afterward.

Erica would never be a casual hookup—the kind he was used to—the kind he preferred. Through the years, he'd hooked up with plenty of beautiful women, but none even came close to her. Plus, she'd managed to do something they couldn't. She'd cracked his hardened exterior and gotten under his skin like a bad case of poison ivy. And the itch to be with her was driving him crazy. Almost crazy enough to forget the promise he made himself a long time ago? *Don't get too close, keep feelings out of it, and never give them your heart.*

No, nothing about Erica was casual. So he felt damned if he did and definitely damned if he didn't. Where was the relief in that?

Erica came back to the table with the tray. "Did you leave any room for popcorn?"

Sawyer's eyes widened. "Yeah, this is fun, isn't it, Dad?"

Reese sighed, trying to shift his thoughts in another direction. "Yup. Now, let's help Ms. Erica get these dishes inside."

Erica opened the screened door and pointed toward the sink. "You can set that down over there. Thanks."

Reese sat the tray on the counter and stepped out of the way to take in his surroundings. The interior of her kitchen came as no surprise. If the patio graced the magazine's cover, then this room alone would fill the rest of the glossy pages. The well-maintained oak cabinets hanging on the walls looked original, as in over one hundred years old. Only they'd been reconfigured with modern-looking hardware and special lighting. In the center of the room was a hefty-sized antique butcher block built into a custom island. It was worn and stained, nicked and tattered, but it fit the space perfectly.

A wide arch led into the hallway. From here, he could see the front door and the main staircase. Erica was by the sink, showing Sawyer a plant on the windowsill that ate flies. No doubt he wouldn't hear the end of it until they had one, too. Reese walked toward a second archway at the far end—the dining room. Standing at the threshold, the faint aroma of cloves lingered with a hint of charred wood. Along the outer wall was a rustic fireplace with an inset mantel made of stone. Growing up, his parents had a wood stove. Nothing was more comforting on a cold day. However, it felt like a safe bet that the fireplaces in this house burned more for ambiance than heat. But, he could be wrong.

In the center of the room, eight high-back chairs with brightly-colored upholstery surrounded a long shaker-style table. Sitting in the middle of the table was a vase of wildflowers, probably gathered during her rides.

But the focal point had to be the gigantic mural covering the main wall behind the table. It was an extraordinary rendering of rolling hills and countryside. He was no artist, but it looked old, as if it had been discovered underneath decades of decor like a missing Rembrandt.

Everywhere he looked screamed sophistication and the chic style that belonged to her. His paper napkins didn't quite measure up to any of this.

## Chapter Fourteen

Erica glanced over her shoulder. Reese was coming back to the center of the room. He'd been quiet throughout dinner, like he had something on his mind. His ability to control what he did and didn't want her to see was incredible. At times, there was no mistaking the desire in his eyes. It closely reflected her own. Other times, he put up a wall, and she could only speculate what might be churning away behind that sea of blue.

Kara wandered next to her. "Can I use the bathroom?"

"It's, 'may I.'" Erica corrected without thinking.

"What?" Kara asked.

"Sorry. Yes, there's a bathroom off the pantry and one down the hallway by the main stairs." Erica pointed to each. Kara chose the small pantry washroom next to her washer and dryer. "Sawyer, since Kara picked the movie, can you be in charge of the popcorn?"

"All right!" Sawyer pulled a chair from the small kitchen table toward the counter.

Erica plugged in the hot air popper and filled the top cup. "Give it a few minutes to heat up, then lift the lever and dump the kernels."

Reese leaned against the butcher block island. His arms were straight, with his hips jutted back. Standing that way, she'd have just enough room to bend over in front of him and the island.

The telephone rang, and he straightened. She had to be spending too much time around Janine. It rang a second time. The machine would pick up on the fourth.

*But what if it is Janine?* Definitely not worth the risk. "I should get this. Excuse me." She raced down the hallway to answer the landline, a novelty 1940s telephone that sat on the small table in the front foyer. "Hello."

*Silence. It's a telemarketer.* She was about to hang up when a recognizable voice greeted her from the other end.

"Erica."

She blinked slowly, stunned and even a little confused. "Davis?" She paused. "Is everything all right? Is Lauren all right?"

He chuckled. "Everything is fine. There's nothing wrong with Lauren. It's just you told me to call first."

"Oh." She lowered her voice and glanced toward the kitchen. Reese had moved into her line of sight, near the counter next to Sawyer. His butt was phenomenal.

"I thought maybe I could come over."

It took a second for his words to register. Her eyes widened with realization. "What? Why?"

Sawyer let out a playful scream when Kara rejoined and threatened to dump the popcorn too soon. The sound must've carried.

"Oh, you have company?" His voice rose higher with the question.

"Yes, Davis, I do."

His disappointment came out like a child pouting. "Is it him?"

Just then, Reese glanced over his shoulder, his blue eyes smoldering with interest—and concern. He pushed away from the counter and took a few steps in her direction. "Yes, it is. I need to go. Goodnight, Davis." She hung up.

Reese strolled into the hallway and stopped in front of her. "Is everything—okay?" His barely-there smile was one of her favorites. And if there was such a thing as the Vee gene, it was cascading off him in droves.

"Yes. Everything is fine." Right now, she'd give

anything to kiss him, maybe lead him upstairs, and turn her island and barn fantasies into realities.

They silently eyed each other like a hunter and prey. Only it was hard to tell who was who. She'd never experienced desire like this before. She felt it in her bones, and if her instincts were right, and they usually were, it was the same for him.

His smile disappeared, and a deep line formed on his forehead. He stepped around her and peered into the main living room. "Your home is beautiful, Erica. It's like you."

"Thank you." The children were still in the kitchen chatting over the growing popping of kernels. The smell drifted into the hallway.

His gaze flickered toward the kitchen. "You really are good at this entertaining stuff."

"Thank you. Maybe I should write a book. Oh, wait."

"You're hilarious. But it's not just the meal, although that was delicious…everything was great. What I'm trying to say is you have a way of making people feel comfortable, especially the kids. Thank you." As his eyes skirted away, he did a double take over her shoulder into the sunroom. "Is that a new bike?"

"It is." She led him into that room. "I just got it today. Marcus helped me get a terrific deal. I couldn't pass it up."

He gripped the front handles, squeezing the brakes. "Your friend's gay, isn't he?"

Erica balked, somewhat surprised. "Why would you say that?"

"I don't care one way or the other, but I'm right, aren't I?"

"Actually—yes, but not many people know, and right now, he prefers to keep it that way. Have you meant him?"

"No." Reese crinkled his brow. "I just can't imagine a straight man would only want to be your friend." One of his eyebrows arched higher, and the shimmer in his eyes left her feeling hypnotized. He took a tentative step closer just as Kara came around the corner searching for them.

"The popcorn's ready."

"Good timing." Erica sighed. Her gaze wavered between Reese and his daughter. "Let's have some popcorn."

Outside, four carefully positioned Adirondack chairs faced the end of the barn. Twilight bled the skies into darkness, and the movie started. The awe of watching a film outdoors was enough to silence Kara and Sawyer. Even the crickets took a break, or maybe their chirps only faded into the background when Bill Murray appeared larger than life on the side of her barn.

****

Erica turned the projector off and then rejoined everyone on the patio.

Reese steered his son away from the glowing embers in the firepit. "Come on, sleepy head."

Sawyer let out another yawn and rubbed his eyes. "That was really cool. We should watch the other movie now."

Erica tossed Sawyer's soft curls. "How about we watch it another day? Okay?"

Reese's gaze shuffled over his surroundings—and her. "It's getting late. I should probably get the kids home. Did you need help with anything?"

"Nah, but thank you."

Kara had laughed during the movie, but now she'd converted back into a rebellious teenager, perhaps remembering that she wasn't supposed to be having fun.

"Kara," Reese called. "What do you say to Ms. Erica?"

"Oh yeah, thanks." Kara glanced up from her phone and flashed a half-hearted smile before grabbing Sawyer by the shoulder to drag him toward Reese's truck.

Erica lifted her chin. A mischievous smile pushed its way onto her lips. "I guess this is that part of the evening where I tell you I had a really nice time."

Recognizing his words and understanding their meaning, he chuckled. "Is that right?"

"Yup." Erica stepped closer, allowing her breasts to graze against his chest. No one had ever accused her of being timid, and the time for being subtle had come and gone. "I had a really nice time tonight."

The playful glint in his eyes became a fury of hunger when his mouth lowered to hers.

****

Erica's eyes flinched against the bright rays of the sun peeking through the curtains. Something had awakened her. "Witchy woman" blared again.

She grabbed her cell phone from the bedside table. "Hello."

"Finally. Did you just get back from your ride?" Janine's tone was extra loud and perky.

Erica glanced at the clock before scurrying off the bed. It was 8:20 AM. *What?* "Um, no...I haven't gone yet." She threaded her arms into a terry robe and tied the belt.

"You sound exhausted. Are you just getting out of bed?"

"I didn't fall asleep right away." That was true. She spent most of the night reliving the most tender, sensual kiss she'd ever experienced.

"Oooohhhh! Do you need me to call back? Is he there?"

"No, Janine, I'm by myself." She trotted down the narrow spiral stairs leading into the kitchen.

"Oh. Well, do you, you know, need me…to…call back so you can be—by yourself? Janine said in a leading tone.

"What are you talking about?" Erica screeched.

"That thing in your drawer, the thing you need batteries for…."

Erica huffed. "No! God, no. I don't have—a…one of those."

"Not even a dildo? Sorry, I just assumed you needed something like that when you were with Davis," Janine said defensively.

"No. But I wouldn't discuss it with you even if I did."

"I have three. Of each." Janine giggled. "Anyways, I was calling to see how your dinner went."

Erica grabbed a cup from the cupboard and filled it with some *cold* coffee. The coffee pot timer had clicked off hours ago. At this point, it was more for the caffeine. "It went…fantastic. Everyone had a nice time, I think."

"What about his daughter? You said she might be a challenge."

Erica strolled up the hallway. She opened the front door to take advantage of the fresh morning air. It truly was a beautiful day. A piece of paper flapped next to the handle of the screen door. "Kara is just a typical teenager." Erica pulled the paper from the crease.

"I wanted to let you know, too, that I'll be home tomorrow, so I thought we could have dinner if you don't have plans."

Half-listening, Erica unfolded the paper. "Sure." She read the note: *Saturday.* Signed with a big "R."

"Hey, are you listening to me?" Janine asked, sounding somewhat irritated.

"Oh yeah. I'm free tomorrow, but I have plans for Saturday."

# J. ALISON COLE

## Chapter Fifteen

Last night, after they kissed, Erica whispered, "I want you." She showed him no mercy by rubbing her body against him. Reese almost lost it right then and there. And the huskiness of her voice was dredged with so much longing that his dick stayed hard for hours. But having two kids in a house with thin walls, relief had to wait until morning when he jumped into the shower and took matters into his own hands.

After breakfast, he dropped Sawyer off at Robin's, then headed straight to Erica's with a note. She'd know what it meant. The hardest part of this plan was having to wait until Saturday. The next few days might require a record number of showers.

Reese glanced at his watch. It was 11:15 AM, and he was headed back to the Koontz's main farm with about fifty bags of feed piled up in the back of his truck.

His phone dinged a short musical melody on the seat next to him. Kara's name appeared on the screen. He set it on speaker. "Hey, Kara. Don't tell me that you're just now getting up."

"No, I've been awake for a while. And it's not even lunchtime yet."

"Well, there's a dozen eggs in the fridge or a loaf of bread and some peanut butter in the cupboard if you want to make yourself a sandwich instead."

"Oh, I'll make something." Kara's tone sounded uncharacteristically cheerful. The lengthy pause that followed made him instantly suspicious. "Can I ask you something?"

Reese's instincts switched to high alert. "Sure?"

"I know that I'm grounded right now, but my

friend Lisa was wondering if I could spend the night at her house this Saturday. And before you say anything, Lisa isn't the girl from the liquor store thing, and her parents will be home the whole night. It's her birthday, and we're just going to hang out…and stuff."

"Yeah, it's the *stuff* that has me concerned." Even as the words left his mouth, he saw this as a godsend. He'd already arranged for Sawyer to stay with Joey on Saturday, so knowing that Kara wouldn't be home alone, his night with Erica could last until morning. Was that selfish of him, or just poor parenting? Instead of giving her an immediate answer, he had to let her sweat a little. "Well, I need to think about it." *This is fuckin' perfect.* "We can talk about it this evening. Or you could always try to beat me in bowling tomorrow night."

"Oh my god, you were serious about that? I've never been bowling in my life."

"I was serious. And you haven't lived until you've eaten pizza from a bowling alley.

"Sounds gross."

"Gross and delicious." The long breath he took was for both of them. "Just give it a chance, Kara." *Give me a chance.*

"Whatever. Me and Sawyer get to use those bumper things."

"No bumpers for anyone." Reese crested a hill between a large pasture and a Christmas tree farm that had row after row of three and four-foot trees. He'd taken these back roads on purpose, and it paid off. "I have to go now, but I'll be home in a few hours. Make your bed and wash any dishes you dirty. Okay?" Behind the "okay" was an empty gap. It was for the space of *I love you, Kara.* But those words couldn't come out because of what he did, just like it was too hard for her to call him Dad yet and mean it. Most of the time, she danced around calling him anything, which was fine for now. He didn't want his daughter calling him Reese. But they'd get there, and then he'd say how much he loved her all the time, whether she wanted to hear it or not.

"Okay. Bye…." *Dad.*

"Goodbye…" *Kara. I love you.* He pressed the button on the phone.

They'd get there.

Reese stretched his neck to see further ahead. Up ahead, a spectacular woman on a bike swerved to the edge of the road and coasted to a stop sign. He'd never been so happy to be driving on the back roads of Southern Pennsylvania.

Erica removed her helmet and grabbed a water bottle from the bar above the gears. She squirted a stream across her face and forehead. The final squirt went into her mouth. Her head swiveled as he pulled up next to her. The smile on her face nearly smacked him senseless. Besides Sawyer, he couldn't think of anyone who looked so happy to see him. He really was one lucky son-of-a-bitch.

She pushed the matted hair away from her forehead and studied him with a coy smile. "Hello, Reese."

Reese pushed the brim of his mesh ball cap further back on his head. "Erica." Even a sweaty mess, the woman was still sexy. Tiny droplets of water clung to her face and neck. What he wouldn't give to lick every single one of them off.

*I want you.* The words echoed again. How in the hell was he going to make it two whole days?

She propped a hand on the passenger door through the open window to balance herself without getting off the bike. "I haven't seen you in a hat before."

"I can take it off if you want."

"No. It looks good." She studied him for a moment. "I like it."

"I could say the same about you." Her laugh was humbling, but he meant it. "Hey, I wanted to make sure you got my note?" He really wanted to say, *I'm going to give you what you want. You'd best be ready.*

"I did." The sultriness in her eyes practically answered for her, *And I'm ready.* The woman looked like she was ready to eat him alive, and he couldn't wait.

"Sawyer's spending the night with Joey, and I'm allowing Kara to go to her friend's house. I thought maybe this time I'd take you to dinner." *And then take you again and again.* He kept his left wrist draped over the steering wheel and extended his right arm along the top edge of the bench seat. It felt like a subconscious invitation of sorts. *Or I could take you now.*

Erica's eyes darted from his chest to the dash, then back again. He'd push the seat back the whole way and make it work.

Her weight shifted on the bike, and a bead of perspiration trickled down the front of her neck. He followed the glistening dew until it disappeared between her breasts. *Fuck me. I'll rip the seat out if I have to.*

"Dinner sounds fabulous. I'd love that."

A truck coming from the other direction turned into the intersection. Reese ripped his gaze away from her when it stopped beside them.

Steve Koontz rolled down his window. "Hey, Erica. Hello, Reese."

Erica bent lower to view him through the windows of his truck. "Hello, Steve. How's Robin?"

Steve yanked his hat down further. "Fine, just fine." He stared at her for a moment and then at Reese. "Joey's excited for Saturday."

"That's good." *And he's not the only one.* Another

awkward moment went by—then another.

"Well, take care, Erica." Steve's smile faded. "Paul is probably waiting on that feed."

"I'm headed there now." Reese watched Steve pulling away in the rearview mirror. "You're going to get me into trouble." His attention returned to the lady steadying herself with his truck.

"I don't think you need me for that." Her eyes skirted away like she hadn't meant to say that aloud.

He took his right arm down from its resting spot along the top of the seat and gripped the wheel. "Hopefully, we all stay out of trouble. I'm doing something special with the kids tomorrow night, but I'll pick you up Saturday around seven."

She let go of the edge of the truck door. "I'll be ready."

His focused stare didn't waver, and he couldn't help but smile. "So will I."

**J. ALISON COLE**

## Chapter Sixteen

Erica took another sip of wine and checked the time. Janine's flight was supposed to be in at three o'clock, and they'd planned to meet at Nicco's around 5:30 PM. Janine was rarely late, and it was almost six o'clock. A second later, "Witchy Woman" bellowed from her cell phone.

"Hey, are you almost here?"

"No, that's why I'm calling. I got my period last night, and these cramps would kill an elephant. I should've called you sooner. I'm sorry, Erica. I thought the Midol would kick in, and then I fell asleep. I feel like shit."

"No problem, maybe we can get together on Sunday. Do you want me to bring you anything?"

"Oh...oh, that was a big one." Janine let out an exasperated sigh. "I just stood up, and a clot gushed out. I always have the biggest clots on the first day. Are yours like this?"

"I'm not answering that. You're so disgusting, but I hope you feel better. Let me know if you need anything. I'll call you in the morning."

"Oh, here comes another one. Damn, I think that one is going to bleed through. Yup. Shit! My panties probably look like I used them to clean up a slaughterhouse."

"I'm out of here." Erica ended the call and reached for her purse hanging on the back of her chair to put her phone away, when her elbow almost whacked a man walking by.

"Oh my God, I'm so sorry. Her gaze shifted from the man's crotch to his face only to discover Davis smiling back.

"That might have drastically marred my evening." He stepped to the opposite side of the table. "I was coming up to say hello, but I couldn't help overhearing. It sounded like you just got stood up."

*What in the world?* "I *was* waiting for Janine. We eat here all the time."

A perceptible shimmer appeared in his eyes. "I know. And...what, she can't make it now?"

"No, she's not feeling well."

"There is a god. Would you mind if, perhaps, I join you instead?" He tilted his head, gesturing toward the empty seat. "You know I'm only joking about her not feeling well.

*Was he though?*

The surprise pop-in, the unexpected phone call, and now this quasi-stalker-ish move. For some reason, she thought of the first time they met in a coffee shop. He'd approached her in a similar way—minus the near-miss crotch shot. Something was going on, and it was time to find out what.

"Be my guest." She sipped some wine as he settled into the seat.

Wendy materialized next to the table. For such a large woman, she had the stealth moves of a ninja. "Hello, Dr. Gebhart. How nice to see you again. May I get you something to drink?"

Davis leaned back in his chair, collected and relaxed—as usual. "I'll just have cranberry with lime." He gestured toward her. "Would you care for another glass of wine, Erica?"

"You know what, I think I'll have a gin and tonic. Thank you." *Just one.*

Erica eyed the man sitting across from her. Davis wore his confidence as well as he wore his jeans.

Although tonight, he looked equally dashing in a crisp navy blazer and Dockers. He'd already removed his tie and unbuttoned the top of his shirt. They called him "McDreamy" at the hospital for a reason. As a couple, they made a dynamic duo, respected, revered, and envied by all. But that was then.

"Cranberry juice?" Erica asked.

"I'm on call at the hospital."

Erica balked, semi-confused. "I didn't think you had to do that anymore with your new position."

"I volunteered because I *hate* my new position. It's too much paperwork and posturing for the administrators. I hardly get to see patients anymore."

"I'm sorry to hear you say that." She finished the last of her wine. "But you are a wonderful doctor." No one could deny that, not even Janine.

Dark lashes framed his sage green eyes as his attractive smile became the focal point of his clean-shaven face. "Thank you."

Wendy returned with their drinks. "Are you ready to order?"

Davis nodded and gestured to her.

"I think tonight I'll have a Caesar salad with grilled chicken." Erica wasn't in the mood for shrimp.

"Oh, something different." Wendy gave a curt nod of approval.

Davis closed his menu. "That sounds good. Make it two."

She gathered the menus from the table and vanished into the crowded restaurant. All that was missing was a puff of smoke.

Erica surveyed the nearby tables. When Davis sat down, chins lifted, eyes darted, and gossipy whispers hummed behind the clatter of glasses and silverware. Seriously? What was so intriguing about her eating dinner with someone? Granted, someone who just happened to be her ex-husband. What was the big deal? She despised the unwanted attention and ignored it the best she could.

"So, Davis, what brings you to Kensington's finest eating establishment?"

Davis propped his elbows on the table, seemingly prepared for her line of questioning. "Before you jump to conclusions, I spoke with Lauren just yesterday. She's happy and healthy and doing well in her summer classes. My mother is still contrary and judgemental. And yes, I can safely say that Bethany has a pretty good idea of where and what I'm doing."

"What *are* you doing, Davis?"

He removed his elbows from the table and reached for his drink. "I sold the condo." He said it as if she should've already known. "I hated living there." He smiled over the edge of his glass. "By the way, who mowed your grass?"

She stirred her drink. "Did you need a bigger place?"

His brows arched higher. "No. I just needed a place of my own." He gave ample time for that to sink in. "Bethany and I are not together anymore."

"Oh. I see."

Now, things were starting to make sense. Davis was forty-three, and if he was having relationship problems on top of work issues, it made sense that he would turn to someone he felt comfortable and familiar with—her. They had a mutual respect for one another. And if he needed help, she'd listen. "For your information, I mowed the grass." A satisfied smile beamed on his face.

For the next hour, she kept the conversation focused on his work problems. Erica purposely avoided anything to do with relationships, his and hers. That's if what was happening to her could be considered a relationship. Or merely relations. After tomorrow, she'd have a better idea.

Their daughter would always be the common ground they shared. It was inevitable that Lauren came up in the conversation.

Davis laid down his fork and leaned back in the chair. "I'm just grateful that she has your temperament."

"I'm so proud of her. We did good."

Davis disappeared into his thoughts, his eyes chasing memories that she couldn't see. Then he cleared his throat. "Yeah, we did. Hey, I'm thinking about getting a new car. Do you think Lauren would want the BMW? Or is it too much of an old-man car?"

"Old-man car? It's a sports car. Now if it was a Volvo…I'd say no way."

"What's wrong with a Volvo?"

"Your mother drives a Volvo." A playful snort escaped.

"Oh, I see how it is." His smile mellowed and his gaze intensified.

*Whoa, whoa, whoa.* She knew that look all too well. *Not happening, buddy.* "I'm only joking about your mother. I know that Lauren likes her Subaru, but you can always ask."

"I'll do that." He looked down and chuckled. "You always know how to make me feel better. Thank you. I needed this. I haven't relaxed or laughed like this in a long time."

"I'm glad you feel better. And you're right. It was a very nice evening."

"Although, I have to ask, should I be worried? Do you always drink this much now?"

Erica stared at her empty glass and snickered. Her

third, no, fourth, gin and tonic. How did that happen? *Dang Wendy's treacherous ninja skills.* She failed to contain a fit of giggles. *Crap.* "No, you know I don't. And it used to take more than this to knock me on my butt."

"You're a lightweight now, Erica. No wonder the grass was all wonky."

Erica cupped her mouth to stifle another round of bubbly laughter. "Hey, I think the grass looks pretty good."

"How many drinks did you have that day?" Her mouth opened in playful horror. "Come on now, Erica, I've seen you drunk, and this might be a good time to get you out of here."

"I'm not drunk, but I'll give you tipsy." Her cheeks hurt from smiling. "But yes, I think it's time to leave."

Davis was about to signal for the check when Wendy's broad hips and shoulders loomed over the table. "Oh, there you are. We're ready for the check, please."

Wendy curtsied. "Of course, Dr. Gebhart."

Erica waited until she was gone. "Janine thinks she's a man."

"What?"

She covered her lips with her fingers. "Actually, she thinks they're all spies." She snorted, and her shoulders started to shake.

"Your sister is an idiot." Davis shushed her and leaned over the table. "If you keep that up, you'll give those old men at the hardware store a week's worth of fodder."

He wasn't wrong. Erica inhaled, then exhaled. *Nope, still tipsy.*

Once Davis paid the bill, Erica rose to her feet. The floor had a gentle sway like that first step onto solid ground after being on a boat all day. She felt drunk, so when he offered his arm, she took it. In her mind, she sashayed through the restaurant with the grace of a runway model. God only knows what she really looked like. And He was the only one who mattered.

Stepping outside, Erica sucked in the aroma of charbroiled meat and French fries. "Can you smell that? Why does the food always smell better when you're outside of the restaurant." Next to Davis's car, she closed her eyes and inhaled again.

"I have no idea."

When her eyes opened, either the ground was a few degrees off, or she was. The sway carried her sideways, but her feet didn't get the same message. Davis reached for her, and instead of hitting the pavement, she landed against him.

"Oops." Her feet finally caught up and moved, but the tip of her heel became entangled with a shoelace of his brown leather shoe. "Oh, the heel is—" She tried moving her foot from side to side. "How is it hooked?" She lifted her knee forward and tried again.

"Whoa, watch it. Stop, stop, stop."

She froze. Her shoe was still stuck, and somehow in her struggle to get free, her thigh was now directly between his legs.

"Just calm down. I got you." His hands moved to her hips, and the sage in his eyes sparkled from the accidental cozy contact. "You know I'm going to have to take you home, right?" Davis said, half laughing.

A dim light bulb went off in her head. He tried to kiss her the last time he was at her house. "No. I don't think so." Holding on to his forearms, Erica craned away from his body and carefully detangled her shoe from his. "There. I got it."

"Erica, I can't let you drive."

"Um, I'll call Janine."

"I thought you said she wasn't feeling well."

*Dang, he's right, and Reese is doing something special with his kids.* "Lauren, I'll call Lauren." She swayed just a tiny bit. He reached for her again, but she raised her hands to ward him off.

"All right," he said in mock surrender. "But I'm right here Erica, and it doesn't make sense to bother her. Plus, it defeats that whole good example thing."

Davis had a sound argument. But he was also dangerously handsome, and his eyes twinkled more than the sequence dress she wore to the gala the night they opened the new wing at the hospital. She huffed loudly and unladylike.

*Shiitake mushrooms.*

"Erica, if I didn't know any better, I'd think you were afraid to be alone with me." He caressed the side of her forearm.

She swatted his hand away. "And if I didn't know better, I might think you ordered all those drinks for me on purpose," she bluffed. Davis would never have to get a woman drunk to seduce her.

"You ordered your own drinks."

She did. Another colossal breath came out. "Fine. You may give me a ride home." *But that's all.*

He opened the passenger door of his BMW, and she not so gracefully flopped onto the seat.

When the car started, "Feel Like Making Love" by Boston vibrated through the speaker against her knee. She eyed him suspiciously.

"What? It's still a good song." He didn't look so innocent.

"Just drive me home."

"With pleasure, my dear."

## Chapter Seventeen

"You'll be back home before your kids wake up." Paul attached several hoses to another cow.

Reese didn't know the first thing about milking cows, but thankfully, "the ladies," as Paul referred to them, did most of the work, and the machines did the rest. Electronic sensors identified the tag of each cow and measured their production. Dividers separated long concrete columns with dangling hoses and pipes running overhead. The raised level of the dairy was spotless. The pit in between was an oozing stream of waste.

The first three ladies understandably didn't appreciate his inexperience. By the fourth cow, things seemed to go a little smoother.

Paul hollered over the churning pumps and compressors. "Hey, you doing okay?"

Reese glanced over his shoulder. "I think I'm getting the hang of it."

"I sure do appreciate you filling in for Bob. I owe you big time, but that's not what I meant. You kind of look like somebody pissed on your Pop-Tarts. If this messed up your morning, hey I'm sorry man."

"No, it's not this." Reese dropped his gaze. "I, uh, just didn't sleep well."

Paul nodded. "Sorry. Something on your mind that you want to talk about? I'm a hell of a listener."

"It's nothing." The cow behind Reese released a funnel of poop over the railing, splashing all over his boots and pants. He stepped away from the slippery pile. No one liked getting shit on. And that was exactly what was on his mind. "Hey Paul, what do you know about Dr. Gebhart?"

Paul peeked from behind the back end of a cow

and grinned. "I knew it. You're thinking of tapping that ain't ya? Erica, I mean, not him, although I can admit he's a fine-looking man."

Reese's jaw tightened from Paul's immediate assumption about Erica, accurate or not. He took a calming breath. "I was just wondering why they got divorced."

Paul casually scrapped the cow dung caked on the sides of his boots onto the concrete lip of the dairy. "Don't get me wrong, there isn't a man in all of Somerset County that wouldn't give his left nut to be with someone like Erica Gebhart, but why they got divorced, hell, that's what everyone wants to know."

"Do you think he cheated on her?"

"Nah. He's a pretty decent guy, and everyone would've known if that happened." Paul nonchalantly placed a pinch of chaw inside his bottom lip. "It was almost a year before he started seeing a woman from the hospital where he works. They shacked up in some condo outside of Somerset."

Reese hesitated before asking the next question. "Could she have cheated on him?"

"Her? I doubt it. The scuttlebutt was after the divorce. She started spending a lot of time with some young teacher from school. But they were just rumors, you know, stuff people said." Paul checked the overhead line. "Look, I'd like to tell you that Davis is a son-of-a-bitch, but the truth is, I like him, and so does Bob." He glanced away for a second. "Steve, not so much, but you can guess why. He's had a stiffy for Erica since she moved here, not that he'd ever have the balls to cheat on Robin. It's just something he likes to think about. Hell, who doesn't?" Paul spit a rocket of brown juice to the floor. It blended right in. "Dr. Gebhart is successful, good-looking, and charming as all hell. Isn't that what every woman is supposed to want? Some might even say he was the perfect man for the perfect woman." He shrugged. "But for some reason, it didn't work out. Maybe he has a little dick. I don't know."

A half-hearted chuckle escaped Reese.

Paul gave him a crude smile. "Tell you one thing. I wouldn't mind banging Erica's sister. Have you met her yet? She got some big titties." His hands formed invisible melons in front of his chest. "Just like these ladies. Come on, we're not even halfway done." Paul went back to work.

Reese lost count after thirty-six, no, thirty-seven. The mindless work and endless parade of cows let his mind drift back to the chance sighting from the night before. He'd taken the kids bowling in an attempt to create family time. That part of the evening went great. Leaving the bowling alley was a different story. He nearly tripped over his feet when he spotted Erica coming out of Nicco's holding onto a man's arm. It had to be her ex. They looked cozy standing next to a sporty black BMW, precisely the kind of car one would expect a doctor to have, spoke for a moment, and then left together.

"My place or yours?" A classic scenario Reese knew all too well. Shit, a lot of people hooked up with their ex, not that he ever would, even though Stephanie made herself available more times than he could count since moving here.

A gnawing hurt tried to claw its way out of his chest from the cavern where he buried it. Erica didn't seem capable of that. She was nothing like Stephanie. And if anyone deserved the benefit of the doubt, it would be her. Right? There had to be an innocent reason for her to leave with her ex-husband.

Instead of getting too far inside his own head,

there was one thing he could do. He'd just ask her.

"Last run." Paul popped up behind him.

"What?" Reese came barreling back to his immediate surroundings.

"This is the last run. Just a few more, then we're done."

"Great."

The moment they finished milking, Reese jumped in his truck and headed for Erica's. The streets in town were bare as the rising sun sprayed over Nicco's empty parking lot. The Jeep was gone. That was a good sign, wasn't it? Maybe he got himself all worked up over nothing.

Five minutes later, Reese turned onto their road. She was usually riding by now, so he left the truck running and jogged up the stone walk to leave her another note. Standing on the front porch, Reese scribbled a quick message: *Call Me. R.*

As he reached for the handle of the screened door, the main door opened. A rush of promise filled his lungs. But the person that greeted him may as well have punched him in the gut.

## Chapter Eighteen

"Can I help you?" At six o'clock in the morning, the same man Erica left the restaurant with was standing in her doorway. His shirt was unbuttoned, and he was sipping on a cup of coffee.

Reese glanced away to recover from the numbing blow. That's when he caught sight of the back end of a BMW parked on the *far* side of the garage. If he'd looked around better, he would never have stopped and been in this position. He shoved the note back into his pocket. "No, thanks."

The man pushed the door open and joined him on the porch with his right hand extended. "Dr. Davis Gebhart, call me Davis." The doctor surveyed him with an icy stare all the way down to his cowshit-covered boots.

Acid, putrid, and bitter filled his stomach, but Reese shook the offered hand. "Reese Mailing."

Davis pointed toward his pocket. "Erica's not here, but I can give her a message if you want."

Reese's head felt like a grenade, ready to explode. His anger grew by the moment, more at himself than at the man standing in front of him wearing the congenial, overly triumphant smile. The urge to throw a good right hook was overwhelming but would solve nothing. "It's all right. She'll get the message." Reese turned and lumbered down the steps. *Fuck me.* He climbed behind the wheel of his truck and threw it in gear. *And fuck you, Erica.*

## Chapter Nineteen

Erica cleaned the house, changed the sheets, and fluffed the pillows. Then she showered and shaved everywhere. Her lady garden (Janine's polite description) was groomed and ready for action. *So was she.* If they made it to dinner, she'd be surprised.

Looking out of her bedroom window, a trail of dust kicked into the air. Erica checked the time. It was seven o'clock on the nose. She skipped down the main staircase like a lovesick, horny teenager and darted onto the front porch. Her heart was racing, but a second later, it slowed when clanking metal drowned out the squealing axle. A few seconds later, Bob Koontz zoomed by in his old, gray truck.

Erica settled onto the porch swing. It swayed back and forth. Fifteen minutes passed, and no other vehicles came or went. Maybe he had to work late, or something happened with one of the children again. Hopefully not. Another ten minutes went by. It didn't make sense to worry. she'd just call.

She opened the screened door just as the phone rang. Adrenaline filled her brain with hope as she raced in and answered the telephone in the foyer. "Hello?"

"It's me," Janine replied from the other end.

"Oh, Janine, I thought you were Reese. He's not here yet."

"That's why I'm calling Sweetie."

Why was Janine's voice a pitch higher than usual?

"What do you mean?"

"I told you this morning that I had to go to Pittsburgh to sample this little Indian place. It's not bad. They have wonderful tikka masala."

"Okay," Erica said, partly irritated.

"Well, it happens to be right across the street from this little dive bar, and if I'm not mistaken, I just saw your man and one of those Koontzs walk inside. What the hell's going on, Erica?"

*Reese is in a bar in Pittsburgh? That's forty-five minutes away.* A frigid wave washed over her. Did she get the day wrong?

"Erica? Did you hear me?"

Erica flinched. "I'm here, and yes, I heard you. I don't know what's going on. Let me call you later." She hung up the phone. Something wasn't right. Her fingers shook as she scrolled for Reese's number.

Three rings. Four. Five. *Six will go to voicemail—*

.

Only it didn't.

"Yeah." Reese snapped.

"Reese?" Muffled music and bar noise eeked through the phone. *He is in a bar.*

"What do you want?" The coldness in his voice felt like a spear jabbing her in the ribs.

"Where are you?" she squeaked.

"I made other plans." His reply had the same aloofness as his swagger.

"Why?" The question popped out faster than she could stop it. It made her sound...desperate. More desperate than she dared to admit.

The twang of a country song lengthened the moment—before he *finally* answered. "Because... I don't want to be with someone like you. You're not worth it.

*Click.*

\*\*\*\*

The smallest amount of light drifted into the window from the beckoning sunrise. Erica rolled onto her back and flung an arm over her eyes. She hadn't meant to fall asleep on the sofa. But her mind never stopped hashing over the unrelenting questions. *What happened, what changed, why would he say that?* Exhaustion finally claimed her in the wee hours of the morning, right where she lay.

She swung her legs over the side and sat up. Her shoulder ached, and her fingers tingled with pinpricks from being pinched between the side of her jaw and the stiff embroidered cushion. She rubbed her scalp. Her brain felt like oatmeal.

*Coffee.*

Filling the carafe, her blank stare ventured through the window above the sink. The rooster crowed inside his pen, and two deer nibbled at the tall grass along the trees next to the fence.

Beams of sunlight sprayed across the open field and flashed off the windshield in the distance. It was too early for the regular Sunday morning churchgoers, and the sound wasn't a truck. The vehicle hit the straightaway and sped on by. Sitting behind the wheel of a silver Honda with a green door was a dainty blonde.

Erica's mushy brain took several seconds to process this information.

*Stephanie and—.*

The coffee pot landed in the bottom of the sink and broke. Erica's hands flew to her mouth as a wallop of bile threatened the back of her throat. She took a quivering breath. "Oh, my God." *How could I have been so wrong, so naive, so stupid? He's everything they said he was.*

Erica raced upstairs and changed out of the clothes she'd slept in. She didn't bother to shower because nothing would make her feel any less dirty, and no amount of riding would help her today.

She drove straight to her sister's apartment and

banged on the door. Two hours later, after Janine called Reese every despicable name she could think of, the new king of a-holes was crowned.

****

A week passed. That Monday—forgotten. Tuesday, the miles were more of a blur. Wednesday, Erica would've ridden to Alaska, but a month ago, she'd agreed to stand in as interim committee chair for the town's beautification and revitalization group, the very program she'd helped start years ago. Millie Brown, the current committee chair, was expecting her third child any day.

Erica dabbed on some lipstick and checked her reflection in the mirror of the little bathroom in the hallway. The thought of being around people today made her nauseous. But the committee was counting on her. Letting them down because her pride took a hit didn't seem like a good enough excuse to ditch the meeting. She smoothed a hand over her dress.

The one and only upside in doing this is that it would keep her mind occupied on other things for at least an hour or two. She got into her Jeep and headed for town.

The group met in an empty office inside the same building of the Kensington Bank. Walking into the meeting room, an unwanted sense of déjà vu washed over Erica. As if she wasn't stymied enough right now, her old life was rattling at the windows, trying to shake her foundation.

Millie had neatly arranged everything for Erica in a bedazzled project tote. She opened the "Meeting Agenda" binder to check off the members as they arrived. Ten women and five men made up the committee. Erica knew most but not all. Their ages ranged from early twenties to late seventies. Some were bored homemakers, while others held a unique connection to the community. Two of the older men were frequent faces in Jackson's Hardware.

The old geezer had a network of people everywhere.

The last woman to enter the room squealed in a shrill voice. "As I live and breathe."

"Hello, Claire." Claire grabbed Erica by the shoulders and gave her a mock kiss and a pretentious hug.

"Oh, we've certainly missed you." Claire Simmons was a lawyer in her mid-fifties. Her husband was a city councilman.

When Erica was in charge, she encouraged Claire to join the group. Having a lawyer on a committee such as this seemed beneficial. Those with spouses in positions of power, even better. *Two birds, one stone.*

"Thank you, but I'm only here—temporarily." Erica surveyed the smiles and expectant faces of the members. "Have a seat, and we can get started." *Let's get this over with.* "This meeting is called to order."

The agenda consisted of three topics: Review minutes from the last meeting, budget report, and progress report. The first two items on the list took a surprising thirty-five minutes. It shouldn't have taken more than ten. Erica's patience was holding on by a thread.

"All right, let us proceed." She opened the "Project Binder."

Two years ago, right before stepping down, Erica suggested getting a clock or a fountain for the park entrance. Raising funds took a little longer than she would've thought, but the project in the works now was a combination of the two, apparently by accident. Millie confessed to not understanding the notes she handed over. At least, this was a happy accident.

"Okay. The progress report. So, I reviewed the notes, but I couldn't find the projected completion date."

Claire tapped her pen against the table. "Oh, we don't have a date. They told Millie two months ago that it might take three to four months to get approved."

"Hold on, that can't be right." Erica flipped three pages back and reread the blurb from the city council meeting. "March 15th, Park and Rec division, BR group, clock fountain project. Motion passed." She scanned the committee. "The project is approved. So what's the holdup?"

Four women spoke at once. Two started to argue with Mr. Wilson.

Erica used her most assertive but pleasant voice. "Let's quiet down." The room fell silent. She was in no mood to play referee, which must've shown. "How about you all take a quick break? And I'll make a phone call."

Erica dialed the town office and pushed a series of buttons to navigate the many automated options. Eventually, she reached the zoning officer and explained the situation.

"Why yes. I was at that meeting." A series of rapid pecks on a keyboard resonated through the phone. "Ah, here it is. Looks like a permit from the Department of Public Works is waiting for a signature from the Mayor."

Bureaucracy and the DMV had a lot in common. "All right, could you please transfer me to the Mayor?"

"I don't usually transfer the calls, but I think I know how to do that. Just call back if you get disconnected."

*Yeah, and waste another fifteen minutes of my life pushing buttons.* "Thank you." She held her breath, praying she didn't get a dial tone. Her prayer was then answered with scratchy, old music that sounded like it was being played on the oldest tape player in existence. After a full minute, someone picked up.

"Mam, I'm told that the mayor is in a meeting. I can take a message if you'd like."

"Sure, have her call Erica Gebhart at 717—"

"Excuse me. Did you say *Erica Gebhart*?"

"Yes. That's right."

"I'm so sorry. Please hold."

Erica's brow arched. Evidently, being somewhat of a small-town celebrity had some perks. Seconds later, the mayor took her call, apologizing for the mix-up. Three minutes later, Erica received an email with the electronic signature on the permit.

Several committee members stared at her like she just parted the Red Sea.

Ignoring their wondrous stares, Erica resumed the meeting. "I need two committee members to contact the contractors and give them the green light." She selected two of the five hands that went up, then circled a date for completion on the calendar in the front of the Project Binder. Give or take, the work could be done by the end of summer. At least this way, they had a goal. "I know Millie has her hands full right now, but I'll fill her in on everything that happened today, and you'll all be contacted with a date for the next meeting by her. Thank you so much for your time. Meeting adjourned."

Newly motivated committee members filed from the room. The last woman to leave stopped and eyed Erica with conjecture.

"Your name comes up a lot around here. It's nice to finally meet you. I'm Juanita Fleagle." She extended her hand.

Erica took the offered hand, feeling like she'd just passed some kind of test. "It's nice to meet you too. I understand you're a landscaper."

"I am. You know, this project may actually get done now. I'm impressed." Juanita laughed before explaining. "Most of our meetings are spent trying to decide when to have the next meeting. Thanks again." The woman nodded and then walked away.

Erica slowly reentered the room. All said and done, the meeting was successful. The stalled permit crisis was resolved, and momentum on the project was now moving forward. How easy would it be to fall back into her former life? This would've made her happy back then and given her a sense of accomplishment.

But that didn't happen today. Why? Because her heart wasn't in it.

*No, it's lying in little pieces at the bottom of the trash can with the coffee pot.*

Her eyelids lowered, and she took a long breath. *Stop being angry. Stop being mopey. Stop trying to figure it out.* She'd been wrong about him, and that's all there was to it.

Glitter covered the table where Erica gathered her notes and packed the binders into the large bedazzled tote. She flung the bag over her shoulder, turned the lights off, and left a trail of blue rhinestones following her.

Her high heels clicked on the black and white marble tiles, echoing off the high ceilings and walls of the empty hallway. Walking on the slick surface of the marble was like walking on ice. Why did she wear high heels anyway, or a dress for that matter? She could've worn slacks or even jeans. It was just a silly meeting. Guess it was safe to say that old habits die hard.

Erica scanned ahead to where the carpet runner started at the corner of the hallway. A few more steps and she'd be on the rug.

Eyeing the thin metal strip that separated the carpet from the tile, she never expected a towering figure to come barreling around the corner at the same time.

*Omph!*

The collision emptied the oxygen from her lungs and sent her body flying backward. As her arms cartwheeled, the bag smothered over her face, and a high-pitched squeal pierced the air from somewhere.

But she didn't hit the hard marble. With the bag draped over her face, her vision was limited to the adjacent wall and a person wearing black leather shoes. Her gaze trailed higher. The shoes belonged to Patrick Lambert, the balding bank manager. He had folders clutched to his chest. The squeal that sounded more like a frightened Chihuahua must've come from him.

She pushed the tote aside, and warm, minty breath tickled her nose.

Her eyes shifted.

*Reese.*

His massive form was huddled over and around her body. He had one strong arm curled around her waist and the other braced against the floor like a tripod holding them both.

Reese jostled her weight from the awkward pose and hauled her upright onto the carpet in one seemingly effortless move. He released her and stepped back, but not before his gaze raked over her dress, which had ridden up and splayed open where it overlapped. It was only instinct that had her tugging the fabric back in place.

Mr. Lambert started waving the folders in front of his face. "Good heavens, are you all right, Mrs. Gebhart?"

Reese huffed. "Are you—all right?" A mixture of emotions flashed through his eyes, everything from concern to longing and—what looked like *disgust*. He drew another breath and lowered his eyes.

Erica adjusted her dress again. "Yes. I'm fine." She turned to the bank manager. "I'm fine, Mr. Lambert. The marble floor is slippery."

Mr. Lambert continued to fan himself in an overly dramatic fashion. "For years, I've told them they need to put tread on this floor. I slip all the time. Thank goodness you weren't hurt. You're lucky Mr. Mailing has such quick reflexes."

Erica adjusted the handles of the canvas bag back onto her shoulder. More blue rhinestones fell to the floor. "Well. Thank you, Reese." His jaw tightened.

Mr. Lambert stopped fanning himself. "Oh, do you know Mr. Mailing?"

*Only by reputation.* "Um, he's my…neighbor." She forced a smile.

Reese created some distance between them and placed his hands on his hips. She almost missed his attire because of his stance. A black pinstriped shirt tucked into a pair of indigo jeans. He wore it well.

Mr. Lambert opened one of the folders, and briefly scanned some information. "I guess he is your neighbor, for now, at least. That's good to know."

Reese fired a sharp look at the man before turning it toward her. The crease on his forehead deepened. "Well, if…*Mrs.* Gebhart is okay. We shouldn't detain her." Pure disdain turned the silver flecks in his eyes into icy daggers. "Erica."

Mr. Lambert snapped the folder shut. "Of course, by all means. I'm so glad you weren't hurt, Mrs. Gebhart." Reese glared at the bank manager again.

*I wouldn't say that.* "Yes, thank you, Mr. Lambert." She stepped backward. "Goodbye, Reese." A scowl marred his features. "Please say hello to Sawyer and Kara for me." That brought his eyes back to hers.

They only softened a small amount, if any.

"Yeah...I'll do that." It sounded more like, *"Auh, no."*

*So be it.* Erica turned away from the harsh reply, taking a cautious step. Each one that followed came quicker. Heck, she was on carpeting now. She could run if she wanted.

**By the time she reached the end of the hallway, she practically was.**

J. ALISON COLE

## Chapter Twenty

Reese followed the ditsy bank manager into an office. The man was still rambling about the near-miss fiasco with Erica. Reese wished he could tune him out.

*Of all the people to run into, why did it have to be her?* Christ, he almost fell on top of her. And that dress. Hell, if she wasn't wearing that navy blue wrap-around dress. It had fallen open at the slit revealing her long, trim, gorgeous legs. *Fuck.*

Lambert took a seat in a high-back leather chair and organized more papers from another folder. "Have a seat, Mr. Mailing. I just need a minute to get this organized. Then we'll get you all taken care of."

Reese sat in an ugly green wing-backed chair opposite the wooden desk. The padding in the chair was hard and uneven and about as comfortable as a wooden church pew. He leaned forward and shifted on the seat. Doing so, he glanced out the large picture window. Erica was crossing the parking lot. Watching her was disturbingly addictive. She stopped at the Jeep and just stood there. Her head slowly drifted forward until it came to rest against the vehicle.

*Wait...was she hurt?*

*No. She looks upset.*

*Why would she be upset?*

"Shit." He spewed under his breath and sat up taller. After a moment, Erica straightened, tucked her hair behind her ear, and finally left.

Reese slumped back against the shitty chair and scrubbed at the whiskers on his chin.

Mr. Lambert leaned forward and rested his folded hands on the paperwork, finally ready. "Now, Mr.

Mailing, I guess now is the time to decide if you're ready to move forward?"

Reese chuckled sarcastically, more so to himself. *Move forward?* Four days ago, he knew exactly what he wanted. Now, he didn't want to stay in the same town if it meant having to randomly see Erica every fuckin' place he went.

He should've followed his first instincts and left her alone from the beginning. He should've dropped her off at her house and never gone back. *I thought she was different, and look what it got me.*

Patrick plucked the top sheet of paper from the folder and slid it toward him. "It's now or never, Mr. Mailing, but of course, it's up to you."

Reese skimmed over the loan document. If he let this deal get away, he could lose his entire down payment, which was a sizable chunk of his savings. It would also forsake the very reason he moved here: to plant roots and make a real home for both of his children once and for all. He picked up the pen, but it just hovered over the paper.

"Fuck!" His roar filled the office, the hallway, and the whole damn building.

## Chapter Twenty-One

The desolate road was a scene right out of any scary movie. The nearest driveway was a mosaic of fist-sized rocks and broken blacktop. A small brick rancher barely visible from the road was hidden by a rotten tree, downed limbs, and tall weeds. Everything screamed, there's a creepy pit in the basement where they hid the bodies of wayward passersby.

And she was, once again, without a cell phone. She could almost hear Janine's whiny voice. *I told you so.* Erica limped toward the house and knocked on the door.

An older woman peeked from a window a few feet away.

*Well hello, Clarice.* "Hello. Is it possible I might use your phone?"

The curtain floated back into place. After a moment, the door opened—just a crack wide enough for the old woman to hand her a filthy and, *yuck*, sticky cordless telephone.

"Thank you." Erica hopped to the edge of the porch and dialed Lauren. "Pick up, Lauren, pick up."

"Hello."

"Lauren? It's Mom."

"Oh, hey, Mom, I didn't recognize the number. Can I call you back? We're getting back on the bus to head to the hotel. This class is so much fun. We're in Ohio."

"Your summer class. That's right." *Great, Lauren's not even in the same state.*

"Yeah. We'll be back tomorrow night. Is it something important?"

"No, it's nothing. Be careful, honey, and have a

nice time. I'll talk to you tomorrow night."

She dialed Janine's number next. It went straight to voicemail. That usually meant she was in meetings. It could be hours, so leaving a message wouldn't help. The older woman spied on her again from the window.

Erica rubbed her thigh. At least thirty-seven miles away from home with a pulled hamstring, she had to mentally run through the list of other people to call. Marcus was on vacation in the Florida Keys with his boyfriend, and she didn't know Steve Koontz's number off the top of her head. And after how Reese acted at the bank, she doubted that he'd be interested or willing to assist her with another roadside rescue.

That only left one person. She dialed a number she knew by heart.

"Davis, I'm sorry to bother you, but I need your help," Erica explained what happened and gave him the address.

"I'm glad you called, Erica. I'm leaving now."

"Thanks, Davis." Erica returned the phone through the narrow crack in the door and then limped back to the road to wait.

Her breath hitched with each step from the throbbing muscle in her leg. The pain dragged her to the group next to the possible serial killer's mailbox.

As it happened, the first vehicle to pass by was a silver Honda. It didn't have a green door, and the driver was a teenage boy, but the irony left Erica feeling angry, lonely, and chilled.

She hadn't cried in a very long time, and it took all her resolve to keep from doing so now. Nothing made sense, and crying wouldn't fix it. A single tear landed on her thigh.

Nearly an hour later, a black BMW stopped next to her.

\*\*\*\*

Davis was her crutch limping up the front walk. "This is good. Thanks, Davis."

"Do you want me to look at it, maybe wrap it for you?" He was in doctor mode. His concern was sincere and touching. But unwarranted.

"Thank you, but no, I'll be fine."

"Put some ice on it. And here," Davis handed her a small orange bottle of pain meds. "Lay off the bike for at least a week. Two would be better."

Erica nodded automatically.

"Erica, you know, if you want to talk about anything, I'm here for you. You didn't say much in the car. What's going on?"

She shook her head and shrugged. "Nothing."

"Bull shit. Does this have anything to do with Reese Mailing?"

*How does Davis know Reese by name?* "Why would you ask that?"

"You know I had a few psychology classes in school, too. I told you before that I don't want to see you get hurt. All I've ever wanted is for you to be happy."

Davis's gaze was so earnest that she had to look away. Consequently, his arms came around her in a warm embrace. It was consoling and reassuring.

She closed her eyes, mindlessly allowing herself to nestle in that secure place, if only for a moment.

The roar of a truck splintered the moment away. Erica squirmed out of Davis's arms just as Reese turned onto their road.

Davis glanced at the blue truck going past her house. "I guess that answers my question."

"You should go, Davis." Her brows knitted, more annoyed with herself than him.

"I meant what I said, Erica." Before leaving, he

placed a soft kiss on her cheek.

Davis offered solace but nothing more. Even as confused as she was, moving backward was not the answer.

\*\*\*\*

For two days, Erica rested, read a book, and caught up on the last season of Yellowstone. On the third day, she busied herself by cleaning out closets, reorganizing the kitchen cabinets, and gluing blue rhinestones back onto Millie's bag.

By day four, she'd rather tackle the pain than let her mind fester anymore. The sun sprayed light over the horizon. She wrapped her thigh nice and tight, popped a pain pill, and coasted onto the old dirt road. This direction would take her past Reese's house, but it was the least strenuous and smoothest way to get to the main road.

At the crest of the last curve, her gaze hunted down the three tenant houses, and her heart skipped a beat. Reese's truck was still parked out front. Erica glanced at her watch. it was ten minutes, 'til six. With any luck, she could whiz by without being seen.

Twenty yards to go, Sawyer darted from the side door and spotted her. Reese was a mere step behind. The little boy ran toward the edge of the road, and Erica felt compelled to stop.

"Ms. Erica. I miss you." Sawyer's enthusiasm flowed, unencumbered by the early hour, his youth or innocence.

"Good morning Sawyer. I've missed you too." From the corner of her eye, she peeked at Reese. He— was not as thrilled as Sawyer to see her. She had no reason to hide or be uncivil, and she could get through this *unpleasant* situation by focusing on Sawyer. "How's your hamster?"

The little boy laughed. "Two days ago, he got out, and we couldn't find him. Kara didn't want to go to sleep until we did. It took a while, but Daddy found him in the back of the closet."

"Thank goodness."

The morning breeze carried a hint of Reese's unmistakable scent, and her disobedient gaze drifted to his formidable presence brooding near the back end of the truck. By standing there he safely split the distance without having to come any closer. But she could tell that he was freshly showered, his hair still wet and curled on the tips. He wore a plain white tank top. The USMC tattoo was fully exposed, nestled over the swell of his bicep, and his ratty, super faded, worn thin, and frayed at the thighs blue jeans gave a whole new definition to the word "shredded." Her stomach dipped, blatantly ignoring the supposed warnings her fragile mind tried to set.

"Good morning, Reese." She cursed the slight hesitation in her voice.

The chill from his arctic persona could have left a trail of frost on the grass. Although, he didn't look angry like he did at the bank. But he wasn't happy either. Just cold.

"Erica."

Sawyer touched the handle of her bike. "Maybe one day, I can ride with you."

Reese snorted. Which meant he was never going to let that happen.

"We'll see, maybe when you're older."

Sawyer pointed toward her bandage. "What did you do to your leg?"

"I pulled a muscle."

"Does it hurt?"

"Not too bad. I'm keeping my ride easy today along Lincoln highway. It's nice and flat."

Reese lifted his chin. "Say goodbye, Sawyer. We need to get going." His tolerance and cordial attitude was obviously spent.

"Bye, Ms. Erica." Sawyer gave her one of his beautiful smiles before running to the passenger side of the truck.

Erica should have taken off then, but the sight of Reese sauntering to the driver's door held her attention. Pulling the door open, he turned and glared. The contempt in his eyes nearly knocked her off the seat.

## Chapter Twenty-Two

The concrete floor of the equipment shed held the cold like the lining of a refrigerator. Reese lay underneath the hay baler, on a rug of dirt and oil, staring at vibrant green gears, hoses, and pumps. "What am I looking for again?"

"Steve said it was rattling near the cylinder rakes. Look around that bar that goes the whole way across. Look for something that could've...I don't know...wiggled loose." Paul squatted and peeked around one of the big tires.

Reese grumbled. "You know that's not overly specific." Running his hand along the bar, he gave it a gentle tug. Near the middle, buried in a glob of grease next to some gear housing, he found the culprit. "It looks like a sheared bolt. Maybe 9/16." It took him a minute to pry the fragmented pieces free. And then he crawled out from under the equipment.

Paul snatched the top half of the bolt and tossed it back and forth between his hands. "Shazam. Now I can tell Steve to suck it. Hey, what time you got?"

Reese threw two wrenches into an open toolbox before glancing at his watch. "10:35 AM. Why?"

"That's close enough for me. What do you say we head to town and grab a bite?"

Reese held in a grimace. "It's a little early for lunch, or would this be considered a late breakfast?"

"Either or." Paul shrugged. "There's a new lady working at the gas station. She ain't no nine like Erica or that sweet tail like your ex, but she's a solid six, hell, maybe even a seven. I got to get a good look at her in the daylight."

Reese slowly wiped the grease from his hands

onto an old rag. It was odd that Paul, of all people, didn't see Erica as a ten. He knew better, but curiosity got the better of him. "You think Erica's only a nine?"

Paul pushed away from the baler. "Well, it's like this. I have a very stringent scaling system that involves, shall we say, intimate knowledge and qualifiers, like whether or not she'll swallow, or if she'll let me in the backdoor, you know, shit like that. Since I'll never have a chance with her, I can only call her a nine." A glint of mischief danced in his eyes. "So, what do you think she is?" Paul tossed the bolt again.

His chest ached and tightened. Reese snatched the bolt from mid-air and walked to the workbench to find a replacement. "I think it's none of your damn business." Paul was like everyone else in town. To them, Erica Gebhart could do no wrong. "What I think about Erica doesn't matter, but as for Stephanie, trust me, she doesn't even rate."

"Damn, man." Paul let out a defensive laugh. "Somebody's got your nuts in a vice."

Reese dumped a rusty coffee can that held different-sized bolts. "No, no one. Just drop it."

Shoving through the pile on the counter, Paul wiggled his eyebrows suggestively. "I know we're looking for a bolt, but here, you might need this." Paul held up a long screw.

It was difficult to stay mad at Paul. "You're a real dick. You know that?"

"Actually, most of the ladies love me for that very reason. Don't ask me why." Paul abandoned his lackadaisical search for the correct-sized bolt and relaxed against the counter. "I hear you went ahead with the property deal. Congrats."

"Yeah." Reese held up three bolts that could possibly work. He laid them side by side before leaning against the counter, the same as Paul, glad to talk about something other than Erica or screws. "You knew from the beginning that I wasn't a farmer, and this was only temporary."

Paul eyed him from head to toe. "Look like a farmer to me."

Reese shook his head. "Don't worry, I've already talked to Steve about leasing the ground."

"Oh, it's not that. We'd love to keep you around. You're a hell of a handy guy. It's hard for me to believe that you're really a cop."

"I met with Chief Snyder the other day. He's giving me a referral with the state boys."

"State boys, what, you don't want to serve with Kensington's finest?" Paul's mildly sarcastic tone made it clear he lacked respect for the local department. "I suppose it wouldn't be enough to entice a badass like you. only a few loud drunks and some dim-witted squabbles now and then."

"If all the drunks were like you, then yeah. I'd still have you locked up as drunk as you got a couple of weeks ago." Reese lifted a disapproving brow at the man next to him.

Paul replaced the chaw in his lip with a quick swipe of his finger. "Hey, I wasn't expecting to drink my shots and yours too. I figured one of us needed to get drunk that night. Thanks for being the DD. I know it was late. Thanks for hanging around."

"Yeah. I didn't want to wake up the next morning to hear about you choking on your own vomit."

"I only puked twice."

"Twice? Maybe twice when you got out of the truck and two more times before you made it to the door. There was a trail of, I don't know, noodles, maybe carrots. What the hell did you eat that night? No, wait. I don't want to know."

Paul laughed silently. "I didn't take you for being squeamish." He shook his head. "But really, thanks. I'm sorry you had to sleep on the couch. I've been told it's not exactly comfortable."

"I was more concerned with the crusty stains all over the cushions." Paul was about to explain, but Reese held up his hand. "Just get a new couch. Hell, I'll give you my old one when I move."

Outside of the shed, truck tires skid to a halt. A second later, Steve raced through the side door.

"Do you have the scanner on?" he shouted, charging past them.

"Yeah, I think it's on." Paul stared at his brother, concern replacing his grin.

Reese straightened, suddenly uneasy. "What is it?"

Steve adjusted the volume on the scanner. "Who the fuck turned this down so low?"

All the muscles in Reese's jaw tightened. In the short time he'd worked for the Koontz brothers, he'd never seen Steve so agitated or heard him use profanity of any kind. Something was definitely wrong.

Reese studied the running lights on the antiquated small square box. Differential tones played high and low before a woman's monotone voice broadcast. "Rescue nine-one. Life flight two-seven, please respond to 4918 Heprend Road. 2 MVC with cyclist. Possible DOA. Time ten forty-seven."

*Cyclist and DOA.* A cold chill sank into Reese's spine. "Where the hell is Heprend Road?"

"We call it Lincoln Highway." Paul's answer confirmed his worst fear.

Steve locked eyes with Reese. "Is she riding? Do you know where she is?"

*Lincoln Highway.* Erica's soft voice from earlier

echoed in his head. "Dammit." Reese managed a diminutive nod.

"It might not be her." Paul offered a sense of hope. "Cyclist could be a motorcycle. Hell, it could be anyone. She's usually home by now anyway."

Steve grabbed the phone from his pocket and started dialing.

Reese didn't wait. He darted from the shed and ran to his truck.

*She looked so confused this morning, just like at the bank.* His foot landed on the accelerator and shot gravel against the side of the metal building. He had to check her house and see for himself.

Speed and a rough patch in the road sent the truck's back end into a fishtail. "Dammit." He cursed the road, not wanting to slow down. But if he wrecked, then what?

Reese swerved wide and hit the straightaway, frantically searching along the back of Erica's house. He spotted the Jeep in the driveway, like always. Sometimes, she parked her bike on the patio, if not near the garage. He didn't see it in either place.

He slammed onto the brakes and skidded onto the grass edge of the front yard. Then, he threw the truck in park and left the door hanging open to sprint toward the front of Erica's house.

He knocked and turned the knob at the same time. The house was unlocked. So he charged inside. The heavy wooden door banged against a coat rack by the wall.

"Erica?" A telephone sitting on the narrow table rang until the machine picked up. *Had to be Steve calling.* The greeting was cut short with a click, but no message was left, then the ringing started again. If she were here, she would've answered. "Erica!" Reese dashed up the hallway toward the kitchen, glancing into the side rooms.

Nausea filled his stomach. Lincoln Highway, Heprend Road, whatever the fuck it's called, couldn't be that far away. A few strides carried him back toward the door.

Reaching for the handle, a creak on the main staircase pierced his rambling thoughts. Did he imagine it? Could it be? A sickening fear almost kept him from checking over his shoulder.

Standing midway down the stairs from the second floor—Erica, dripping wet from head to toe, tying a short white terry robe around her waist.

Reese all but sank to his knees with relief. "You were in the damn shower."

## Chapter Twenty-Three

The telephone started ringing again. What on earth was going on? Erica hurried down the remaining steps, hoping to catch it before the fourth ring. Nothing but a dial tone buzzed in her ear, and it didn't ring after that.

Reese stood like a statue in the middle of the foyer with a bead of sweat across his forehead. "What's wrong, Reese?" Erica stepped closer and reached for his cheek. "My god, you're shaking. Tell me, please."

Without warning, he pulled her into his arms and buried his face in the wet hair at the base of her neck. His body trembled against hers.

She wrapped her arms around him, hoping to soothe and comfort whatever had him so upset. His faint whisper reached her ears.

"I thought I lost you." His fear resonated in the tight grip he had around her waist.

She ran her hands over his shoulders and stroked the fine hairs on the base of his neck. "I'm here, Reese. I'm here."

She held him that way until his tension waned. The vibe shifted at that moment, and the air crackled with sudden awareness. Heat from his breath seared over her collarbone, and every part of her body that made physical contact, the front of her thighs, breasts, arms, and fingertips, started to tingle. She inhaled his manly scent and nuzzled against the skin just below his earlobe.

Reese sucked in a shallow breath and, in one startling move, spun with her in his arms. His towering frame pinned her flat against the wall and planted one hand beside her shoulder. A hardened bulge in the front of his jeans nudged against her pelvic bone. Desire racked her body, and the thudding ache between her legs pounded in rhythm with her beating heart.

A low growl vibrated from his chest, and his eyelids lowered. "Erica, if we don't stop now, I won't be able to." A combination of hunger and turmoil dogged his voice.

Erica held him in place by the waistband of his pants and shifted her hips, grinding against him. Reese released an animalistic groan, trying to resist the stimulating contact. She undid the button on his pants, and his long lashes lowered. Reaching for the tab of the zipper, he captured her wrist. The smokiness in his blue eyes gave her fair warning. *Last chance.*

Erica's gaze fell to the enticing tendons below his jaw. God, she wanted to do this for so long. She kissed the shallow cords below his chin, savoring the feel of his whiskers on her lips.

Any restraint he might've had left disappeared. He claimed her lips with fury.

Spurred on by the scorching kiss, she inched his zipper lower and freed his cock. His shaft was lengthy, thick, and hard as granite, yet silky smooth. It thumped against her palm as she stroked him. Another ragged groan rumbled from his chest.

Reese tugged on the robe, baring her breasts. She arched away from the wall to meet his hungry lips. He devoured the tender flesh of her breasts, mouthing and sucking her nipples into ripe berries.

Mini shocks and a trail of fiery heat followed his hand, skimming down her stomach. He reached between her legs and found her velvety core.

She lifted one leg onto his hip, granting him better access. Ready and wet, he spread her juices and circled her opening before sinking one of his long fingers inside.

"You're so wet for me."

"Uh, Reese. It feels so good." Her head fell back as she rocked against his hand.

Reese branded kisses up her neck and nipped at her earlobes. A second finger merged with the first as his thumb strummed over the sensitive crux. Her body heaved against him with every swipe. The climb had never been so good.

Reese withdrew his fingers from her core, secured her leg on his hip, and wheeled away from the wall. She landed on the entryway table by the main staircase. He yanked her robe open the rest of the way as she pushed his jeans below his hips and spread her legs.

His broad hands scooped under her thighs and hauled her to the edge of the table. He channeled his penis against her slickened folds and then dipped so she was poised just over the tip of his cock. Her mouth fell open, and her body flooded to another level of want.

She held onto his shoulders and stared into the fiery opal depths of his eyes when the tip slowly entered. She sucked in a breath with every inch that followed until he was buried. Her lungs and body had never been so gloriously full.

The first stroke—Reese drew out most of his length before driving into her again. Pleasure hurtled through her limbs. Intensity filled his eyes. Focused, he gripped the banister over her shoulder, gearing up for the next.

He pumped again, and her legs locked around his waist as a demanding and steady rhythm developed. Her body harmonized with each plunge, finding that perfect spot inside.

Tremors from some forgotten place came to a boil, ready to seize her. The muscles in her legs quivered and tightened around his hips. He shifted lower, and the thrusts that followed were harder, deeper, and more demanding than the ones before.

Her orgasm hit with shattering spasms and bolts of pure bliss. She was obliterated.

Reese drove again—the muscles along his back constricted, and his thighs and backside went rigid. A moan vibrated from his torso as tapering pulses warmed her inside.

Erica floated, suspended in the staggering shockwaves coursing through her body. A lengthy sigh left her lips when his weight sagged against her. After a handful of moments, her eyes opened and she met his gaze.

## Chapter Twenty-Four

Reese stared into Erica's cinnamon eyes. They held that contented *You fucked me senseless* look. And damn if it wasn't better than he imagined.

But her lips were puffy, and her delicate breasts were marred and rosy where he'd taken his pleasure. He hadn't meant to be so rough. But, god, she was beautiful. As if she hadn't just rocked his world. He couldn't think of a time that he'd ever come that hard before. His legs had turned to jelly. Even now, they were still weak and a little shaky. *Thank god for the railing.*

Erica's satiny thighs were still wrapped around his waist, and she smelled like honeysuckle, sweet meadows, and sex. When he had her against the wall and found her so ready, so wet for him, he nearly lost his load right then.

A board on the front porch creaked. Both of their heads swung that way.

Standing on the other side of the screened door was Steve, flushed and wide-eyed, as if he couldn't comprehend what he was seeing. *Shit, shit, shit.* When the shock finally sank in, Steve turned and walked to the edge of the porch.

Reese yanked Erica's robe onto her shoulders to cover her the best he could, and her legs loosened from around his waist. He eased from her luscious warmth, but inner muscles clamped around him.

Resisting the urge to pump her again took everything he had. "Christ almighty, Erica." From somewhere, he found strength that allowed him to dip free of her body. Then he blew out a hollowed breath, tucked his dick away, and zipped up his pants.

Erica hopped down from the table and cinched the

belt on her robe. She should've looked mortified, but all he could see was the afterglow of satisfaction.

He'd store that look away for the lonely nights ahead, because right now, he had to talk to Steve. "Stay here." Reese stepped onto the front porch.

Steve stood next to the railing, staring straight ahead. A steady whistle fumed through his nose from heavy breathing. The poor son-of-a-bitch had been worried and frightened, too.

"Steve, I...uh."

Steve turned to face him. His gaze skirted toward Erica, standing in the shadows inside the foyer. His lower jaw twitched, and he gave his hat a swift tug before rearing back and swinging.

Reese took most of the right hook, unable to dodge it entirely. It took him a second to regain his balance. That was the last thing he expected from the mild-mannered farmer, even though he probably deserved it. He rubbed his jaw.

Steve's fist opened and closed like he was contemplating taking another swing.

*Fuck that.* Reese broadened his stance. "I'll give you one, Steve, but only one."

Steve's hands came together, and he rubbed his knuckles. His gaze scurried in the general direction of the door again. "I'm glad you're okay." The whistle from his nostril fumed one last irate breath as he left the porch. In the yard, Reese's truck was still running, with the door hanging open. Going by, Steve slammed it shut and then jumped into his own truck and took off like a bat out of hell.

The spring on the door squealed as Erica stepped onto the porch. Her footsteps were soft as a whisper, but her presence hit him like a dart between the shoulder blades.

Her robe was hugged tight around her slender curves. "Are you going to tell me what's going on now?"

Her disheveled appearance and the hoarseness of her *just-had-sex voice* had Reese momentarily mesmerized. He cleared his throat in a lame attempt to clear his mind. "There was an accident on the highway. Everyone thought it was you."

"Oh." A light wind swirled, carrying a hint of honeysuckle.

*Fuck.* Reese stepped toward the railing and haphazardly shoved his shirt into his jeans. He needed space to rebuild his shattered defenses. But the luscious scent followed him. Hell, he was covered in it. He'd need more than a shower to remove her from his skin.

He'd messed up big this time.

From a safer distance, he turned. "Look, Erica—" His concentration stalled again when his gaze landed on the rosiness on her cheeks left by his whiskers. "I didn't mean for any of this to happen." Yeah, he'd ravished her lips, her neck, her delicate breasts. He cleared his throat again. "I'm sorry if I was a little rough." Anguish punched him in the gut.

A tempting smile curved her lips upward. "I'm not complaining."

Her simple smile nearly unraveled him. Was this what it felt like to drown? "This, it—shouldn't have happened."

Her vixen smile altered into a strenuous stare. "It's a little late for that, don't you think?"

His chest tightened. "What I'm trying to say is that I didn't want it to happen."

She flinched, almost indignant. "You could have fooled me."

Maybe so, but a few days ago, Erica was standing in that very spot in the arms of her ex-husband. Everyone in town was talking about the two of them being back together. The thought of her entwined around the good doctor the same way she'd been with him practically ripped out his guts. *She's no better than Stephanie.*

"Look, I should have stopped—but I didn't." Glancing away, he had one last issue to address. "I don't normally—well, I'm not ordinarily this reckless." A deep breath filled his lungs. "I need to know—are you on anything?"

Erica's face blanked. It took a few seconds more before his question became clear. Her light brown eyes widened, and her hands flew to her mouth. "Oh my God, I—no. I'm not on any birth control." Another muffled gasp slipped out.

Reese dragged a hand over the scruff of his cheeks. "I sure as hell wasn't expecting something like this to happen, and well, I didn't exactly hold back." He gave her another moment. "If you're worried, maybe you can take that morning-after pill, but just so you know, I've been tested, and I'm clean." He paused. "Are you?"

Her mouth fell open, clearly insulted by the question. "Wha... Seriously?"

He shrugged. "Hell yes, I'm serious. How am I supposed to know how many other men you're sleeping with?"

Erica's voice and entire persona shrank. "I've only... Davis is the only other person I've been with."

*Fucking figures.* His cynical laugh recaptured her attention. "Well, don't worry, I won't tell anyone. And I seriously doubt Steve will say anything to sully your pristine reputation." Her gaze locked onto his. "Look, it's not that big of a deal. We fucked—"

Her hand scorched across his face faster than lightning. Reese grimaced from the sting, letting a self-loathing smile consume him. His remark was callous, and he knew it.

All the color drained from her face, and her bottom lip started to quiver. "I think you should go."

There it was, his getaway. It wasn't clean or pretty or—even welcomed for some goddamn reason. Every instinct Reese had said to take it, run, and not look back. Only his feet felt like they were nailed to the floor.

This wasn't the first time he trusted a woman who dicked him over. But by god, it would be the last. "Damn you, Erica."

## Chapter Twenty-Five

Erica didn't wait for Reese to leave. She charged inside and slammed the main door closed, hoping to shut Reese out—in more ways than just her home.

*Wham bam, thank you, ma'am.*

Those foolish words ricocheted through her mind. Erica closed her eyes and covered her ears, trying to drown out the sound of his truck—roaring away from the house. After a minute passed, her eyes opened.

The small space of the foyer would never be the same. The narrow hallway table sat askew, and the telephone had been knocked over. If the phone made that annoying beeping sound, she never heard it. She'd been busy. She calmly set the receiver in place, leaving the cord a tangled mess to unravel later.

She'd had sex with Reese, or as he put it, "fucked." Unprotected, uninhibited, mind-blowing, light her soul on fire—sex. She never quite understood how people could be so reckless and find themselves in a position like this. But, now she was one of them.

*Potent.*

What if Reese really was potent?

Erica hadn't worried about getting pregnant since before Lauren was born. She and Davis had tried to have another child over the years, but it never happened, even though multiple tests proved them both healthy.

*Tested.*

Good grief. Reese said he tested clean. The fact that he needed to be tested—was unnerving. And then, for him to question the number of men she'd been with, huh. He was the one with the reputation. And now, ironically, more than ever, she had first-hand knowledge of how he'd earned it.

Erica slid down the wall in the hallway and pulled her knees close to her chest.

He stated quite clearly that he didn't want her. Now, he'd said it twice. So he certainly wouldn't want a baby. Where did people even get those morning-after pills, and how did he know so much about them? Would she need a prescription? She could just hear herself asking Davis for one. *Oh, by the way, I accidentally screwed the Koontz's handyman, and he doesn't want to add to his hoard of children. He probably does have seven kids.*

But even if this 'pill' was over the counter, it wasn't as if she could just pick it up at Jackson's Pharmacy. *What are you buying there, Mrs. Gebhart? Oh, hey, everybody, guess who succumbed to the Don Juan manwhore, Reese Mailing?*

The telephone rang, jarring her away from her derailing thoughts. Erica crawled toward the table and answered the phone. "Hello."

"Mom! Thank God."

"Lauren." Erica paused briefly to reset her frame of mind. "What is it, honey?"

"Dad called. He said he's been trying to reach you, but the line was busy."

Erica cringed in silence. *Yeah, it was off the hook, physically and literally.* "Uh, yeah, sorry."

"Apparently, there was some kind of accident involving a bicyclist. I told him it couldn't be you if you were on the phone."

"I—no, Dear. It wasn't me."

"I'll let him know that I got a hold of you. Could it be any of your friends?"

"Ummm, I don't know. Marcus is still in Florida."

"Are you all right, Mom? You sound—different."

Boy, was she. Erica tried sounding less different. "I'm fine, really. Tell your father I'm fine." She was anything but fine.

"Good. Hey, I thought we could have dinner soon."

"I'd like that." She praised her automatic responses.

"Okay, great. I'll talk to you later. Bye, Mom."

"Bye, sweetie." Erica hung the phone up. Her hand barely left the receiver before it rang again. "Lauren?"

"No, it's me." Janine spat through the line. "I'm coming over."

"Janine, this really isn't a good time, I—"

"No. I'm coming now. In fact, I'll be there in ten minutes."

Erica was in no condition to deal with Janine. She was about to protest, but Janine cut her off.

"Erica, I know what you did."

*Click.*

A chilling numbness consumed her. How could Janine know? The loud beeping began. The irony was almost too much. Erica slammed the phone down and raced upstairs to get dressed.

Six minutes later, Janine burst through the kitchen door and tossed her purse onto the island. She eyed Erica with disdain, then marched to the cupboard, grabbed a glass, and poured herself some tea from the fridge. It was all very methodical and assertive.

Erica sat quietly at the small table by the window, curious to discover *exactly* what Janine thought she knew.

Her sister flopped onto the chair opposite hers. She leaned back with a snide and disapproving glare in her eyes. "You had sex with him."

Erica was totally dumbfounded. "How?" She shook her head. "How in the world did you find out already?"

Janine sat her drink down. "It's all over town."

"What?" Erica squeaked. "That's impossible."

Janine clucked. "I was really hoping it was all some ugly, disgusting rumor, but you're not even trying to deny it. Hugh, the thought of it is just so gross. I think I might puke, and if I do, you'll have to clean it up because I can't handle vomit, even my own."

*How...how...how?* Erica stared at her sister, trying to get her brain past that word. Steve must've driven directly to the hardware store, but even that would have taken time to circulate. Was there a skywriter flying over Kensington that she didn't know about? *Erica had sex with Reese.* "How? I don't understand how you found out already."

"Does it matter? I just can't believe you'd do that with him again."

Erica chewed on the side of a jagged fingernail, something she *hadn't* done since she was fifteen. She stopped and jerked her hand away from her mouth. "Wait, what do you mean again?"

Janine shivered in open disgust. "Well, like I said before, Lauren came from somewhere."

"You're talking about Davis?"

Janine squinted bizarrely. "Yes."

Erica jumped to her feet. "What exactly did you hear?"

Janine's demeanor turned judicious. "I heard it from Tom. He said everyone saw you and Davis having a delightful dinner, and then you climbed in his car and left the restaurant together.

Erica shook her head. "What? No."

"Are you telling me that you weren't at the

restaurant with him and that your car wasn't in the parking lot all night? Everyone already knows he's moved out of his condo." Janine jumped from her chair. "Hold on! Who did you think I was talking about?"

It didn't take long for Erica to fit the pieces together. If that rumor was all over town, then Reese could have heard it. The timing, his reaction toward her. She had dinner with Davis on Friday. A day later, Reese canceled their date. That was too much to be a coincidence.

Erica sank back into the chair and covered her face. "Reese. I was with Reese."

An unusual span of silence followed as Janine articulated her reaction. "Reese! You went to pound town with Reese. When did that happen?"

"Don't you see Janine? Reese thinks I slept with Davis, too. That's why he made other plans." *That's why he turned to Stephanie.* Erica rubbed her scalp.

Janine rose from her chair. "So you really, you know, got his hot beef injection?"

Erica sighed. "You're so crude, Janine." First things first. "What do you know about morning-after pills?"

Janine's eyes couldn't get any wider, even on top of everything else she'd just learned. "Holy shit. You did it raw. Wow! I'm in total disbelief right now. His loads are probably massive." Janine's excitement took ample time to dwindle. "I just realized something. This is usually the other way around, huh?" Her sister knelt in front of her chair. "Don't worry, honey. I got what you need in my medicine cabinet, and I know a lady."

Erica let her hands fall onto the table.

"I'm sorry, Erica. I'm sorry men are such dicks, even if *his* was probably really nice. It was nice, wasn't it?"

She could only shake her head. "Shut up, Janine."

"Come on, let's go."

"Where are we going?"

"We're going to take care of business."

\*\*\*\*

At Janine's apartment, the afternoon became a whirlwind of Twinkies, pizza, two bottles of wine, a pill from Janine's medicine cabinet that was beyond its expiration date, and a dose of non-prescribed, anti-pregnancy herbal tea from some old hippie woman that lived in the apartment building. It looked like a mixture of cilantro and pinkish-gray sand.

"If I die from drinking this, tell Lauren it was from the alcohol."

"You're not going to die. I drank it once." Janine shoved a glass of water closer toward her lips. "You'll need to chase it down with this because it tastes like shit."

And it did.

Spiced Rum and some kind of coffee liqueur quenched her evening thirst, and with that, Erica settled into a contented level of inebriation.

"Maybe Davis should be worried." Erica scoffed when Janine's face twisted. "I was buzzed that night at the restaurant, that's why he drove me home, but that's all that happened. So, technically, this is your fault."

"How do you figure that?" Janine refilled her glass.

"You bailed. Davis showed up along with too many gin and tonics."

"Bastard probably ordered them on purpose. I wouldn't put nothing past him."

"I ordered my drinks. Me, I did that." She eyed Janine curiously. "When were you weethhh Tom?"

"I wouldn't say we were *together* together. Uh, it was after I got back from Chicago. He wanted to show me his kitchen after hours."

"Gross. You did it at the restaurant?"

"Noooooo." Janine stumbled against the chair next to the sofa. "But, I did find one thing out. I don't think he's circumcised, not that it matters."

"If you didn't do it, then how—would you? Oh, gross, never mind."

"I didn't blow him if that's what you're thinking. We were in the little office area, and I just, you know, felt—over his pants. It was kind of stubby and felt different."

Erica choked, trying to hold her laugh inside.

"What?" Janine asked.

"Maybe he's a *they*."

Janine's head flopped against the cushion. "Maybe, but it doesn't matter. Little Shit can cook.

Erica gulped some syrupy, sweet, clear liquid. It had a name made up of too many 'H's and 'R's' for her to try to pronounce when she was sober, much less drunk. The alcohol numbed her mouth with a cooling peppermint sensation.

"Reese said we *fucked*." Erica blurted. "He said it was no big deal." She took another swig before offering the bottle to Janine.

"And what do you say?"

A drunken laugh popped free. "I say, it was incredible, and it was a *big* deal to me, at least." She held her hands apart for Janine. "About *this* big. He's much bigger than Davis." She sank back onto the sofa, letting images of Reese warm her insides. "It was the best sex I've ever had."

****

"Rise and shine, Lady." Erica flinched at the light shining behind Janine, sitting on the coffee table holding a glass of water and two aspirin. "It's morning. Here, take these."

Erica's head felt like a block of cement, and her mouth had the unsavory taste of wet cardboard. Sitting up, her body resorted to slow motion. "Thanks." She took the pills and drank the entire glass of water.

"I take it *all* back," Janine said.

"What are you talking about?"

"You don't have to share details ever again. You were pretty explicit."

Erica eyed her sister skeptically. "Why, what did I say?"

"Along with the length and girth, you pretty much described everything from the grip he had on your ass to each thunderous pump, thrust, and shudder he gave you. You sounded like a damn porn star. I don't know if I can look at you the same way ever again."

Erica chuckled and immediately winched from the horrendous pounding in her head. "Now you know what I go through. I'm sorry, Janine. Maybe this got him out of my system."

"Honey, that put him in your system, bodily fluids and all. You know that pill you took and that tea you drank aren't one hundred percent effective. Just saying."

She could've done without the subtle reminder. "He's probably screwed so many women. It makes me feel tainted. And the worst part is, I doubt it meant anything to him."

"What did you do to his taint?"

Erica scoffed. Of course, Janine honed in on that word. "Good Lord Janine, not that kind of—never mind."

"Look, I get it. I know what this is. This is the *Angry, and I'm so stupid* stage."

"I'm not angry because I did it."

"Oh, I know."

Erica rolled her eyes, flinching from the pain it

added to her head. "Really? Please do share your infinite sex wisdom."

"Okay. You're angry, not because it happened, but because it did—and you liked it anyway. Therefore, you feel stupid. It happens to me all the time."

*My sister is a genius. Good grief.*

It was true. Erica more than liked it. Reese had pushed her aside and even tried to stop her, but she wanted him anyway, probably more now than before. How pathetic.

Janine gave her a condescending smile. "Come on, Skank. I'll take you home. Just don't breathe on me. You need to brush your teeth."

****

The red light in the center of town finally turned green. Janine eased forward, waiting for the oncoming traffic to pass so she could turn left. Of the three vehicles going straight, the third was—blue and—a truck. A rod entered Erica's spine. How many blue Chevy trucks, like Reese's, could there be in Kensington? A grumble shouted from her gut.

At least he wouldn't recognize Janine's beige Lexus.

*Why should I even care?* Sweat broke across her forehead as her noisy stomach churned with a mixture of apprehension, betrayal, and Snapps.

The glare on the windshield didn't hide Reese's stern expression when he rode by. Today was probably just another day for him, unchanged by their recent encounter. He probably didn't get drunk last night or fall asleep dreaming of her. She was just another notch in his belt.

The truck roared by. From what she could tell, Reese was alone. Erica didn't see the children or a dainty blonde in the seat curled beside him. Her stomach bubbled again, forcing her to swallow.

Two more cars went by before Janine could turn. She seemed unaware of the person who passed by.

"Tell you what, Erica. I have to go to San Diego on Friday. Why don't you come with me? We can make it a long weekend, maybe even one or two days beyond that. It's a private charter for the company, so it won't cost you a thing."

Erica relaxed her shoulders into the plush seat. "Can I let you know tomorrow?"

"Sure."

****

Erica stepped from the shower. The toxic soup in her stomach frothed, creating a slight tickle in her throat. Several gulps forced it back down. She only had a split second to decide. Fight it and pray that the feeling goes away, or throw up to rid the poison from her system?

She took long, soothing breaths, but her head pounded, hovering over the ivory porcelain bowl. Drinking that much last night was stupid. Almost as foolish as drinking some foul-tasting concoction…that may or may not keep her from getting pregnant. Why did she listen to Janine? But, as bizarre as that was, it still wasn't the dumbest thing she had done in the previous twenty-four hours. Her stomach settled, and she laid her head against the cool seat.

So much for being classy.

Five minutes later, Erica threw on a sweatshirt and some black leggings. Downstairs, she checked two messages on her machine, one from Claire, informing her that Millie had given birth, and the second was from Lauren. She dialed her daughter's number.

Lauren picked up after two rings. "Hello."

"Lauren, I just saw your message."

"Hey, I heard you stayed with Aunt Janine last

night."

Erica really had to start slapping her sister. "Yes." Hopefully, that was all she heard. "Did you need something, honey?"

"I was hoping we could have dinner tonight, maybe, The Olive Garden?"

"Tonight?"

"Yeah, if you're not busy."

Erica didn't feel like going anywhere, but milling around the house wasn't exactly appealing either. She could barely step foot in the foyer without seeing images of Reese. "Sounds good. I can pick you up around six."

"Actually, I'll meet you there, but six is good."

"Okay, I'll see you tonight." Erica hung up and headed to the kitchen for a glass of water. She needed to flush her system sober. Standing at the sink, waiting for her glass to fill, a trail of dust chased a vehicle coming up the road. A minute later, a silver Honda zoomed by. There would be no holding it back this time. She raced into the bathroom and threw up.

\*\*\*\*

The smell of oregano, onions, and garlic hung thick in the air. Her squeamish stomach gurgled. Erica should've told her daughter another day, which would have been better. Just then, she spotted Lauren waving from across the restaurant. So she maneuvered through the crowd but came to a sudden stop when *Davis* rose from the hidden side of the booth.

If he intended to blindside her, he succeeded. "I'm so glad you could make it." He planted a light kiss on the cheek.

Erica remained standing and openly stared at Lauren.

"Dad said you wouldn't mind."

"Please, Erica, I thought we could have a nice

dinner—as a family."

Family dinners were usually discussed—in advance. Erica's mood was already dismal, of course, all by her own doing, but this unexpected gathering was like poking the bear. With some reserved malice, she slid onto the bench beside Lauren.

"Dad ordered you some wine."

"No, thank you. I'll just have water."

He smirked at her from his side of the table. "Not drinking tonight?" He said it in jest, lightly referencing the last meal they shared—which ironically started the erroneous gossip all over town.

Erica was tired of being polite, proper, and predictable. She leaned toward Davis and began her interrogation. "Tell me that you didn't start that rumor."

Davis didn't display a flicker of surprise, only a sly smile. "No, I didn't start it. I swear. And if you must know, I just heard it myself."

"Did you at least deny it?"

"What rumor?" Lauren exchanged looks between her parents.

"I thought there might be a chance I wouldn't have to." Davis met her intense gaze head-on.

"You've got to be kidding me." Erica lowered her chin. "How do you know Reese by name?"

His green eyes tightened right before his gaze scurried away. "I met him."

"Wait, Dad knows about Reese?"

Davis glanced at Lauren.

"Where?" Erica's tone started the volley.

Davis took a heavy breath. "At your house."

"At my house? When?"

Davis fiddled with his napkin, smoothing it over his lap. "That morning after—we had dinner, and I drove you home." The pounding in Erica's head grew stronger.

She was unable to make sense of this. He quickly perceived her confusion and huffed. "I came by to give you a lift to your car. It was early, very early."

"You guys had dinner without me?" Lauren questioned, trying to keep up.

Erica's face scrunched. "Wait, where was I?"

"You'd already ridden your bike in town to get the Jeep yourself."

"I told you that's what I was going to do. I couldn't have been gone that long." Erica collapsed against the back of the cushioned seat. "Tell me exactly what happened."

"I got to your house and poured myself a coffee, but I'd spilled some down the front of my shirt. I was in the middle of unbuttoning it when he pulled up. It looked like he was leaving you a note, so I answered the door and introduced myself."

So not only did Reese have to hear the rumors floating around town, he found Davis at her house at an ungodly hour with his shirt undone. Anyone would jump to the same conclusion, true or not. "Davis, you are an asshole." Erica jumped up from the table. "I'm sorry, Lauren, I'm not feeling up for this. We'll have to have dinner another time."

Davis stood. "He's not the type of man you should be with. Seriously Erica, do you really think he could make you happy?"

"The type of man? You don't even know him." Why was she defending Reese? Disheartened, she forced the lump of heartache that was lodged in her throat back into her gut. "None of it matters now."

J. ALISON COLE

## Chapter Twenty-Six

Clouds covered the sunrise, and rain pelted her face. It would've taken a hurricane to keep Erica from riding this morning. She pedaled into a driving wind up a long, steep hill. She stopped when she reached the top. From this vantage point, the land resembled a patchwork quilt of rich, multi-colored fields. Rain-soaked earth darkened some, making the rows of bright green sprigs of new corn look like the stitching. The overcast sky made the view hard to appreciate. And her thoughts were as gray as the sky.

The rain conveniently hid her tears. She needed a good cry and was tired of fighting it. Everything changed the moment that rumors started circling about her and Davis. They weren't true, but Reese believed them *and* moved on easily enough.

*We fucked.* It was just sex for him.

The memories flooded her mind, and her body hummed, remembering his tongue lapping on her breasts, the friction of his thrusts, and the throbbing inside her when he came. Reese touched more than her body, more than her skin. He branded her soul.

Logic dictated everyone in town was right about Reese. Her mind was telling her to accept that, but a nagging uncertainty in the pit of her stomach refused to let her. How could she be so conflicted over this?

Maybe a couple of days away in San Diego with Janine would help.

The ride to reach this spot took almost an hour. Returning home would only take half that. From here, it was all downhill.

\*\*\*\*

"It's a late flight, ten or eleven, so I'll call you around six to let you know. I'm so glad you're coming. We're going to have so much fun," Janine squealed.

Erica didn't feel the same level of enthusiasm, but her sister meant well. "Okay, I'll wait for your call." The screen door squawked, and Lauren entered the kitchen. "Oh, hey Janine, Lauren's here. I have to go." She hung up.

"Hi, Mom, are you feeling better?"

"Yeah, and I'm sorry I left so abruptly last night. Things between your father and I…well, he and Bethany have separated, and apparently, a rumor started that he and I were getting back together. Honey, it's not true, and that's never going to happen."

"I didn't think so. Is that because of Reese?"

It made perfect sense for Lauren to assume as much. But, in this case, Erica had the truth on her side. "No. Reese and I aren't… He and I are…well, no, he's not the reason." Saying it aloud sliced her heart into ribbons.

"He seemed like a nice guy. I actually thought that the two of you had something. But, I guess it would be weird for someone like you to be involved with a guy like Reese."

Her daughter's comment sparked that inner need to defend him again. "Guy like Reese? What do you mean, Lauren?"

"I'm sorry, Mom, I don't mean it—in a bad way."

"Is there a good way to say something like that?"

Lauren shook her head. "It's just that last week, I saw Grandmother Gebhart, and she asked if you were seeing anyone. At the time, I told her about Reese. And then she asked me what he does for a living. I said that I wasn't really sure. But you have to admit that it's odd to see someone like you involved with a man who probably has more pairs of jeans in his closet than suits."

"Someone like me? Are you saying I'm a snob?"

"No, Mom. It's just how society is."

"Society? And here, I thought that I taught you better. Hard work and success are what you make it, and love in its purest form isn't defined by the clothes you wear, the job you have, or even the amount of money you have in the bank."

Erica's throat tightened. When and how did *love* enter her tattered thoughts? Her face scrunched with a self-loathing, sarcastic smirk. "Well, I'll bet your grandmother was grinning ear to ear."

Lauren laughed. "Not really," she paused. "I think she finally understands now."

"Understands what?"

"How incredible you are. Grandma said Dad was an idiot, and she called Bethany a bitch."

****

Erica packed herself a small bag for the weekend and then poured herself a bowl of cereal for dinner. Using the last of the milk would be one less thing to go bad in the fridge until she returned. She rinsed out the bowl and placed it on the drying rack just as the telephone rang. It had to be Janine letting her know when their flight was leaving. She picked up the phone in the kitchen, trying to sound more cheerful than she felt. "Hello."

"Erica. Don't hang up, please." Reese's baritone voice steamrolled over her.

"Listen, I need you to pick up Sawyer."

"Reese, I'm...getting ready to go away for the weekend, and—"

"Erica, I've been arrested. Sawyer's at the police station in Kensington."

"What?"

"I can't explain now, but Robin and Steve are

away until tomorrow. Paul and Bob are at a tractor show in Martinsburg, and I can't reach them. Erica, if there were anyone else I could ask, I would. Trust me, I didn't want to call you." *Why not call Stephanie?* "If you can't do this, they'll call child services. Please, please, Erica. I can't let that happen." The desperation in his voice carved into her conscience.

"Okay, okay. I'll be right there." Erica hung up the phone, grabbed her purse, and raced out the door. Her adrenaline was pumping faster than she could think. She jumped behind the steering wheel of the Jeep and fished for her cell phone out of her purse. Her sister would be pissed, but she had to do this for Sawyer.

*Sorry, Janine, had something important come up, and can't go now. I'll explain everything tomorrow. Thnx. Luv you.*

Ten minutes later, Erica turned into the parking lot of the Kensington police station. Twenty years ago, this building served as the original bank of Kensington. The town acquired this property when the new, bigger bank was built. It was her first year on the revitalization committee, and she'd played a huge part in finding a good use for the building. Basically, making it a police station was her idea.

Erica entered through a set of double doors. Her usual nerves of steel pinged tighter than a bridge cable. Sawyer's tiny frame sat on a metal bench beside the front desk. His feet dangled back and forth, not long enough to reach the floor. His little head lifted and spotted her a second later. He sprung off the bench and raced toward her with all the innocence of a frightened seven year old boy.

Erica gathered him into her arms. His thin frame and bony limbs clung on for dear life. "It's going to be all right, Sawyer. I promise."

"I'll be damned. You do know him. Should've figured. I forgot how you have a soft spot for charity cases." Officer Wendham stood behind the counter with his hands spread wide, and his bloated belly melted over the surface like Jabba the Hut.

Everything about the man was contemptuous. *Janine would've smiled and said, "Fuck you."* Instead, Erica held her ground with a cool, resolute stare until he looked away like a beaten dog. She patted Sawyer on the back, and straightened to her full height.

Chief Snyder stepped from a doorway off to the side. "Wendham, find a desk." The Chief came toward Erica, his weathered face holding a sympathetic smile. "Thank you for coming, Mrs. Gebhart."

"Please, call me Erica."

"All right, Erica. I didn't want to involve social services if possible." He glanced at Sawyer. "Do you think I might have a word alone?"

Erica nodded and reached inside her purse for a few dollars. "Here, Sawyer, go to the machine, pick something to drink, and grab a snack. I need to take care of a few things before we go." He took the money with a wide-eyed grin. "Wait for me on the bench. All right?"

"Yes ma'am."

Chief Snyder led her to his office. From the doorway, she was still able to see Sawyer.

"I thought you might like to know what really happened."

Did she want to know? "Of course."

The Chief crossed his arms and propped a hip on the front edge of a cluttered desk. "It's really just a case of bad timing. I'm afraid Mr. Mailing got mixed up in someone else's domestic dispute. He has a daughter. You knew that, right?"

"Yes, I'm aware."

"We got a call from one of the neighbors. Apparently, the girl's mother and boyfriend were arguing, and somehow, the girl got dragged into it. Reese was there to pick her up. He pulled up about the same time as we did. Needless to say, the boyfriend is a real piece of work and dumber than a mud-oyster. Reese called his daughter just as the dumb-ass boyfriend grabbed her by the arm and called her a little cu— well, something nasty. The next thing I knew, Reese was on him. I'd never seen anyone move that fast. And hell, it took three of us to drag him off the knucklehead. The guy insisted on going to the hospital to get checked out. He was spouting off that he wanted to press charges. I didn't have any choice but to bring Reese in."

"Where is Kara now?"

Chief Snyder lifted his brows. "The mother made the girl stay, but Reese refused to let his son be exposed to that environment—and I don't blame him." The chief uncrossed his arms. "Erica, Reese isn't a bad guy. He actually served with my youngest brother."

"In the Marines?"

"Yeah. I know there's a bunch of scuttlebutt going around town about him, but whatever you may have heard, all that stuff that happened in Michigan, it's not true, well, not all of it. And I know he could use your help with this."

Erica had no idea what happened in Michigan other than what she heard from Herb Jackson and his cronies at the hardware store. "What's going to happen to Reese?"

"Judge Dougherty is away for the weekend on some goddamn fishing trip. It'll be Monday before Reese can be arraigned or have any kind of bail posted." Chief Snyder grabbed a set of keys from the desk behind him. "You can speak to him before you go."

"Is that necessary? I mean, did he ask to speak with me?"

The chief glanced at her, somewhat confused by the question. "Well, no, but I need you both to sign some papers." He stood. "Erica, if this is a problem, just let me know. I was under the impression that the two of you...were acquainted, being neighbors and all. If you don't want to do this, no one would think less of you."

*Think less of me,* as if that were Erica's concern. The chief couldn't possibly know the true extent of her *acquaintance* with Reese. "No, no. It's nothing like that. Sawyer's a wonderful little boy. I'm happy to take him. Just to be clear, Chief Snyder, I've never cared what people think of me."

Chief Snyder gave her a nod of approval. "I'll take you back myself."

From the doorway of the office, she called Sawyer. "Sawyer, I'll be right back."

He raised an orange cheesy curl, dust-covered thumb, and started swinging his feet again.

Erica followed the chief past a series of cubicles. Walking through the station, she became the focal point for several of the officers. She'd been in this building plenty of times, but never to see someone incarcerated, and they all knew it.

At the back of the room, the chief pressed some numbers into a keypad to unlock a door. After a loud buzz, she followed him into a short hallway with three more doors. The first door was a bathroom, with the universal symbol for a man or a woman. The second door had a small sign that read "Storage." The sign on the last door read "Detainees." He pressed a series of numbers into a keypad, and the door opened.

"I'll give you a couple of minutes. Then I need both of you to sign some papers." Chief Snyder stepped aside.

"Thank you." The last few days had done a number on her inner strength and self-confidence, but she mustered what was left and stepped into the room.

Kensington's jail amounted to nothing more than a large room divided into three holding cells. Each cell had a cot and a sliver of walking space. The bars covering the windows along the exterior walls were remnants of the bank, but the bars dividing the cells shined ominous and criminal enough.

The first two cells were empty. Reese occupied the third. He was sitting sideways on the cot with his feet spread and his elbows propped on his knees, holding his head in his hands.

A strip of yellow duct tape on industrial-grade Berber carpeting dictated how close visitors were allowed to stand. Erica stepped up to the line.

She hadn't seen him since. Vivid memories flooded her brain, and the flutter in her stomach nearly choked her. All she could do was stare.

After two breaths, she found her voice. "Reese?" It came out meek and sounded strange to her ears.

His hands fell away from his face, and he looked up. And when he stood, the air in the room disappeared. The blue of his eyes held no sparkle today. The brick wall was up. His brown tee shirt hung loose at his waist with a three-inch tear near the seam of his shoulder. A bluish mark shadowed under his left eye, and a thin split of dried blood marred his bottom lip. Even wild and disheveled, the man was incapable of not being sexy.

Erica stepped beyond the invisible power of the yellow tape and gripped the bars. It somehow drew him nearer. "Are you hurt?"

Reese ignored her concern. "Thank you for doing this." The curtness in his tone was a sharp reminder of why she was here.

*It's not that big of a deal. We fucked.* His words echoed in her mind. "I—of course." She almost said she was glad to help, but he told her he had no one else to call, which made sense. He hadn't lived here long enough to know that many people, and the few he did know were unavailable. She was his last choice. "I know several lawyers. Would you like me to contact one for you?"

"God, no. I didn't want you involved as it is. This isn't your problem, Erica. If Steve and Robin get back and I'm still here, I'll see if they can take Sawyer and maybe check on Kara until I get this straightened out."

"I don't mind."

Reese huffed, shaking his head. "Of course you don't." His deep voice rattled with sarcasm.

Her chin lifted an inch. "What does that mean?"

He gripped the bars below her hands. "Honestly, a *regular* person would have told me to go straight to hell." The crease appeared on his forehead. "I cussed you, Erica. To your face and behind your back. Yet here you are."

The disdain saturating his voice seemed like it wasn't directed at her so much as himself because she showed up.

Her grip around the bars loosened, letting her hand slip lower and accidentally brush the tops of his. The jolt hadn't changed.

Reese jerked his hands away from the bars like he was stung. He took his familiar pose and made a full circle with his head. A storm of derision entered his eyes as he whispered. "I wish to God I had never met you."

Erica's knees almost buckled. Did he mean that? Did he hate her that much?

Chief Snyder cleared his throat and entered the room. "Reese, I need you and Mrs. Gebhart to sign these papers for the boy's release."

Erica didn't bother to read anything or look at Reese again. She scribbled her name where the chief pointed, gathered Sawyer, and fled.

****

The boy who never stopped talking sat uncommonly quiet in the passenger seat of the Jeep. After witnessing his father being hauled off to jail, Sawyer had to feel isolated and a little scared.

"Hey, Sawyer, how about we swing by your house to pick up your hamster and grab some extra clothes and maybe your toothbrush."

He only shrugged his shoulders in a *whatever* manner.

"The way I see it, your hamster might get lonely. This way, you can tell him everything will be okay."

He shook his head, never looking up.

"Are you hungry, Sawyer?"

"Well, we were supposed to go out for dinner, but that didn't happen. I was going to order spaghetti."

"Spaghetti! I love spaghetti. Tell you what. When we get to my house, we'll make some. A big giant pot. And you can help me."

"Can we make meatballs?"

"What's spaghetti without meatballs?"

****

Sitting at the small table in the kitchen, she and Sawyer feasted on Italian cuisine. And slowly but surely, Sawyer returned to his quintessential jabbering ways.

"So, how do you like hanging out with Joey?"

Sawyer had a full mouth. After two chews, he answered. "One time, we made bowls out of popsicle sticks. Mine was bigger than Joey's. He painted his green, and mine was blue."

"Is blue your favorite color?"

"Oh yeah." He described planting marigold seeds in Dixie cups and dream catchers made of yarn and grapevines.

As the list of summer crafts continued in detail, Erica took the time to observe him more freely. The shape of his face, his beautiful blue eyes—identical to his father's. Even his lanky frame held the promise of one day being similar in height and build. He was Reese's son. Only his tawny dark skin and ebony curls would differentiate them. Perhaps Sawyer would grow up and become a lady's man, too, just like his father.

After dinner, they watched the movie *Babe*. It ended around 8:45 PM. "Come on, Sawyer, I think it's time for those Spiderman pajamas."

Erica watched as he washed his face and brushed his teeth. "Now, I'm going to give you a couple of minutes so you can take care of business and change into your jammies. I'll wait for you in the bedroom across the hall."

After a couple of minutes, the toilet flushed, and the small boy darted into the room with the bottom half of his PJs inside out and backward.

"Oh well." She tapped the bed.

Sawyer climbed onto the antique bed and slipped under the crisp white sheets. He looked so small in the double-sized bed. "Ms. Erica?"

"Yes, Sawyer."

"I'm really glad you know my Dad."

A rock landed in her stomach. *He's sorry he ever met me.* "Would you like me to read to you?"

"Nah, I'm good." He let out a long, slow yawn. "Sometimes, when Dad reads to me, he falls asleep before I do."

The image of Reese reading to his son came easy. She never questioned if he was a loving father or not.

That much was evident. "I'm going downstairs for a bit to clean up before I come to bed. Okay?" Seven-year-olds helping in the kitchen equaled mess. But it was well worth it. "Goodnight, Sawyer." Erica swept his dark curls away from his forehead, leaned down, and kissed him goodnight.

"Can you leave the door open?"

"You got it."

Downstairs, Erica loaded the dishwasher, wiped off the counters, and scrubbed the stovetop where tomato sauce splashed when Sawyer added the meatballs. He added them one at a time so the entire surface was covered.

After she had the stovetop shining, she went ahead and prepped her old coffee pot for the morning. It didn't have a timer, but all she'd have to do is flip the switch. Jackson's sold the carafe to her maker. She'd pick up a replacement the next time she went into town.

In the quiet of the house, a noise from outside drew her attention to the window. Through the darkness in the dining room, headlights swerved over her lawn. Could be someone turning around. It happened at least once a week. But after a moment, there was a soft knock on the front door. Erica hurried up the hallway, somewhat concerned by all that had already happened that day. She pulled the door open.

"Kara?" Erica glanced toward the road in time to see red taillights in the distance. The girl was here by herself.

"Hey. I um…wanted to check on Sawyer. I figured he had to be here."

"Yes, he's here, and he's fine. Come inside, please." Kara stepped into the foyer and readjusted the knapsack hanging over her shoulder. "Are you?"

Kara looked surprised by the inquiry about her

well-being. "Oh yeah." She shrugged like it was no big deal and offered nothing further.

Common sense dictated that at thirteen, Kara was not as innocent as Sawyer. There'd be no need to ease into it. "Who dropped you off?"

"Friends."

"You know I need to ask, does your mother know you're here?"

A contemptuous laugh almost covered a hidden hurt—almost. "Nah, Mom doesn't have a clue."

"Maybe we should call her to let her know so she doesn't worry. Is she home, or maybe with her friend at the hospital?"

Kara snorted. "No. My mother is out on the town. She won't be home 'til morning, and then she'll sleep the whole day." Her voice held enough of a bitter edge that Erica knew she wasn't exaggerating.

"What about your other brothers?"

"They're with their real dads this weekend, well, two of them anyway. My youngest brother Donny goes with Jacob, not that he belongs to Jacobs' dad, he just doesn't have anyone else, and the guy is pretty cool. My other brother Terry is spending the summer in North Carolina with his dad." Kara turned around, looking more lost and alone. "Before I moved in with my...father, I usually stayed by myself on the weekends." Kara's carefree manner faltered. "Do you know i-if he's okay?"

Empathy consumed Erica. She wanted to hug the girl, but Kara didn't seem like the hugging type. Her walls were taller and thicker than her father's. "Your dad seemed fine when I picked up Sawyer. And he's worried about you too. Are you hungry? Sawyer and I made spaghetti. There's plenty left over if you'd like some."

Kara glanced at the door and then down the hallway. "Sure. I could eat something."

*One wall down.* "Come on." Erica led the way to the kitchen and heated a plate of leftover spaghetti in the microwave.

"He talks a lot, doesn't he?"

"Sawyer?" Erica laughed. "Yes. He's a sweet kid."

Kara twisted a fork full of noodles. "Curtis calls him a mud baby."

Erica's smile disappeared. "Who's Curtis?"

"Mom's so-called boyfriend. It's bad enough what he called me, but if he would've called Sawyer a mud baby in front of...my father, he might have killed him instead of just beaten the shit out of him." Kara smiled with a mouthful of spaghetti. "It was great. Did you know he was a Marine?"

"Yes. He has that swagger."

Deep in thought, Kara slowed her chewing. "You guys had some kind of fight. Huh?"

*Fight?* How does she respond to that? Thankfully, she didn't have to.

"When my mom called this morning, she said she wanted to take me shopping." Kara snickered over her plate while scooping more noodles. "I should've known all she really needed was an alibi."

She shoveled the last few bites into her mouth and sat her fork down. "You make good spaghetti. Thanks."

"Would you like some more?"

"Nah, I'm good."

Erica rinsed off the silverware and plate and placed it in the dishwasher. Her experience said that Kara opened up and had more to say. She refilled her glass of iced tea without bothering to ask.

A scowl pinched between the girl's delicate brows. This particular expression made her look more like Reese. "Mom just dropped me off at the mall."

"And where did she go?"

Kara shrugged. "I don't know, really, but I can guess."

Had she seen the silver Honda go by today? Of course, her mind went straight to that.

"She's been coming by and trying to get me to go with her or watch my other brothers so she can go out. That's what started the argument. Curtis accused her of horsing around, but she lied and said I was with her all day." Kara's head fell forward. "My dad got caught up in this because of me."

Erica touched the girl's hand. "Kara, you need to understand that none of this is your fault."

Kara half shrugged, half nodded. "You know, when I was little, I actually thought it was possible for my parents," she snorted, "to get back together. But that was just stupid."

"I think it's normal for kids to want their parents to be together. Deep down, even my daughter, as old as she is, still feels that way. It can't always happen, but that doesn't make them stupid for wanting it."

"When he first moved here, Mom tried real hard to get back with him." Her eyes turned dark, and her voice soured. "But after what she did to him, I knew that would never happen."

*Was Kara that gullible or that certain?*

Erica shifted in her chair, suddenly uncomfortable with the conversation's direction.

Kara drained her glass, finishing her iced tea. She reached for her backpack and pulled out a small red wallet. From one of the tight pockets, she pried out a photo. "I have this picture of me when I was little." She handed it over. "That's him holding me next to the sign at Camp Geiger in Jacksonville, North Carolina."

Erica examined the crinkled old photo. A

younger-looking Reese was holding his baby girl on his hip. He looked like a proud poppa. The smile on his face was happy and carefree. Some men grow into their looks, but he was even handsome back then. She handed the photo back to Kara.

The girl stared at it for a moment. "It was taken the day he left on his deployment. He was gone for fourteen months, November to January. I was four years old when he came home, but I remember the day clearly. It was so close to Christmas, and he came through the door with an armful of presents just for me. My favorite was this weird pink sock monkey. Then he hugged me and left. It wasn't like I was used to having him around, so when he didn't come back, I didn't really notice the difference."

Kara fell silent in her thoughts. "When's your birthday?"

The question seemed strange, and Erica wasn't sure how or if it related to the story, but her gut suggested that Kara was skirting around to something else. "July, when's yours?"

"October."

Other than the low hum from the refrigerator, the house was deathly silent. Erica remained quiet, waiting for Kara to continue.

"My brother Terry just had a birthday in May. He turned nine. Would it be okay if I stayed here tonight? If not, I can walk home. It's not that far."

"Of course, you can stay." Erica couldn't let her walk home in the dark or to an empty house. "If you're sure it'll be okay with your mom."

Kara tiffed. "She won't care."

Erica stood. "You can sleep in my daughter's old room. Come on, I'll show you upstairs." Erica led the way up the spiral stairs off the kitchen. She started processing the off-the-cuff information Kara shared. The girl's brother, Terry, had just turned nine. With each step of a riser, Erica ticked off the years and then the months. At the top of the stairs, she figured it out. Stephanie was five months pregnant when Reese returned home from his tour in Afghanistan. *Holy sh.... Well, holy shit.*

Erica pushed the door open to Lauren's old bedroom. Kara glanced inside the room. But the girl's genuine interest lay in whether or not she'd figured it out. Apparently, Kara was pretty good at reading people, too.

Erica nodded her head, and the girl's grin widened. She deserved some credit.

She looked back into the room. "I wouldn't know how to be part of a regular family."

*Regular. Reese thinks he's just a regular guy.* "Sometimes, regular is hard to define." Erica cleared her dry throat. "The bathroom is right across the hall. My bedroom is down there, and Sawyer is in the room right beside you."

Kara glanced at the various doorways before giving her a leveled stare. "I was Sawyer's age when I figured it out. It helped to know why he left." The girl paused briefly. "So, what *did* happen between you guys?"

Kara was a typical thirteen-year-old girl, well, for the most part. Yeah, she had the sass and defiance to get caught smoking near Jackson's Hardware and, of course, lest she forget getting into trouble with older boys at the liquor store that could've landed her in jail. But on the flip side, she'd also had the responsibility of caring for and, most likely, raising her younger siblings for years. She had to learn about deceit and betrayal at a very young age.

A fundamental rule to live by is that children learn by example, and the one Kara had grown up with was horrendous. It was hard to say how much innocence remained, if any.

Erica had one thread of hope for Kara. She came here, which could mean that underneath the pink hair, trashy clothes, and harsh persona, there was a small part of Kara that didn't want to turn out like her mother.

Erica told her the truth. "He thinks I betrayed him too."

## Chapter Twenty-Seven

At ten past eight on Monday morning, Chief Snyder unlocked the door of Reese's cell. "You're free to go."

Reese stood up. "Free to go? What about the arraignment?"

"Charges have been dropped. He's out of the hospital, by the way."

"What did you do?"

"I didn't do anything. I think he figured out that if he pursues this, it might turn around and bite him in the ass. He did grab your daughter's arm, and I agreed that it was probably the wisest thing for him to do." The chief relayed a demure smile.

"So, where's my truck?"

"It's in our lot out back. I was able to waive the impound fees, but you still have to cough up the towing, sorry. They'll send you a bill." Chief Snyder handed over a manila envelope containing Reese's keys, a wallet, a penknife, and a cell phone. "I had to wait for the damn judge to sign off on this. I just now got it faxed. Come on. I'll take you to where we keep the vehicles."

Reese followed Bill down a hallway and through a door off the rear of the building. Officer Wendham was outside, leaning against the railing, smoking a cigarette.

The chief waved his hand through the smoke as he shuffled by the broad officer. "Make certain that butt doesn't land on my parking lot, Wendham." He jogged down the four steps and beckoned Reese to follow. "Reese, I hope you know this doesn't change anything we discussed earlier. I really wish you'd consider the offer the city council made you to work for us instead of the state troopers."

They started across the parking lot. "If I do decide to work here, can I fire that asshole?" Reese nodded over his shoulder toward the dumpy officer. There was something off about that guy.

"Hell yes. You can even fire me if you want. I'm ready to go fishing with Judge Dougherty." Chief Snyder unlocked a chain from a large metal gate and swung it open.

"I don't know about all that. Do you think none of this…" Reese glanced around and then tugged on the front of his shirt. "…will have any bearing on the offer?"

"Nope."

"You sound pretty confident."

"I am."

"How is that possible?"

"Because I say so, Smartass. You did what any man would've done if some moron assaulted their daughter."

Reese snickered. "Damn, now I know where your brother Ryan gets it from. He's just like you."

"The chief chewed on his bottom lip. "Look, you're qualified for the job, hell, probably more than me, and you're already sanctioned. If you want it, it's yours, but you have my endorsement for the state troopers if you think it'll help. I promise none of what happened on Friday will make a difference." Bill readjusted a leather snap on his belt. "So now, I suggest you get cleaned up, pick up your kids, and fix whatever's wrong with you and that pretty lady of yours."

Reese glared at the chief. "You mean Erica?" He received a brash nod. "You may find this hard to believe given the circumstances, but I didn't do anything wrong."

Chief Snyder shook his head to placate him. "Son, in my experience, whether you did or didn't don't matter a lick. If it's something worth fixing, you should try."

Reese unlocked his truck door. "If I end up working here, maybe I will fire your ass." He extended his hand toward the chief and gave it a firm shake. "Thanks, Bill."

"Try to stay out of trouble."

"I will." Reese jumped behind the wheel and cranked the key. The truck sputtered, maybe from sitting all weekend. When the engine leveled off, he left the police yard and pulled onto the main road. It'd be nice to pick up Sawyer first, but he hadn't had a real shower in three days, and he's been wearing the same clothes since Friday.

Going up a slight incline in the road, the fuel light came on. The gauge was sitting on 'E.' "Shit." He'd just filled the tank Friday morning. Someone must've siphoned every fucking drop on the police lot. "Mother Fu—" When a tank gets that low, all the dirt floating around gets sucked into the filter and carburetor. Karma was such a bitch sometimes.

The closest gas station was just a half mile further—if he had enough fuel to get there. Ronny's Automotive was privately owned, and they charged more for their gas than the big chain at the other end of town, but Reese didn't want to risk it. He turned into the station and stopped by one of the three pumps.

Reese dumped the envelope with his belongings across the seat to find his wallet. At the pump, he swiped his card, entered his pin, and proceeded to fill his truck. The loose rubber gasket on the old pump allowed the fumes to waft freely. He stepped away from the pungent vapors and snatched his phone off the seat.

Asking for Erica's help slaughtered the last bit of his pride. But damn, if she didn't come when he needed her the most. It made it that much harder to keep pushing her away. *Fuck.*

Reese stared at his phone, dreading the thought of having to face her again. The right thing to do would be to call first and maybe give her a heads-up. If he had any luck, she'd send Sawyer outside and spare him the turmoil of facing her.

*Just get it over with.* He swiped along the bottom of the phone—but nothing happened. He tried again, pushing a button on the side. "Great." The phone was dead. He tossed the phone back onto the seat and dragged a hand through the three days' worth of growth on his cheeks. "Dammit." His elbows came to rest on the open window of the driver's door.

"You look like hell." A man's voice came from behind the far pump.

Reese straightened and leaned further around the pillars separating him from the person. A shiny black fender was the first clue before he saw the man. A snide burst of laughter escaped. "I'm pretty sure I'm in it. Hell––that is."

Davis pulled a nozzle from his pump and selected the premium gas for his BMW. "Looks like you've been in a fight."

"And?" Reese didn't have time for this shit.

"We had a guy come in the hospital Friday night. Only he looked a lot worse off than you."

Davis lifted his chin, almost mocking him. "What can I say? Some people just have it coming." Getting into some kind of pissing match with Davis was the last thing Reese wanted. He checked the gauge on the dash to see how much gas he had. The overpriced fuel had to be flowing from the world's slowest pump. The tank wasn't even a quarter of the way full. Yeah, he was in hell. "Shit," he hissed.

Davis surveyed his surroundings before an odd grin covered his face. "I can't believe I'm going to do this."

*What did that mean?* Reese took a shrewd stance. "Do what?" He'd already taken a punch from Steve—granted one he deserved, used Curtis as a punching bag defending his daughter, and maybe, if he was being honest—vent a few frustrations in the process. Still, Chief Snyder told him to stay out of trouble. He probably wouldn't appreciate another altercation so soon. Reese loosened his shoulders, just in case.

Davis squeezed the handle twice and put the nozzle away on the pump. Obviously, the man didn't really need gas. He must've spotted the truck and darted into the gas station just to give him a hard time—the dick.

The doctor's eyes darted lower, clearly debating his next move. "I may have," he hesitated. "Misled you before." He cleared his voice with a quick cough. "Small towns, well, let's just say everything you hear isn't always true, no matter how much *I'd* like them to be. It was a Friday night and Erica was supposed to have dinner with her sister, but Janine didn't show. I happened to be at the restaurant and joined her instead. We talked about a lot of things, including our daughter. Erica had a few more drinks than normal, so I offered to drive her home. I went to her house the next morning to give her a lift to the Jeep. She'd already left, so I helped myself to some coffee, which I accidentally spilled down the front of my shirt." He gestured toward his chest. "I was going to rinse it out real quick, but that's when you showed up. I knew what it looked like, and I should've told you the truth then."

It took a moment for everything to sink in. Davis had purposely misled him, arrogant bastard, and now he was coming clean. It took another moment after that before the full ramifications hit. He pushed Erica away because of that. "You son-of-a-bitch."

"I don't think I need to tell you she deserves someone special." Davis surveyed him from head to toe. Given his filthy attire and lack of proper hygiene, it was a bit demoralizing. "All I've ever wanted was for her to be happy."

"Then what happened? Why did you get divorced?"

Davis's gaze shot over his shoulder to a vision that only he could see. "I asked for the divorce because I knew she wouldn't. Erica wasn't happy, but she would have stayed. I can't explain it other than it was the right thing to do." Davis crossed his arms. "She has this light about her. It can make you feel invincible. And I hadn't seen it for a really long time until the other day, and I'm pretty sure she was thinking of you. I'd give anything to be wrong, but I don't think that I am."

Yeah, Reese had seen that light. No one had ever looked at him the way Erica did. "So why are you telling me this now?" Irony slated his voice.

"Trust me, I'm not doing this for you." After several awkward hand movements, Davis reached between the pumps and offered his hand. "Mr. Mailing."

Davis was offering a truce, an apology, and hopefully a goodbye. Reese took his hand, accepting all three. Sadly, it was probably all too little and too late.

\*\*\*\*

Reese marched up the front walk of Erica's house. He was so fucked. At this point, getting showered or cleaned up wouldn't make a difference. He didn't have a chance in hell of fixing what he'd worked so hard to destroy. For now, he'd just get Sawyer, and maybe figure something out later.

A Taylor Swift song and laughter drifted through the screen door from inside. He knocked twice, but it went unnoticed.

He stepped into the foyer and called out. "Hello." Still, nothing. Peering into the living room, sheets and blankets were draped over the cushions and every piece of furniture, creating a makeshift tent city. A flap from one end flew up. Sawyer dove into a pile of pillows lying in the center of the floor.

A few seconds later, Erica flopped onto the rug from the other end. "I give up, Sawyer. You win."

Sawyer rolled onto his back, laughing. When he sat up, his eyes widened. "Dad!" He scrambled to his feet and beelined across the room.

Reese scooped up his son and held him tight. A dewy scent of honeysuckle floated from his skin. *Sawyer smells like her.* "Hey, buddy. God, I missed you."

"Yeah, I missed you too. Look, we made a fort."

"I see."

Erica climbed to her feet. Her hair had that tousled look, and color dappled her cheeks, no doubt from all the clambering on the floor. But she probably looked this beautiful every morning.

A sheet from the middle section of the fort ballooned into the air as another figure emerged from the draping material. "Hey, Dad."

*Dad.* "Kara?" The sofa's cushions had her barricaded on all sides. Reese hiked Sawyer onto his hip and walked toward her with his arm extended. She clambered over the foam walls and dove into his embrace. "Oh my god, Kara?"

She looked down self-consciously. "I didn't want to stay at Mom's." He'd never seen her so humble. "And I didn't want to be alone."

Reese pulled his daughter closer. "I'm so sorry, baby." He found Erica's gaze and mouthed the words *Thank you.* But words would never be enough. How could he have thought the worst? He felt like such a wretch.

Reese released Kara and put Sawyer down. "Look, guys, we need to get home and have a long talk, so get this cleaned up while I straighten some things out with Ms. Erica."

Erica started collecting a sheet from one of the chairs. "I'm sure you're eager to get going. Don't worry about this. I can get it."

Kara maneuvered around the pillows and pulled the sheet from Erica's hand. "Sawyer and I should clean this up. Why don't you guys get some coffee or something?"

Reese stepped toward the hallway. It was wrong of him to even wish Erica would give him this chance, and her hesitation said as much. *She wants nothing to do with me.*

"Please, Erica." He really was a selfish bastard, but what did he have to lose?

When he stepped into the foyer, his gaze combed over the narrow table. A second later, Erica veered out of the living room. Her eyes maneuvered from the table to him to the hallway. The transparency on her face mirrored his thoughts, and her cheeks, already flushed, deepened another shade. He followed her down the hallway into the kitchen.

In the Marines, he'd faced bullets from fifty-caliber guns. As a police officer in Michigan, he dealt with junkies and criminals on a daily basis, but he never felt as skittish as he did right now. "Erica, I don't need any coffee."

"Are you sure? It's still hot." Her back was to him. Not so much of a cold shoulder, more like a *I can't even look at you.* God knows he deserved it.

"Erica, I really didn't expect to find Kara here. Thank you, for that. I know why you did it. You did it for her—her and Sawyer. I can't thank you enough."

"She's a good kid. She's just looking for direction." Erica poured herself a cup of coffee.

"I've got a lot to make up for. And not just them. Erica, I'm so—"

"We ran into Stephanie yesterday," she cut in.

*Shit.* "Oh." She turned slightly. Her profile was pure elegance.

"Yeah, I was out of milk, so we slipped into town to the Sheetz. Stephanie seemed rather curious as to when you were getting released."

He didn't want Stephanie anywhere near Erica. "I would've called this morning, but my phone died, and I had already left the station."

The liquid inside the cup owned her focus. "She said it didn't matter. She'd see you soon enough."

*Great, that's just fucking great.* Once he had legal custody of Kara, he hoped to never have any more face-to-face dealings with Stephanie or her degenerate boyfriends again.

"Erica, despite what you may have heard, I don't normally get into fights or get thrown in jail. The charges were dropped, just so you know." He paused. "Not that it makes a difference now." He'd done enough damage long before that.

"Robin and Steve came by on Saturday and offered to take Sawyer *and* Kara, but I told them I didn't mind, plus I didn't think it would be right since Kara doesn't know them very well. She's struggling enough."

The woman was a Saint, and he didn't deserve her kindness—or her.

Kara and Sawyer entered the kitchen. "Did you tell him what's happening this weekend?" Sawyer hopped in front of him, his enthusiasm undeterred by the thorny current filling the room.

Erica set her cup on the counter. "No, Sawyer, you can tell him later." She smiled sincerely.

"When Ms. Robin came by, she asked when Ms. Erica was going to have a summer movie night, you know, like we did before. They planned one for this coming Saturday."

Erica's gaze skirted in his direction. "It's for all the neighbors and a few friends and family. Everyone's been asking to do it for a while."

Kara's smile was as big as Sawyer's. "She said I could bring a friend if it's okay with you."

"We'll see." *Yeah, I'm a piece of shit.* "Do you guys have all of your stuff? We should get going."

"My bag is upstairs." Kara took off.

Sawyer followed. "Mine too."

After the children disappeared up the stairs, quiet filled the kitchen.

She had yet to look him in the eye. "The hamster is in the dining room." Erica marched into the room with the large mural.

"You thought of everything, didn't you?"

"I knew it would make him feel better."

He'd been a real son-of-a-bitch pushing her away, and apparently, he succeeded. "Erica...I don't know where to begin, but I'll figure this out. Just...don't give up. Not yet."

## Chapter Twenty-Eight

Why did he keep looking at her like that? His eyes seeking…forgiveness, understanding? What was there to understand? Wasn't he the one who said he wished he'd never met her?

Running into Reese's ex-wife at the convenience store stung like lemon juice in an open cut. Only her cut was more like a gaping wound that went all the way to the bone.

Stephanie made no attempt to disguise that she was just coming home from an all-night bender. Her makeup sagged, just like her wrinkled clothes. Everything about her artificially tanned complexion looked blotchy, and her bleached blonde hair hung dull and flat down her back. Stephanie tripped across the parking lot and tried giving Kara a pretentious hug, two days late and lacking any genuine concern. Kara pushed her away, hurt and embarrassed. "God, Mom, you stink and smell like old cigarettes."

Not once had Stephanie inquired about her daughter's well-being or bothered to ask where the girl was staying. Her only concern was finding out when Reese was being released. "Tell your father I've got a surprise for him."

Erica had a stomach ache for the rest of the day.

And now this.

Reese followed her into the dining room—a tall, sexy mess of long whiskers and primal prowess. What was wrong with her? Why the empathy from Reese now? Why so much passion in those sky-blue pleading eyes? *Because she watched his kids?* Her gut said no.

*Don't look at him.* She forced her gaze toward the window. Birds squabbling on the grass made her think of three old men cackling at her expense.

Kara and Sawyer charged down the main staircase and charged into the room. This time, the static in the air slowed the girl down.

Reese cleared his throat. "You guys go ahead and take your stuff to the truck. I'll be right there."

"Sure." Kara paused before crossing the room for a swift, sideways, and unexpected hug. "Thanks—Erica."

"You're welcome, Kara."

Sawyer hugged her next. His tiny arms reached around her waist and squeezed. Then, the boy collected his hamster and followed Kara out the front door.

The screened door banged closed behind them. It felt like a starting pistol going off at the beginning of a race.

But she had nowhere to run.

What if he tried to hug her? Would she push him away or hold on for dear life? She didn't have a clue, which was frightening and infuriating. After everything that's transpired between them, everything that was said, how did this man still have such a hold on her? She was worse than a fool. She was a glutton for punishment.

Erica maneuvered toward the kitchen doorway, needing more distance than the table provided. "What happened in Michigan?" The question popped free before she could stop it. Even with everything going on right now, this question had been on her mind all weekend long.

The scowl above his brow scrunched, and a jagged laugh escaped. "It's...complicated." A flicker of sorrow swept through his eyes before he took an unwavering step toward her. "Erica, the last couple of days have been... Well, right now, I couldn't handle it...if you..." He snickered despairingly, "...thought even less of me. If that's even possible."

*What does that mean?* "I shouldn't have asked. Never mind. It doesn't matter." Reese took another step toward her. He was only an arm's length away.

"Yes, it matters." The opalescence in his eyes started to glow.

Her body hummed in all the places he'd once touched. She looked down and closed her eyes. Feeling this vulnerable was new to her, and she hated it for reasons she didn't want to admit.

The heat from his breath grazed across her forehead, and a whisper-light kiss landed above her brow on the very spot that had been the cause of their first meeting. She drew in a shaky breath.

But by the time her eyes opened, he was gone.

J. ALISON COLE

## Chapter Twenty-Nine

Reese had so much to fix, and quite honestly, he didn't know where to start. He walked out of Erica's house and over the lawn toward his truck. Kara was standing beside the tailgate.

Finding her here was the last thing he expected. But he was more grateful than he could put into words. Reese gathered her into his arms and gave her another hug. They say real men don't cry, but that's not true. Years of bottled-up tears for leaving his daughter trickled into his whiskers. "You don't know how surprised I am to see you here."

"It's okay, isn't it? That I came here?"

"Of course." Her grip tightened around his waist. "What happened the other night will never happen again. Everything is going to be different now. I promise." She leaned away, and the glimmer of the little girl from years ago looked back at him. *About time.* "Let's get home. I need a shower, and you guys can tell me what you did all weekend."

They jumped into the truck and headed back down the road. Rounding the last curve, he spotted a vehicle parked in the driveway of the second house.

Reese jammed on the brakes. "What the fu-udge?"

"Oh my God," Kara groaned. "It's Mom."

He couldn't believe what he was seeing. But sure enough, Stephanie stepped onto the front stoop of the house right next to his.

Reese's knuckles turned white, gripping the wheel. "Son-of-a-bi-squet. What else is going to happen today?" He took his foot off the brake.

Kara looked almost as appalled as he was. "She said she was moving, but I didn't know it was here, right next door." Her voice was full of bitterness and shame.

"Doesn't matter. We won't be here much longer." Reese turned into his driveway and parked the truck.

Two younger boys, Kara's other stepbrothers, raced into his yard to see Sawyer's hamster. Of course, the boys were innocent and couldn't help that their mother was…a fucking whore.

Stephanie held her arms out toward Kara, who ignored the jester and retreated into the side door of his house. Not bothering to acknowledge the slight, her focus shifted, and she slithered toward him. Her hand dragged over the front fender of his truck. "Howdy, neighbor."

Reese checked how far away Sawyer and the two boys were before speaking. "What the fuck are you doing here?"

"Well, since you beat up my boyfriend, I needed a place to stay. Steve Koontz was very helpful."

"There are a lot of places you could rent. Why here?"

Stephanie put on her best pouty face and took a deep breath in an attempt to draw his eyes to her chest to see that she was wearing a very thin t-shirt without a bra—a technique she used to make men notice her. A long time ago, he'd been one of them. But never again.

"You know why. I didn't get to thank you for standing up for us." She ran a finger down the front of his shirt.

He swatted her finger away and huffed sarcastically "You think I did that for you? I beat up that asshole because he grabbed my daughter. I don't want scum like him around Kara. But as for you, honestly, I don't give a rat's ass. You can live with whatever trash you want."

"You can't mean that. Besides, the whole argument was kind of about you."

"What?" Reese sputtered, somewhat confused. He was trying real hard to remain civil, but her mere presence irritated him more by the second.

"You've been so nice to me."

"I prefer to think of it as trying to get along for the sake of our daughter."

"Curtis isn't that bad of a guy. It's just that you intimidate him. When I needed a car, you sold me your old one, and then you helped me with some bills. It made him feel—like less of a man."

"Anyone that would attack a kid isn't a man to begin with."

Stephanie twirled a strand of hair. "Curtis was upset. He just assumed that I was with...you all afternoon."

"Why would he think that?"

"Well, he started following me, driving around to see where I was going."

"So."

"A couple of weeks ago, he and I had a fight. I knew Kara was spending the night with Tanya, so I came here, but you weren't home. No one was. The door was unlocked, and I fell asleep waiting for you. But you never showed."

"You slept here?"

"I left in the morning. Don't be upset, Reese. I can make it up to you." She shimmied closer, trying to press her breasts against his chest.

Reese grabbed her shoulders, holding her at bay. "Not going to happen. I told you that before."

"It'd be so easy now, seeing how we're neighbors and all." Her dainty, pert lips curved up. "I've never forgotten how incredible you are."

"Seems like you did forget—about ten years ago." Resentment from that betrayal boiled up inside of him. "You made your choice then, and now you have to live with it. The only reason I'm here is to make a home for my children and give them the best life possible. I feel sorry for you, Stephanie, because apparently, you don't understand that. And we won't be neighbors for long, so let me be perfectly clear. You keep your rancid pussy away from me and the people I care about, all of them. I've moved on. You should too."

## Chapter Thirty

Marcus rode ahead of her and glanced over his shoulder. "You know how much I love Florida. And I can say, hands down, this was the best vacation Phillip and I have had in a while. I know, I know, I've been going on and on about this. So, fill me in on what's happening with you. Did anything exceptional happen in my absence?" He'd called her nearly every day while he was away, and knew almost everything.

"Oh, you know, stuff. I told you about the accident involving a bicyclist and that everyone thought it was me."

"Oh yeah. Did it happen nearby?"

"Kind of. Thankfully, no one died. But everyone was concerned."

"Who's everyone?"

"You know, Lauren, Davis, the Koontzs...and Reese."

"Huh. So, Reese was concerned, too?"

*Was he?* "Yay, he... came by."

They turned onto her road and coasted right onto the patio. Marcus arched his back and climbed off his bike. "I just love your house. I'd give anything to live here. Hey, you wouldn't happen to have any of your famous green iced tea?"

"Made it this morning. I'll get us some." Erica went inside and poured two large glasses. Returning to the patio, Marcus had unzipped his riding jersey and was doing arm stretches over his head. He was by no means shy.

Janine constantly entertained the idea of one day having the chance to convert him. Thank goodness she wasn't here to see this.

Erica kept her eyes trained on the dark, swirly mass of chest hair above his waist and away from the fruit basket lumps protruding from the front of his spandex rubber-looking, snug shorts. Marcus' bulges weren't sexy, at least not to her.

Along with the glass of tea, she handed him two sugar packets. He pulled another small pack of enzyme supplements from a hidden pocket of his riding shorts and poured it, and the sugar, into his drink.

"Would you like a pack? I have several."

"No thanks, I'm good. No sweaty additives for me. They taste like dirt." Erica sat down on the knee wall at the end of the patio.

Marcus spun one of the lounging chairs and sat down directly in front of her. "I've talked Phillip into coming to movie night. If that's all right?"

"Of course, you know it is."

Marcus studied her and laughed. "I need him to get to know you better."

She tilted her head in his direction. "I'd like that."

Marcus took a sip of tea and laid his gleaming bright smile on her. "He gets so jealous sometimes."

Erica's chin twisted. "Jealous of what?"

"He thinks you're beautiful. So do I, by the way. He knows how much I enjoy the time you and I spend together. Too much time, according to him."

"He could always start riding with us." Erica laughed. "Hey, he knows you're gay, right?" Once they became friends, Marcus's age and sexual preferences were never an issue. They joked like real friends do.

"Very funny, and trust me, he knows."

Erica shrugged playfully. It was nice to laugh again. She'd missed Marcus and the escape riding with him always gave her.

"Don't take it personally. It also bothers him that I

had girlfriends in college, and then there was all that stuff that circulated between us at school he had to deal with."

"He shouldn't worry about what people say. Especially in this town."

"That's what I told him. Heck, I thought it was funny how everyone believed that you and I were hot and heavy. It proves the old saying that things aren't always what they appear."

Erica let the heat of the sun warm her upturned face. "You have no idea how right you are."

"But one thing is for sure. The truth always comes out in the end, Erica." He emphasized her name.

Erica perked up. "Why do you say it like that?"

"Appearances. They can be deceiving. Look, I know the rumors about you and Davis really mucked things up between you and Reese. You told me about the collision at the bank and what he said to you at the jail. But I don't get it, especially after what you learned from his daughter. I do think he was angry and hurt, but I don't think Reese slept with his ex-wife."

"What?"

"I mean, I know I haven't met him, but to go back to someone like her? It doesn't make any sense."

Erica stood and paced to the edge of the patio. "Yeah, welcome to my world."

Marcus swirled his glass nonchalantly, bringing the liquid close to the top edge. "All I'm saying is, maybe nothing happened. You only *saw* her car leaving his house. That could mean anything."

"It's not just that. He said he made other plans. And I know for a fact that the children weren't home, plus *he* has a reputation. I'm not that naïve, Marcus."

"What if you're jumping to conclusions the same way Reese might've? He found Davis at your house that morning... Heck, I've spent the night here. Christ, on some of those road trips we've taken, we shared the same bed."

"Your point?"

"My point is, you're using that as an excuse. You need to ask him point blank. That way, you'll know the truth and can move on one way or another. You said he seemed different when he came to get the kids. Don't you wonder why?"

"You don't understand. It's not that simple. Reese said things I'm pretty sure he meant."

"If he felt betrayed, doesn't it make sense that he'd be mad and push you away?"

"Sure. But it doesn't make it okay to bury his...*sorrows* with someone else. And even if it wasn't Stephanie, I don't think he'd have any problems finding a willing partner." *None whatsoever.* " You know, I've seen other cars on this road that I don't recognize."

"Stop. You can't see this clearly because you have real feelings for the man."

*Feelings for the man?* More like a raging conflict of body versus common sense. Her guts were in so much turmoil she could barely eat, much less think straight. Erica stared into the fields behind her house. Was it possible that Reese said all those hateful things and acted like a jackass just to push her away?

She turned. Marcus had finished his tea and was watching her summarize everything he said. "So tell me, Marcus. When did you get your degree in psychology?"

A smile that would melt the panties off of every woman she knew—materialized on his slender lips. "I know this really cool lady. She's taught me how to be a good listener." He held up his glass. "I could use another."

"I guess you've earned it."

Marcus handed her the glass and then leaned back

in the chair. "When you get back, you can tell me the rest."

Erica stopped in her tracks. "The rest of what?"

Marcus arched and put his hands behind his head, quite pleased with himself. "For starters, I want to know exactly when you realized you loved him."

"Love?"

"Oh, yeah, Erica Gebhart's in love, and I must say it suits you, plus it will please, Phillip."

She and Marcus got along because, other than his age, height, looks, and sex, they processed information the same way. "And after that."

"After that, you're going to tell me about the part you left out. Because I think I know what it is."

"Oh, I'd need something much stronger than green tea before I share that tidbit."

# J. ALISON COLE

## Chapter Thirty-One

Steve had no practical answer for Reese as to why he'd agreed to let Stephanie move into the second tenant house, short-term or not. He figured either Stephanie had manipulated the quiet farmer, or this was Steve's way of getting even for what happened between himself and Erica.

But none of that mattered now.

Fate had intervened for once and helped him out. Tuesday morning, after Stephanie got it through her thick skull and realized he wasn't going to have anything to do with her, she shifted her focus back onto husband number two in North Carolina. The moving trucks showed up on Wednesday, and she left late last night. *Good riddance.* Reese almost felt sorry for the guy. *Almost.*

Friday morning, Reese met with the State police about his new position. He was back to the house by eleven, and figured now was the time to take care of a few other unresolved issues.

"Hey guys, I've got to go somewhere. I'll be back...umm..." He didn't know whether to say an hour or five minutes. "Kara—"

Kara stuck her head out of her room. "Yes, I'll keep an eye on Sawyer, and hey, can Tanya just spend the night tomorrow? I told her about the movie. If we...go."

"Sure, if we go. And hey, don't let Sawyer have any candy while I'm gone." Reese started for the side door of the kitchen.

"Dad," Kara called.

He stopped mid-stride and turned. *Dad.* That sounded nice coming from her. "Yeah?"

269

"Good luck."

He snickered. "Thanks." It seemed Kara knew precisely where he was headed. The girl was tough as nails and very perceptive. It was nice to know she'd gotten that much from him. "I think I'm going to need it."

"Nah, you got this."

Did he?

For years, he let his past consume him. It ate away at him like growth, and he never really cared—until now. He'd tell Erica everything, no excuses, no sugarcoating, just the whole ugly truth. None of what he was about to reveal put him in a good light, and nearly all of it had the potential to push her further away.

But it had to be done, regardless of how this turned out.

The two-minute drive to Erica's house felt more like two seconds. The anxiety in his stomach swelled up like a basketball. A red Prius was parked beside her Jeep—no black BMW or tan Lexus. There was that.

Sitting along the edge of the patio were two bicycles—and a man. It was the same man he'd seen riding with Erica.

*It's now or never.* Reese cranked his neck and headed across the lawn.

The darker young man met him midway. "Hello, I'm Marcus Schuller." He extended a slim hand.

Reese gave it a firm shake. "Reese Mailing."

"It's nice to finally meet you. I've heard a great deal about you. Come have a seat."

"Sure." Reese followed Marcus back to the table and chairs, trying to imagine what Erica might've said about him. *None of it good.*

Before he even made it to the table, the rear door from the kitchen opened, and Erica came out of the house carrying two full glasses of tea. When she saw him, she stopped like a deer in the headlights.

"Erica." Every time he laid eyes on her, she stole his breath and made his words come up short.

Finally, she nodded. "Reese."

An awkward tension filled the next minute before Marcus intervened. "In fact, we were just talking about you a minute ago." Something about the man's upbeat tone gave Reese a fraction of hope that he could be a potential ally.

"Is that right?" Reese studied Erica.

"We just got back from our ride." Erica set the two glasses on the table. "Are the children with you?"

"No, they're not." He sidestepped the table. "Erica, I'd like to show you something. It's not far, and I was hoping you'd be willing to come. We won't be long."

"I'm sorry, Reese, but I have company."

Reese looked to his hypothetical new ally for support. The ball was in his court. Marcus exchanged glances between himself and Erica.

"Don't mind me. I was just leaving. Erica, remember I told you I have to do that thing."

"What thing?" Her lips narrowed into a thin line, questioning the apparent made-up excuse.

Credit to Marcus, he held his ground. "That thing, but hey, why don't you get changed real quick? I'll keep Reese company for a couple of minutes."

Her reply never came, but a grueling length of time passed before Erica turned and headed into the house. At this point, he'd take that for a good sign.

Marcus took a seat on one of the patio chairs like he was gearing up for an interview. "I give her ten minutes. If she doesn't come out by then, you'll have to go in after her."

Reese knew he liked Marcus. It was probably a

safe bet that the man knew everything that transpired between himself and Erica.

Marcus glanced at the rear door before the smile on his face waned. "Erica is an extraordinary lady, and she's become a very dear friend. I'd do anything for her. You, it seems, have quite the reputation, and some people think you've lived up to it."

*Huh, maybe he was wrong about Marcus.* "I'm sorry…I don't understand what you're getting at."

The man leaned forward before squinting and shaking his head. "There's really no nice way to ask, so I'm just going to do it. Are you sleeping with your ex-wife?"

The question caught Reese so off guard it made him laugh. "Jesus Christ!" Only Marcus didn't seem to think the question was so funny. He was about to lay into Marcus for the absurd question when it struck him. Why would anyone think that?

*Wait.* He could see Stephanie going around saying shit like that. Was there another rumor going around town that he hadn't heard? What if Erica heard something along those lines? *Fuck, what if she believed it. Talk about irony.*

"Shit. No. I didn't. I haven't. I wouldn't. I swear."

"I didn't think so." Marcus stood up. "Look, I love Erica, not the same way, say someone like you would."

Of course, Marcus cared for Erica. Davis, Steve, the eccentric sister, and everyone else in town worshiped her. Reese fell victim the moment he first laid eyes on her, long before they ever met, weeks before scooping her up alongside the road, and well before he felt the heat of her legs wrapped around his waist.

"And I don't like seeing her get hurt. And you hurt her. Do you understand?"

"Yeah. I do understand. Better than you know."

"Don't let it happen again."

Reese couldn't make that promise. He'd done his best to drive a wedge between himself and Erica, and now he was about to pound that wedge even deeper. He just hoped he could live with the results when it was over.

# J. ALISON COLE

## Chapter Thirty-Two

Hopefully, this wouldn't take long. Erica tugged on a pair of black yoga pants and a light gray t-shirt she got free as a *giveaway* to promote the Kensington Farmers Market. She couldn't be any further away from her sophisticated, inspired reputation if she tried.

*Marcus and his bright ideas. Who does he think he is?* She searched for a hair scrunchy and slid her feet into a pair of flip-flops.

The screen door swung wide as she walked outside. The two men were standing at the edge of the grass. Marcus had a stern look on his face, talking to Reese. God only knows what he was saying.

Reese offered his hand and replied. "I'll do my best." The two shook hands.

"Make sure you do." Marcus strutted toward her with a tentative smile. Then, entirely out of the blue, he laid a not-so-brotherly kiss directly on her lips. It ended as abruptly as it began. He whispered in her ear. "Don't be mad." The kiss was meant to distract her anger—and make a point. It did both. *Not everything is as it seems.*

"Go home," she huffed.

Reese stepped to the edge of the gravel driveway and waited for her. His jaw was set, and his brows pinched in that way she liked. If she had to guess, he probably wanted to thank her for watching the kids even though he acted like such an a-hole. Maybe spending the weekend in jail humbled him.

Erica followed him to the truck. Climbing onto the seat, she was prickled by a sense of déjà vu. The air inside the cab popped from the underlying friction. Reese looked nervous, which, in turn, made her nervous. She always wanted to believe that everything would make sense and fall into place at some point. And it looked as if they were headed there now.

Reese drove in deafening silence. Determination rolled off of him in waves. He must've been one heck of a marine because the man was on a mission.

His eyes stayed forward, focused, so Erica directed her gaze out the window. She recognized most of the roads he turned on, with the exception of a few. The rural views were exceptional, and after ten minutes, the blinker came on, and Reese turned onto a long fenced lane.

Two proud sycamore trees graced either side of an older two-story brick farmhouse. The grass had gone to seed, and weeds had overtaken the flower beds. A stained glass arch sat above a beautiful wooden door that centered the wrapped-around porch.

Erica leaned forward in the seat. "Do you know who lives here?"

"Yeah." He turned the engine off and exited the truck.

She followed him to the middle of the yard and suddenly remembered the encounter at the bank with Reese and Mr. Lambert. The clues fell into place. "This is your house?"

Reese confirmed her statement with a single nod. "I wanted to show you the house, but that's not why I brought you here." He shoved his hands into his pockets. "Erica, you ask me about Michigan, and I want to tell you everything. Can we, maybe, sit down?"

"Reese, you don't—"

"Yeah, I do." He headed up the walk. The first two steps leading to the front porch looked brittle and warped. "Watch your step."

Erica mimicked his long stride, skipping over one

of the sketchy risers. Other than some gray paint that had bubbled loose in spots, the rest of the porch appeared solid and in good shape. She sat down on the top step a few feet away from him.

It took Reese another half minute to gather his thoughts. "I'll start with Kara."

"She told me, Reese." He looked somewhat surprised. "Kara told me what you came home to. I didn't ask. She started talking, and I think she just wanted me to know. Don't be upset with her."

He shook his head. "No, I'm not upset. She was just telling the truth." He blew a long, nervous breath. "Stephanie and I were young and foolish when we got married. I'd just enlisted, and that didn't help much. It was always chaotic from the beginning. We'd fight, then make up, until we found something else to fight about. Before we made it a year in, we actually separated for about three weeks. But she came back when she realized that she was pregnant. So, I tried to make it work instead of getting divorced." He took another steadying breath.

"It was nice being deployed because it kept us from fighting, and I always thought that when I got back, it would somehow be different. But it didn't work out that way. After my second deployment, I came home, and yeah, Stephanie was pregnant with someone else's baby. I was devastated and angry. I stayed at the barracks for a month, trying to figure out what I should do. It was pretty clear though. So I hired a divorce lawyer and petitioned for joint custody. At first, Stephanie was going to deny me the divorce until the guy who knocked her up became involved. He was another marine from the base." Reese's gaze drifted to his clasped hands." At that point, I just wanted my daughter. But Stephanie wanted to hurt me, so she told me a very convincing lie. She said that Kara wasn't really mine. She said it happened when we were separated, and after what I came home to, I believed her."

Reese made a face that looked like he'd just swallowed razor blades. "My enlistment was over, so I left and moved to Michigan. There, I made myself a promise never to get close to anyone ever again.

"My folks live there. So for a few years, I hung out in shitty little bars and tried drinking my sorrows away. There, I met a woman named Neeka. We'd hook up every now and then. It was nothing serious for either of us. I wasn't in the best place, and she definitely had her own issues. She told me she was on the pill, but—" His brows lifted to the obvious. "Something went wrong, and she got pregnant. But that's not even the shitty part. I didn't find out she was pregnant until just one month before Sawyer was born. As it was, he arrived early, and God, he was so small, but I knew he was mine the moment I laid eyes on him. Anyway, Neeka…uh, figured that she'd just put him up for adoption, and I couldn't let that happen. She didn't want to be a mom and actually signed away all her rights the day he was born." Reese rubbed his hands together and straightened his legs to a lower step. "At the time, I was working for the Michigan State Police. I didn't know how in the hell to take care of a newborn, but I had to figure it out real quick. My parents helped every now and then, and I managed, and things were good for a while. Then, when Sawyer was almost four years old, Neeka showed up out of the blue and wanted visitation. Needless to say, she didn't strike me as an ideal mother. When I knew her, she was only drinking. I found out later that she had some problems with drugs. She argued that she'd gone through rehab and that she was clean, but Sawyer was all I had then, and I wasn't convinced. That's when her family stepped in, came up with some money, and hired an attorney. The courts forced me to let her see him. They said that any decisions she made when he was born couldn't be enforced because of her addictions. Then, her lawyer even went as far as to demand a DNA test. They were hoping maybe I wasn't the father." Reese paused and took a deep breath. "It was all the DNA talk that made me think of Kara. I had this ache in my gut that just never went away. I needed to know for my own peace of mind. So, one weekend, we visited North Carolina to see her. By then, Stephanie was pregnant again and shacked up with somebody else. It didn't bother her when I asked to see Kara." A tender smile entered his eyes. "Kara remembered me. She still had this stupid little stuffed monkey I had given her." His eyes filled with a distant memory. "Anyway, we went to a park, and I saved the stick from her popsicle. Christ, it was months before those results came back. I already knew how Sawyer's test would turn out, but when I opened the results to Kara's test, it proved that she *was* mine." The crease on his forehead deepened. "I hated Stephanie for cheating on me, but that hate resulted in me abandoning my Kara. I can't even make sense of it sometimes."

Erica shifted her gaze to his face. It was easy to see how much he blamed himself for believing Stephanie's lies. "You shouldn't feel guilty."

"Guilt, shame, disgust. You name it, I've been there." He shook his head. "My world was turned upside down. Here I was, living in Michigan with a preschooler and practically a complete stranger to my daughter. I had to get to know Kara better before I'd have a shot at getting visitation, much less any kind of custody. And all of this was happening while I was dealing with Sawyer's mom." More pain entered his eyes. "Anyway, one weekend, Neeka somehow finagled an unsupervised visit with Sawyer. I saw it as an opportunity to maybe spend some time with Kara, but something just didn't feel right when I dropped him off. So, I stayed and even picked up a weekend shift.

"It was late on a Saturday night when Neeka and a few of her friends decided to have a little celebration at her apartment for Sawyer. At least, that's what the neighbor said. After she and her friends drank all the liquor they had, she loaded my son into the back of her car and drove to get more. The manager from the liquor store refused to sell her any because he said she was already intoxicated. He claimed that he tried to stop her from leaving, but she raced out the door and took off. The station received a report of a drunk driver, and I recognized the make of the car and the tag number right away.

"It was raining that night, a hell of a storm just like the one on that day I picked you up outside of town. The roads were a real mess. My partner and I checked her apartment, but she wasn't there. And by that time, the entire precinct was searching for her. Two hours later, the search ended. She'd skid off the road into a swollen creek. The only thing that saved Sawyer was the angle of the car." A tremor entered his voice. "I arrived on the scene, and his little head was barely above the rising water. Hers wasn't."

"Reese, I'm so sorry. You don't have to say anymore."

"Yes, I do. I want you to know everything." His laugh was painfully cynical. "And I wish that were the end, but it's not."

Erica laid her hand on top of his.

He turned his palm up and wove his fingers through hers. He stared at their entwined hands before taking another deep breath. "Neeka's family was understandably upset. Her death created all kinds of bizarre accusations that I was somehow involved or did something to cause the accident." He gave her a sure-eyed head shake. "I was with my partner the entire night. The press stirred the pot with false information until it came out that she had methamphetamines in her system on top of her blood alcohol level. Not only was she drunk, but high as well. After that, her family decided not to challenge me for Sawyer. I offered to let them be part of his life, but once she was gone, they didn't seem to care."

"He was so young when it happened and says that he doesn't remember much from that night, but the accident is why he only takes showers. I had him in therapy, heck, we both went, and believe it or not, he's come a long way."

His grip tightened on her fingers. "Months passed before I felt like I could finally breathe again. I had to get back on track with Kara. It was hard, but I still tried to keep in touch the best I could. And it was on one of those phone calls I found out that Stephanie had moved to Pennsylvania for some guy she met online. That's when I decided to move here and get my daughter." A cynical half-laugh escaped. "*But then,* the very morning I filed the papers for legal custody, I was served with papers of my own." His lengthy pause drew her gaze. "Uum, not one, but two women…" Tension pinched his eyes closed. "Came forward with paternity suits against me."

Mr. Jackson's shriveled features came barreling front and center in her mind.

"They *were* acquaintances, and yes, I knew both of them—like that." He lowered his head in shame. "Goddammit, this is hard." He cursed. "You may not think so because of when you and I—anyway, after what happened with Neeka, I always, always used protection."

Erica believed him.

"My lawyer advised me to hold off pursuing

custody of Kara until I addressed the new charges against me. He said it wouldn't exactly help my case, not that Stephanie's situation was any better, but..." He bit his lip, thwarting any kind of self-pity. "Anyway, one of the women eventually admitted that she knew all along that her daughter wasn't mine, and the test confirmed it. But, the second woman insisted I was the father. She was hoping for a so-called relationship that just wasn't going to happen. And once her baby was born, the DNA proved I wasn't the father of her baby either." Reese released her hand and stood up. He walked to the side of the porch and stopped by the weathered railing. "Anyway, once all *that* was finally over, I packed up all my shit and moved here, hoping for a fresh start." He turned to face her and shoved his hands into his front pockets. "That's everything. All of my dirty secrets." His gaze barely met hers. His eyes, stance, and expression were full of dread. He expected her to hate him.

She rose from the step and approached him. "I don't hate you, Reese."

"How can you not?"

"I don't think you should hate yourself either."

He turned away, trying to close her out. "My past relationships made it hard for me to really trust someone. I honestly believed that part of me was broken and ruined for good. I haven't allowed myself to be close to anyone in a long time. Then I met you, and...well, I fucked it up royally." He shook his head with disgust. "I thought the worst, but I know now that...I should've believed in you."

Reese looked like he had just fought ten rounds of an emotional battle with the champ. Only he was the champ beating himself up. She touched his shoulder. "Reese, we've all made mistakes."

"I've made more than my share. Erica, I

should've never talked to you or treated you the way I did. You didn't deserve that. I don't expect you to forgive me, but please know I'm sorry."

"Reese, it's not my forgiveness that you need. Lies and rumors have a way of distorting the truth. You need to forgive yourself." He turned to face her, and she reached for his hand. "I always knew you were a good man. I saw it that day we met." His eyes narrowed. "How about you show me your new home?"

# J. ALISON COLE

## Chapter Thirty-Three

How could she think he was a good man? Did a good man return home after a deployment and lose all faith in people? Did a good man abandon his daughter, albeit because of a lie, but a lie that took too many years to question? Did a good man consort with countless women of questionable character because he gave up caring?

Right now, the way Erica was looking at him made him feel like anything was possible.

*Invincible.*

She asked to see the house, maybe as a way to let the dust settle. Or perhaps she needed time to process all the shit he'd dumped on her. *And then what?*

Reese led her inside. The emptiness of the house echoed strangely. She commented on how the light entered each space from the windows as they walked through the different rooms. In the dining room, she remarked on the arched molding and the beauty of the pocket doors being oak. Upstairs, she noted the lack of closets in the bedrooms and laughed at the size of the enormous tub in the bathroom.

Driving her home, a whisper of hope teetered in his gut. It was selfish to think she'd give him a chance to redeem himself, but it would rip him apart if she didn't. He deserved and expected the door to fly open when he stopped. He could almost imagine her gracious tone and polite goodbye.

He slowed and turned into her driveway, but the door didn't open. Instead, she turned to face him.

"I've never seen an entirely green kitchen. The appliances, the walls, the cabinets. It's a lot of green."

He chuckled. "That's what you've been mulling over on the ride home?"

"Among other things." She shrugged with a smile. "You're lucky though. That shade is quite trendy right now. I'd leave the cabinets and appliances as they are but lighten up the walls. Maybe even have an accent wall where the table would go."

Hope inched closer. "You would know far better than me." His fingers closed tight around the steering wheel in an effort to get a grip on his nerves.

"So, what do the children think of the house?"

"Oh, they haven't seen it yet. I was going to surprise them last week, but I got detained."

She exchanged his timid smile. "I think they're going to love it."

He stared at her for a handful of moments. "I spent most of this week getting all my certifications in line to accept a position as the resident State Trooper for the area. Working for the Koontz brothers was always temporary."

Her face brightened. "You know everyone in town believed your ties with the law meant you were some kind of criminal, not that you were an officer of the law."

A cynical smirk replaced his scowl. "Getting thrown into jail probably didn't squash that notion."

Erica leaned across the center space and placed a kiss on his cheek. Before he had time to react, she scurried from the truck but took a second to prop her hands on the frame of the open window. "Let Mr. Jackson think what he wants. The truth always comes out in the end. It's just takes a while to get there sometimes." A beautiful smile spread over her lips.

"Erica... I haven't been with anyone but you since I moved here."

She held his gaze and took a prolonged breath. "I hope you can make it tomorrow."

"I'll do my best."

# J. ALISON COLE

## Chapter Thirty-Four

"Plastic forks, paper plates, and one extra ketchup." Erica crossed off the remaining things on her list and pushed her full cart to the front of the grocery store.

The belt started moving as her items crossed over the red lasers. "Hi, Mrs. G." The young man behind the register greeted her with genuine enthusiasm.

She was so busy getting her things out of the cart she hadn't looked up, and when she did, she had to do it twice. "Travis?" He was clean-cut, wearing khakis and the standard dark blue polo. And the name tag he had on, verified it. "I didn't realize that you worked here."

"It's been about two weeks. My uncle got me the job. I've moved in with him." He held up a box before running them over the lights. "I love these cookies. They're my favorite."

"They're for movie night tomorrow at my house. If you're not working, come by and bring your Uncle. I'd like to meet him."

Travis looked up in surprise. "You're inviting me? I've heard people talk about how you show the movies outside on the side of your barn. Right?"

"Yes, and you're invited, Travis. You can help me eat those cookies. If not, I might eat the whole box myself. They're my favorite too."

His hesitant smile nearly broke her heart. "I'm pretty sure I'm working. Newbies get all the crappy weekend hours, but thanks."

He really was a handsome young man full of potential. "Maybe next time. And Travis, I like the haircut. It makes you look older." She didn't think Travis

289

Baker was capable of blushing. But she was wrong.

\*\*\*\*

Saturday evening, promptly at six o'clock, Bob Koontz and his family arrived first. He lumbered over the lawn carrying a giant cooler filled with hot dogs and hamburgers. He always supplied the meat for movie night and insisted on working the grill.

Not long after, a few more pickup trucks started rolling in, followed by a mini parade of cars. Juanita Fleagle and several women from the fountain committee strolled over the lawn. Some toted lawn chairs and blankets, while others brought offerings of potato salad, broccoli raisin salad, and buffalo chicken dip. Those were usually the front runners of what people brought, and it never failed to have two or three varieties of each dish.

Erica grabbed another bag of ice from the outdoor fridge. When she stood, she found herself face-to-face with Steve Koontz brandishing a crudité of cut-up vegetables. His lips were pressed so tight they looked white, and his gaze was glued to the tray.

"Um, um, Robin asked me to give this to you." His cheeks glowed with discomfort. She couldn't blame him, really. The last time they saw one another, her legs were wrapped around Reese, reveling in the best orgasm she'd ever had. So, this reunion was just a tad bit awkward, embarrassing, uncomfortable, and delicate. *Pick one or all of the above.*

Erica took the tray. He repositioned his hat nervously and spun away without saying another word.

Over his shoulder, a small red car turned onto her road. Marcus's Prius zoomed into the designated mowed area of grass behind the garage. A moment later, he and Phillip came around the corner.

Erica met them halfway across the lawn and greeted each with a hug. "I'm so glad you could make it."

She'd only met Philip in person on two separate and very brief occasions. But this time she noticed something peculiar. His auburn hair was a bit longer than it had been before. Heck, it was nearly the same length as hers. And standing next to him now, they were about the same height. Plainly put, she and Phillip shared a remarkable resemblance to each other. A stranger could theoretically mistake him for her younger brother if she had one.

*Humph. Figuring this one out may take a few miles.*

Marcus handed Erica a bowl of sliced strawberries. "Once this one found out you were showing *The Wizard of Oz*, he couldn't say no. It's one of his favorites."

The smile on Phillip's face vanished. "Nice, Marcus, nothing stereotypical about that." He was holding an Angel food cake covered in clear cellophane.

"Don't mind him, Phillip. It's one of my favorites, too. And thank you for the cake. I know Marcus doesn't cook, and this looks homemade."

"Yes, it is." his smile returned. "I made it from scratch, with gluten-free flour. It's my mother's recipe. The strawberries are organic, but to be fair, Marcus did help cut them up."

"I'm sure it's all delicious. Thank you again." Erica took the cake and found a spot on the granite counter, sliding a few things around to make room for the strawberries.

Lauren raced up behind her. "Mom, I forgot to bring a blanket for my friends and me—"

"Hello to you too." She kissed her daughter's forehead. "I set a few old blankets on top of the dryer. Take as many as you need."

Lauren gave her mother a quick hug. "Thanks, Mom."

"You girls remember Mr. Schuller. And this is his friend, Phillip Bowman." Lauren and her friends fell under the effortless charm of the two handsome men, seemingly ignorant of their connection to each other. The young women probably only saw two gorgeous guys who hung out together. Maybe it was her trained eye that caught the subtle glances and the indiscriminate smiles. Because what she saw was two people in love.

Janine charged up beside her in a cloud of *Coco Mademoiselle* and grabbed her by the arm. "Is that Paul Koontz over there?"

Her sister never went for the typical All-American Marlboro man, plus Paul didn't have an accent. "It is. You don't remember him?"

"I don't remember him looking so…what was the word you used before? Rugged? Look at the bulge in the front of his pants. Do you think that's all his dick or just something in his pockets?"

"You could always ask him." Erica caught herself. Janine might actually do it. "No, please don't. I was joking. Here, food queen, arrange the counter for me."

The sound of another truck door closing drew her attention toward the driveway and her makeshift parking lot. Erica's heart stammered when she spotted Sawyer racing down the hill toward Joey. Kara trailed behind him with a friend, thankfully *not* the girl from outside the hardware store. Then there was Reese.

A kind of calmness washed over her. All of the turbulent seas and misunderstandings from before were far behind her. Everything made sense now, and only one direction remained. Forward.

Reese was somehow that last piece of the puzzle falling into place.

He strolled down the hill by the driveway wearing

a simple black tee that stretched tight across his chest and showcased his biceps. His jeans—perfect, tight, and saggy in all the right places. And yes, that was all dick in the front of his pants.

He didn't make it to the patio before Robin snagged him for introductions to one of their neighbors who lived on the other end of Roop Road. Charlie Dickinson was eighty-three years old and a frequent coffee drinker at Jackson's hardware store. The older man was accompanied by his eighty-two-year-old lady friend, Blanche Simmons. Both seemed utterly smitten by the handsome Reese Mailing.

Erica watched him exchange polite greetings with the older couple. His gaze, however, combed over the picnic tables on the lawn and the different groups scattered by the flower beds. Finally, he looked toward the rear of the house. The smile on his face could've harnessed the sun, and his eyes lit up as blue as the Morning Glory's that grew along the side of her chicken coop.

The day she dropped off the hamster cage, he came out of the side door of his house wearing the same smile. A reflection of her own feelings. Feelings that never really went away.

After exchanging a few more niceties, Reese excused himself and came toward her with a tray of sliced cantaloupe and honeydew melon.

"I can take that from you."

"Thanks." Reese humbly scanned the guests in their proximity. "I had to stop Sawyer from eating all the cantaloupe before we got here."

"I'm glad you were able to come. So, did you finally have a chance to show Kara and Sawyer the house?"

"I did, and I think they're both ready to move

now." The temperature of his smile never fluctuated from scorching.

She stepped closer. "I've had some more time to think about it." A flash of panic gripped his features. "No, no, no...about the house." The crease over his brow relaxed. "What are you going to do about the wallpaper in the living room?"

"You got something against blue and gold roses?"

"I think my grandmother had the same print in her house from the forties."

"I've never tried to peel wallpaper before."

"I can show you how."

A boisterous voice burst from behind them. "There he is." Bob Koontz clambered toward them with a foil tray of cooked burgers and hot dogs. "Did he tell you that he's moving?"

"Yes, Bob. He did."

"It's a nice piece of property. I'm anxious to see what grows."

"Me too, Bob." Erica exchanged the full pan for an empty one, but her smile belonged to Reese.

## Chapter Thirty-Five

"Sawyer, if you have to go, then let's go now."

"I'll be quick."

It must be something all seven-year-old kids do. They wait until the movie starts before deciding that they have to pee. The half-bath tucked under the main staircase of Erica's house had a door that looked like part of the wall. Even the handle was somewhat hidden, and Sawyer insisted upon using the "secret" bathroom. It was odd to think his son stayed here. Hopefully, he didn't break anything.

Reese crossed his feet at the ankles and leaned against the wall in the hallway. His gaze soon trickled toward the narrow table a few feet away. Memories of his encounter with Erica slammed into his groin. The warmth of her skin, the firmness of her breasts, and the moans that escaped her lips when he buried himself inside of her.

Memories that he cursed—until now.

Yesterday, he'd spilled his guts, and Erica didn't hate him. In fact, she looked at him like she did in the beginning. And for the first time in god knows how long, he felt worthy of happiness. Maybe he did deserve her. He spent too many years living in the past. He was ready for the future.

Reese tapped on the door. "Come on, buddy, are you almost done?"

The door flew open, and Sawyer darted out.

"Hey!" Reese yelled after him. "Did you at least—"

Sawyer pushed on the front screen door and was gone.

"—wash your hands? God, I hope so."

Shaking his head, Reese pushed away from the wall to follow his son just as someone entered the door off of the kitchen. It was Erica balancing a sizable empty bowl with one hand and a melting lime Jello ring with the other.

He headed in that direction instead.

Entering the kitchen, he spotted her bent over in front of the refrigerator, moving things around. He stopped next to the center island to admire her shapely bottom. "Can I help you with something?"

Erica yipped in surprise and bolted up. "Uh, no. But thanks." She closed the door and rinsed her hands off at the sink before joining him at the island. "Hey." Her low, sultry voice matched the hungriness in her eyes. She stepped closer and practically devoured him with nothing other than her presence.

"Hey, yourself." *God, she's beautiful.* Reese ran a finger over the remnant of the tiny scar above her brow. Her eyelids lowered midway from the soft caress. A more perfect moment didn't exist for a kiss.

Their lips met. His tongue brushed over the inner rim of her velvet lips before sliding into her mouth. He enjoyed her soft whimper.

Erica dragged away from the kiss. Her fingers curled into the front of his shirt. "Come with me." Walking backward, she silently lured him toward the narrow spiral stairs off the kitchen.

Reese willingly fell under her spell and followed her to the second floor into a spacious bedroom. Large windows allowed reflections of light and shadows from the movie playing outside to bounce off the walls and ceiling. Dorothy was singing *Somewhere Over the Rainbow.*

Erica created a step of separation to slowly undo the buttons on her shirt. A white lacy bra displayed her perfect breasts. Reese watched, mesmerized until the shirt floated to the floor next to their feet. He tugged his shirt free from his jeans, and it joined hers. He pushed the straps down her shoulders and replaced them with light kisses. A quick pinch on the hooks and the bra joined their shirts. The woman was radiant.

"Erica, are you certain you want to do this?" he whispered against her lips.

Her breasts landed against his chest. "I'm very certain, and...I'm prepared," she answered without hesitation.

A scant laugh escaped. "Really?"

She nodded. "How many condoms come in a box?" she questioned playfully.

"I guess we'll have about an hour or so to find out."

Walking backward, she tugged him by the waistband of his jeans until the back of her thighs hit the tall mattress.

Reese wanted to feast on her body and explore all of her desires, but most of all, he wanted to make love to the woman who lit the fire in his cold stone heart.

****

"There's no place like home. There's no place home." Dorothy tapped her heels together. Sitting on the side of the bed, Reese threaded his legs into his pants.

Erica leaned up, letting the sheet fall to her waist. "Turn this way. I want to watch."

Her pose and the sight of her bare breasts were enough to make him hard again. "People usually get turned on when the clothes are coming off."

"What can I say, Reese? You just have that kind of effect on me. And you look good in jeans."

He granted the request by standing and turning to face her. He slid his black underwear up first, then *slowly* maneuvered his pants over his hips. Before reaching for the tab of the zipper, his hand eased down the front to position his junk in the right place.

Her velvety soft lips parted, sending a quiver down his spine along with a reminder of what they felt like around his dick. "Erica, if you keep looking at me like that, we'll never make it back outside." His hips jutted forward to hook the top button, and the zipper came up.

The sparse light in the room didn't hide Erica's modest grin. "Is that such a bad thing?"

"Trust me, I'd like nothing more, but the movie is almost over, and unless you plan on saying goodbye to everyone from your bedroom window naked, you need to get dressed." Reese gathered their other discarded articles of clothing. The mattress sank when he leaned over and placed an attentive kiss upon her waiting lips. "God, you're perfect."

Erica looped her arms over his head before he could get away. She stole another kiss, a soft, sensual kiss. He could kiss her all day long and never tire.

But, he pulled away. "My reputation is one thing. Yours is something else." Someone might've already noticed their absence, and he respected her too much to risk that kind of savage gossip.

Erica tossed the sheet aside and crawled to the edge of the bed on all fours. "Maybe I should go down there right now and tell everyone how I coerced you into my bedroom and had my way with you."

*Damn.* Seeing her on all fours was putting ideas in his head. "I... uh... you're killing me here." Reese flipped his shirt over his head and pointed to an imaginary watch on his wrist.

"Fine." She scooted from the bed and got dressed in a matter of minutes.

She joined him at the door, but he didn't open it right away. "Wait. Before we go, I wanted to clarify one thing." Her caramel-colored eyes drizzled over him, momentarily scrambling his thoughts. She had the same sultry look in her eyes when he was ravishing her pussy. The woman tasted like heaven. And by god, she knew how to suck a dick. She brought him to the point of coming repeatedly, and the anticipation never felt so good. An hour and a half wasn't nearly long enough to explore this woman properly.

"What is it?" Her eyes brightened.

Reese took a sobering breath and gave her a playful smile. "I like the tattoo."

Her laugh was a shy rumble. "I told you I had one."

"*Seize the Day?* It's written so small, barely an inch long, and way below your bikini line. It's practically scandalous. I never would've guessed."

"Unbeknownst to my parents, I got it when I was sixteen at the beginning *and* end of my rebellious phase. A teacher inspired me with those words of encouragement."

"It makes me wish I would've tried harder that first night to get you inside."

She shook her head, letting out a *tisk, tisk, tisk.* "Do you really think I could be that easy?"

He almost lost his footing when she pushed him back against the doorjamb unexpectedly. Her hands slid up his thighs, over his jeans, purposely massaging the mass in the center. Erica wasn't shy, not even a little. Nope, she never failed to surprise him.

"All I can say is—" She dashed away. "You were closer that night than you think."

# J. ALISON COLE

## Chapter Thirty-Six

Erica wedged her scraper under the last bouquet of *blue* roses on the wallpaper in the living room. She wiped the surface clean with a rag and then swept the doughy remnants into a pile. With this chore done, the room would be ready to paint.

For the past week, she and Reese made significant progress with each other and the house.

Reese was upstairs in one of the bedrooms, framing out a closet. She raced to the second floor and followed the sound of hammering. At the doorway of the last bedroom near the back of the house, she found him shirtless, wearing a tool belt over the super-faded shredded jeans. Sweat glistened over his arms and back. Not that she'd ever watched much porn, but this scene had all the makings of a sensational storyline.

Erica had the urge to lick the saltiness from his skin. "Wow, don't you look—hot. And I mean that in more ways than one." She leaned against the door jam.

Reese glanced over his shoulder. "Well then, that makes two of us." He tossed the hammer on top of the tool bag. "I could use a cool down. Care to join me."

"What did you have in mind?"

"The kids are with Robin for a few more hours, and you have seen the size of that tub, haven't you?"

"Really?" Erica's appetite for Reese was insatiable. If her sexual awareness was peaking, then she was soaring into the stratosphere. Maybe even the moon. "It is a very large tub."

His devilish smile appeared, and their cooldown turned into an afternoon generating a different kind of heat—and water all over the bathroom floor.

\*\*\*\*

The following Monday, Reese started his new job with the State Police. To celebrate, Erica made dinner for him and the children. Her jaw nearly hit the floor when he walked into the house in his uniform. The man looked good enough to eat. Dark gray was a good color on him, and the rest of it with all the belts, buckles, and handcuffs had her squirming in her seat throughout the entire meal.

Erica put the last plate into the dishwasher. "Thanks for helping me get the dishes cleaned up, Kara. Did you like the salmon?"

Kara added two forks to the bin. "You know, I didn't think I would like it, even though I've never had it before, but it wasn't that bad."

"I liked all of it." Sawyer bounced across the kitchen, full of energy.

Reese came from the dining room with two half-empty glasses of iced tea. "That was a fabulous meal, Erica. Thank you." He leaned over her shoulder and brushed a kiss along her cheek. It was his way of respecting the children being present. His eyes said *I'll make it up to you.* "I wish we could stay longer, but I promised the kids they could ride their bikes home, and I don't want it to get too dark."

"I'm glad that they like riding. Come on, I'll walk you out."

Walking across the lawn, Reese placed a hand on the small of her back. The warmth branded her skin the exact same way it did on their first date, which felt like a lifetime ago.

Kara pushed the kickstand up on her new bike. "Can we make it a race?"

"A race?" Reese cocked his head to the side.

"But we get a head start." Sawyer was already on his blue bicycle doing circles on the patio.

"How much of a head start?" Reese propped an elbow on the hood of the truck.

"Ten minutes." Erica flashed him a smile.

His gaze connected with her and pinched with understanding. "Ten minutes?"

She slowly moistened her lips, ready to drop to her knees and rip open his zipper. The uniform was really doing it for her.

"Fifteen!" Sawyer hollered.

"Even better." Erica wiggled her eyebrows.

Reese raised *one* of his alluring brows. "If it's a race, I think ten is all I'll need."

Kara and Sawyer headed to the edge of the road. Reese stared at his bare wrist like he was wearing a watch. "Ready, set, go!" Sawyer and Kara took off.

"Get in." Erica jumped into the passenger side of the truck.

"What are you doing?" Reese pretended to be confused.

"The clock is running."

He climbed in behind the wheel and closed the door. His eyes filled with curiosity and excitement.

Erica shimmied her sundress up and straddled his waist, first checking the distance behind her before grinding her pelvis against him.

Reese lifted his hips to meet her. "Aaaaah, yeeaah."

Erica checked over her other shoulder and felt for the wheel again.

"Is something wrong?" Reese questioned with mock concern.

"No. It's just I knew there was enough room." She let go of the steering wheel and rubbed her hands over his chest and shoulders.

His brows lifted in genuine surprise. "You've

been wondering if there was enough room for this." His hands landed on her hips.

"As a matter of fact, I have."

"Really?" His mouth found her breasts over the material of her dress.

"Yes, really." Erica arched and guided his face to each one. She reached for the zipper of his pants. Together, they shoved them lower. "The moment you walked in wearing this uniform, it's all I've been thinking about."

"I'm here to serve you." He scooted his pants lower to free his cock.

She gripped his hard length and pressed it against her core through the thin fabric of her very damp panties. The friction was electric.

Reese popped open the front buttons on her dress and nudged her bra down to expose her breasts. His teeth grazed the nubs while his tongue lapped all around.

She rocked against his erection with another slow grind. His strangled moan stirred more heat into her belly.

"Hooooolly shit Erica, you're amazing. If someone would have told me two months ago that you and I...that you'd be giving me a lap dance in my truck, I never would've believed them."

"Well, for those two months, that's all I've been thinking about." She nuzzled against his neck and pressed against his dick again.

Reese reached for the pocket in his scrunched-up pants.

She stopped him. "If you want, we don't need condoms anymore. Reese, I went on those shots, and I'm ready now, and you're down to about seven minutes."

The glow in his eyes turned feral and matched his rogue smile. He reached between her legs, hooking the edge of her panties to the side. Erica guided his penis into her core. She rode him fast and furious, never hit the horn once, and they made it with a minute to spare.

# J. ALISON COLE

## Chapter Thirty-Seven

"It usually takes me two hours to mow the yard." Erica walked towards the garage, where she kept the mower. Travis followed her. "I've been so busy lately helping Reese at the new house. There just aren't enough hours in the day. Are you sure you don't mind?"

"Mind? Heck, this will be the easiest forty dollars I ever made."

"Fabulous. You can see where I typically mow. But feel free to ignore the crooked lines."

"No sweat, Mrs. G. This mower is almost like my uncle's." His gaze combed over the levers. "You have it all gassed up. Looks like I'm good to go."

"Thanks again, Travis." She pulled her bike out of the garage. "I should be back before you get finished. I'm taking Reese's kids into the hardware store to pick out paint, so if you want, I can take you home and save your uncle the trip." For some reason, she couldn't wait to see the look on the senior Mr. Jackson's face when she walked in with the children.

He gave her a thumbs up and put earbuds in. "Works for me. Don't worry about anything. Enjoy your ride."

\*\*\*\*

Erica chose one of her shorter routes. With so few problems to hash out anymore, she made good time. Her happiness was at an all-time high. She turned onto her road and coasted into her driveway.

*That's odd.*

The lawnmower was sitting in the middle of her mostly-mowed front yard. Did Travis run out of gas? Or, god forbid, did the mower break down? She parked her bike on the rear patio and looked around.

"Travis!" she called, scanning the side yard and the back of the house. Nothing. Maybe he needed to use the restroom. She entered the back door of the kitchen and called for him again. That's when she spotted a scrap of paper wedged between the screen door at the front of the house.

It took her a moment to decipher the hastily written script.

*Took Sawyer to hospital.*

Gasping, her eyes darted through the window toward the garage. The Jeep was gone. She hadn't even noticed. Erica hurried down the hallway to the kitchen and grabbed her purse. She rummaged for her cell phone and found one missed call from Kara. When would she learn to take her phone with her? Surely, they contacted Reese. She pressed his number, but it went straight to voicemail.

"Reese." She tried to keep her voice level. "I just got back to my house." She paused. "Call me."

Next, she grabbed the keys to the Porsche and raced out the door. She must've just missed them.

The powerful engine hummed to life inside the garage. Erica backed out of the garage and headed toward the highway.

She tried Kara's number.

"Erica." Fear strangled the girl's voice.

"Kara, what happened?"

"It's my fault. We were walking to your house, and he got stung by a bee. I didn't know. We called 911, but they said they were already on a call and it might be thirty minutes before they could help. Could he really die, Erica?" A huge sob poured through the phone.

"What hospital are you going to?"

"Somerset. Travis said he knew how to get here.

Sawyer doesn't look right. His face is puffy, and he's having trouble breathing."

"Have you gotten hold of your father?"

"Yes, I called him. He's going to hate me. I just know it. Are you coming?"

"He's not going to hate you, Kara. I'll be there soon." She ended the call and stomped on the accelerator. The car hugged the road, testing her limits to get to the people she loved.

Erica passed other cars on the highway, cruising at seventy and sometimes eighty miles per hour. The minutes ticked away. Somerset *was* the closest hospital, although it was much smaller than Westmoreland, where Davis worked. The exit approached fast, and she swerved onto the ramp. A few horns blared behind her. Five more minutes, and she would be there. They were the longest five minutes of her life.

Pulling into the emergency entrance, Erica surveyed the area. The Jeep sitting in the middle of the drop-off bay was definitely hers. She found a parking spot near the curved drive-thru and charged through a double set of retracting doors, scanning the room. Kara sat in a chair close to the desk with her arms and legs buried inside her sweatshirt. The girl sprang from her seat and raced toward her.

Erica put her arms around the young girl. "It'll be okay. Tell me what happened." Kara's tears soaked through the front of her shirt.

"We were going to surprise you and be at your house by the time you got back from your ride. I didn't feel like riding my bike, so we walked. Sawyer was whacking the weeds alongside the road with a stick and got stung by a bee. He started wheezing, so I ran to get help. Travis jumped off the mower and carried Sawyer back. After I called 911, Travis thought we couldn't risk it, so he put him in your car and drove us here."

The emergency room doors slid open. Reese raced inside, searching the room. He started in their direction just as a nurse came out of a different set of wide metal doors calling for a Mr. Mailing. He raised his palm toward them but followed the nurse through those doors instead.

"They'll let us know something as soon as they can. Let's sit down." She guided Kara toward a row of blue vinyl chairs that connected on the arms like a sideways train.

The rest of the room was nearly empty, except for an elderly woman and a younger woman holding a baby. All three were coughing. Erica didn't know if they were waiting to be seen or if they were here to see a loved one.

The cooking channel was on a television in the corner, but there was no volume to hear how to make the lemon blueberry pie.

Erica sat down next to Kara and looked around. "Travis? Kara, where is Travis?"

Kara surveyed the room as if she expected to see him. "He *was* here. I don't know."

Erica combed the designated waiting area again. "Let me see if I can find anything out." She gave Kara a soft kiss on the top of her head. A month ago, she wouldn't have been able to do that, but things had changed. It had become something regular between them.

Erica approached the woman behind a U-shaped desk. "Excuse me, ma'am, do you know what happened to the young man that came in with that girl over there? He brought in the young boy with the bee sting."

"Yeah, I saw him." The woman rolled her eyes. "He needs to move that car out there, or I'm going to have security tow it." The woman clearly hated her job.

"So, he went back outside?"

"Yup, that cop was irate."

"Cop?" *Did she mean Reese?* "Do you mean Mr. Mailing, the little boys' father?"

Erica received another eye roll. "No, I mean the first cop, the one that came in right behind that young boy driving that Jeep. Are you going to move that car?"

*Straw meet camel.*

Erica reached her limit. "I'll move the fucking car!" Janine would be so proud.

Outside, Erica scanned the parking lot. She walked toward her Jeep and found the keys still in the ignition. Something didn't feel right. *Where are you, Travis?* She moved the Jeep to a spot near the Porsche before returning inside. No one seemed to know where Travis was or why he wasn't answering his phone.

Two hours later, Reese pushed through a set of double doors. The worried look on his face had softened, and his calm demeanor said it all.

Erica and Kara met him in the middle of the waiting area.

Kara immediately broke down. "Is he dead?"

Reese gathered his daughter into his arms. "No, no, sweetie, he's going to be fine. He's asking for you. We can all go back and see him in Room 21A."

"I'm so sorry, Dad. I didn't know."

"None of us did. Why don't you go on back?"

Kara sniffed loudly and pressed the button to open the doors. Reese waited until she was gone before he extended his arms toward her. She couldn't begin to imagine the extent of his fear.

"Oh, Reese. Thank God, he's going to be all right." His relief collapsed onto her shoulders.

"We had him tested before, and he didn't have a reaction, certainly nothing as severe as this. I need to thank Travis. The doctors said if he had waited for the ambulance, it might have created complications. He might've saved Sawyer's life. Where is he?"

"I've been looking for him. I don't know where he is. The woman said a police officer followed him in. But that woman is gone now. Is there someone you can contact, maybe find out who that police officer was?"

"I'll make some calls." Reese released her from his loving arms. "Come on. He's asking for you too."

## Chapter Thirty-Eight

Kara grabbed the remote from Sawyer's hand. To be safe, the hospital wanted to keep Sawyer overnight. "I told you that's the volume button. These channels are different from the ones at home."

"Hey, I'm the one that got stung. I get to pick what to watch."

A light tap on the door made Erica turn. Davis stepped into the room wearing his full doctor attire of khakis, dress shirt, and tie. He looked every bit the prestigious professional he was. She stood up, surprised to see him at this hospital.

Reese met him at the end of Sawyer's bed and extended his hand. "Thank you for coming. I just wanted to make sure that they didn't miss anything."

For a brief moment, Erica was invisible to the two men standing in the room. Davis shook Reese's hand.

"Certainly, I've looked over his chart. Everything looks good, and I went ahead and put together a list of Allergists for you that I would recommend." He handed Reese a folded sheet of paper. "I trust them all."

*Reese contacted Davis on his own.*

Davis shifted his gaze and acknowledged her with a pleasant smile. It was his way of letting her know he was "okay" with this.

A sense of liberation and understanding washed over her. After two long years, she might have figured it out.

*He let her go to find happiness.*

Davis turned to Kara. "I understand your fast thinking helped save your little brother."

Kara actually blushed. Davis could charm any age. "Yeah, I ran to get Travis."

"You did really well. Time played a big part in this. Every second counted."

Sawyer sat up away from the pillow. His eyes and cheeks were still puffy, but not enough to distort his beautiful smile. "I know you. I saw your picture at Erica's house. You're Lauren's dad. I like her. She makes me laugh, and she likes my hamster. My hamster's name is Sonny, but Lauren said she thinks Sonny is a girl. But that still works. She found frogs with me one day down by the creek. It was lots of fun, but she didn't want to hold one. She said they were gooey."

"Frogs are gooey," Kara sat on the foot of Sawyer's bed with her legs crossed like a pretzel. "I didn't want to touch them either."

Davis kept both children in a relaxed conversation while he examined Sawyer. The man had an excellent bedside manner. Reese took Erica by the hand and led her into the hallway outside the room.

"I just got a text from Chief Snyder about Travis. There was only one call all morning of a speeding vehicle. It would've been around the same time Travis was going through town. He didn't know who called it in. There have been no other reports, but I had an APB posted across the region. You're right. Something doesn't feel right, but we'll find him. Do you know of any other place he may have gone?"

"I've called his uncle twice. He's contacted a few of Travis's friends but hasn't heard anything either. It's too far for him to walk, and I'm certain I got here not long after them."

His blue eyes grazed over her. She was still wearing her bicycling gear. "It's getting late, but I'd like to stay here a little longer. Can you take Kara with you, and I'll meet you at your house in a little bit?"

"Sure." Erica stepped into an offered embrace.

"I'm so glad that everything worked out and that he's going to be all right."

Reese let out an exhausted breath. "Me too. Thanks for being here."

She leaned back far enough to see into his eyes. "I love you all."

Reese slid his arms further around her. "And we love you." He placed a light kiss on her waiting lips.

A discreet cough came from behind them.

Davis was standing at the threshold of Sawyer's room, with his hands behind his back and his gaze thoughtfully directed toward the floor.

Reese released her and created a respectable amount of space—for all three of them.

"Thank you again for coming. I know you're a great doctor. Everyone says so."

Davis gave him a curt nod. "When they release Sawyer, they should give you instructions and an EpiPen. You'll probably have to have one with you from now on. Tests aren't always accurate, but now you know. Believe it or not, it is possible that he might outgrow this, but better safe than sorry."

"I agree."

Davis's eyes drifted to her. "Do you think I might have a word alone with Erica?" It sounded odd for him to ask permission.

"Certainly." Reese graced her with a loving smile and stepped back into the room, leaving her alone in the hallway of the hospital with her ex-husband.

Davis took a few steps further away from the doorway. He turned, coaxing her to join him. "He's a funny kid."

A twinkle flashed in his sage green eyes. It made Erica smile. "Yes, and very energetic."

"Lauren has spoken of him and the girl." A

faraway look entered his eyes. "I think if we'd ever been lucky enough to have a son, he would have been like that." He cleared his throat and straightened, trying to conceal the disappointment that flickered over his face. "I know this might not be the best time, but I wanted to let you know that I am considering a position in Chicago, and if I take it, I'll be leaving next month."

"Chicago?"

"Possibly. Nothing is finalized."

"Why, there?" Erica didn't want to think her newfound happiness was the reason he might be leaving. She glanced toward the doorway.

His focus landed on the floor. "Lauren's in college. I just feel that it's something I need to do. For myself and—all of us."

Despite what some people may think, she *and* Davis made sacrifices to be the people they are today. A part of her would always love him for that. He was the man who had made her a woman, the father of her child, and her partner for nearly twenty years. Nothing could change the past, not even Reese. But that was the past.

"You're a good man, Davis, no matter what Janine says."

He reared back and laughed outright. "You tell your sister that she's the one person I won't miss."

"Why are you guys like that? I don't understand."

He lifted his brows in surprise. "Come on, it's obvious."

Erica didn't have a clue.

He stepped closer and gazed directly into her eyes. "She never thought I was good enough for you."

"Nu-uh," Erica huffed.

His chin lifted. "Think about it. You're special. I kind of feel sorry for Reese. Does he even know what he's in for with her?"

Telling Davis that Janine and Reese actually got along might hurt his feelings.

"You know how she is."

"Duh, yeah."

"Have you talked to Lauren about this move?"

He ran a hand through the side of his peppered hair. "I was hoping we could tell her together. You have a better way of explaining things. I guess, basically, I'd like your help."

"Sure. We can make that happen. Just let me know when you'd like to do it." Laughter erupted from Sawyer's room. She and Davis briefly glanced in that direction. When her eyes came back, Davis was watching her.

He took her by the shoulders and placed a light kiss on the cheek. "I'll have Lauren call you."

J. ALISON COLE

## Chapter Thirty-Nine

Kara fell asleep on the ride home from the hospital. They had all been through a traumatic experience today, no one more than Sawyer, but panic, fear, and anxiety had taken their toll on everyone.

Turning onto her road, the headlights grazed over the mower still sitting in the middle of the front lawn. It could sit there until morning because the first thing Erica wanted to do was soak in a nice hot tub.

Erica parked the Jeep in front of the garage and tapped Kara on the shoulder. "Kara, we're home."

They entered the house through the rear door. Erica flipped on the kitchen light, but a shadow moved from the corner of the room. Travis startled awake where he was huddled on the floor by the sink.

"Oh…Oh my God, Travis." Her surprise wasn't just from seeing him but also from seeing his condition. One eye was nearly swollen shut, and a trail of dried blood ran down his face from a cut across his nose. A tear in his shirt exposed a huge gash on his arm. Someone had done a number on him. Handcuffs bound his hands and rubbed his wrists raw.

"Is Sawyer okay?" He tried to straighten himself but winced, favoring one side.

Erica rushed to his side and knelt down. "Yes, he's going to be fine. What happened? Who did this? Let me call an ambulance." She went to rise for the telephone on the wall, but Travis seized her arm.

"No." He grunted from the pain caused by the sudden movement. "Don't call an ambulance. He'll be waiting for that."

She knelt next to him. "Who, Travis? Who did

this? And why?"

Travis's eyes shifted to Kara and then back to hers. He swiped at the dried blood under his nose and looked down. It became clear he didn't want to say too much in front of the girl.

Erica rose and spoke softly. "Kara, go ahead upstairs and get cleaned up. I'll get this straightened out. Don't worry. I'm going to call your Dad."

Kara's gaze trailed over his battered body as tears welled thick in her eyes. "You saved Sawyer's life. Thank you." She touched his shoulder. "I'm sorry this happened to you."

Travis attempted a smile through a cracked lip. "I'm glad he's okay."

Kara raced up the spiral staircase off the kitchen as Erica dialed Reese's phone and grabbed a throw blanket from the laundry room.

Reese picked up on the first ring. "Hey."

"Reese. Travis is here at my house, but you need to get here as soon as possible."

"Is he all right? Where was he?"

"No, he's not, and I'm about to find out. So just come as soon as you can. Hurry, please."

"I've already left the hospital. I left not long after you. I'll be there soon."

Erica tossed her phone onto the center island. "Travis, can you sit at the table?" He grimaced but rose to his feet with her help. She pulled out a chair and wrapped the blanket snuggly around his shoulders. "We'll call an ambulance once Reese gets here. Let's see if we can get you cleaned up some." It might help to assess his condition. She wet a cloth and cleaned the blood from his face. "I don't have anything to undo those cuffs. They look so tight."

Travis glanced at his wrists. "Yeah, they work

really well too. It's hard to fight back with your hands hooked together."

She shook her head despondently. "I knew something was wrong when I couldn't find you. Tell me what happened."

He took the cloth from her and wiped it under his nose and across his jaw. The story entered his eyes with a mixture of anger and reserve long before actual words left his mouth.

"It was that dickhead Scott Wendham. He followed us the whole way to the hospital. After I carried Sawyer inside, he came storming in behind me. He said that I was speeding through town, and then he accused me of stealing your car. I guess, technically, I did both." Travis gulped and shifted again from an unseen pain. "Once the people from the hospital took Sawyer, he grabbed me by the collar and dragged me back outside. I tried to explain, but he was acting crazy. I wasn't resisting or anything. I figured he'd take me to the police station, and it would all get worked out somehow." He snorted. "At worst, a speeding ticket was worth a little boy's life, and I was extra careful with your car." Travis set the wet cloth on the table and leaned back in the chair, curling the blanket around his shoulders. "Only he didn't take me to the police station. We ended up on some bum-fuck back road in the middle of nowhere. That's when I knew my ass was in real trouble." Travis's voice grew small. "He hit me upside the head with that bully stick and took me inside some kind of hunting cabin and tied me to a chair. He told me I had two ways to get back home: Suck his dick or take it up the ass." Travis's eyes shot off to the side. "Motherfuckin' pervert." He sniffed louder and wiped his nose. "I told him I wasn't doing either, so he slammed my ribs with the stick and punched me a couple of times. I guess he thought he could beat me into submission." A sarcastic laugh escaped him. "You see, he was wrong about that because I've been beaten a lot worse than this, and I ain't never sucked anyone's dick or had to get bung holed."

"How did you get here?"

"The prick pulled down his pants and started to jack off. He wanted to jizz in my face." Travis blinked, momentarily embarrassed, realizing that his depiction was very explicit. "Sorry, but that's what he tried to do. Anyway, he did a shitty job tying my feet, and I got one foot loose, so I kicked him in the jewels, hard. I think he passed out for a bit. The door to the cabin was locked, and he had the keys, but I just wanted out of there. So I crashed through a window still tied to the chair. Mrs. G, I don't think he was planning on me leaving that cabin. I guess he figured no one would care if I went missing or believe me if I told anyone. Because if you think about it, he *couldn't* risk letting me go, right?" Travis went silent, and his gaze drifted downward.

"You have people that care about you, Travis." She placed her hands over his.

He gave her a timid smile. "I know. He was wrong about that, too." He sniffed again. "After I crashed through the window, the chair came apart. It's how I cut my arm. Anyway, I got my hands to the front and just started running. I stayed to the sides of the roads until I saw one I recognized. I figured he'd be waiting at my uncle's, so I came here."

"Reese has everyone looking for you, Travis. You're right about that." Headlights from outside swirled through the kitchen windows. "That's him now. We'll get to the bottom of this and get you to the hospital safely. Let me get you something to drink." Footsteps echoed over the front porch, and the door opened.

Returning to the table with a glass of water,

Travis sprung from the chair, his face bleached white with panic.

Erica turned. The glass slid through her fingers and shattered over the floor. It wasn't Reese standing at the entrance of her kitchen. She raced toward Travis and scurried them to the far side of the room.

"Yahtzee." A twisted sneer distorted Scott Wendham's face, and his eyes had that crazed look of a madman. "It took me a while, but I figured it out. Who would help someone like him?"

Flee or fight. Travis was in no shape to run, plus Kara was upstairs. Erica had no choice but to hold her ground. "Don't make this any worse on yourself, Scott."

"Worse? How could it get any worse?" He laughed like an evil villain. "I suppose he's already told you his version about our afternoon." His face scrunched, like someone with a migraine. "Nothing went like it was supposed to." His hand came to rest on the butt of his gun.

Travis tried shouldering his way around her. "She doesn't have to be a part of this. I'll go with you."

"It's too late for that. I maybe could've convinced them that you were lying, but not her, not the respectable Erica Gebhart." He stepped closer to the butcher block island. "I'm curious, Mrs. Gebhart. I'm always so careful, so how did you know? You talked about the clubs in Pittsburgh, but I can't imagine those are the places you acquaint yourself with." He shook his head scornfully. "You're always acting so high and mighty, but maybe you're just a nosy bitch." He unsnapped the holster on his hip.

"Did you ever stop to think that no one would care if you're gay?"

A look of pure disdain entered his eyes, and his face turned blood red. Wendham shouted his fury at her from across the room. "I'm not gay!"

*Oh, no.* Now Erica had a better understanding. Scott Wendham was struggling and confused with feelings and urges he clearly didn't understand. There was no way to reason with someone in this current frame of mind. Travis was right to believe that he may have never made it out of that cabin alive.

"Just calm down," she soothed.

Wendham's lip curled with uncontrollable anger. A psychotic breath preceded the next outburst. "Shut the fuck up!" A loud bump came from the second floor, drawing Wendham's eyes upward. His gun came free of the holster. "Who else is here?"

"It's an old house. It creaks. It's just Travis and me." Erica tried speaking loud enough, hoping Kara would stay where she was.

Scott's head tilted to the side. He didn't believe her. "Come down here, now!" His lips wrestled into a horrific grin. "Or I will kill them both." He sang the last part of his twisted request.

Less than a minute went by, and the door to the spiral staircase creaked open about a foot. Kara peeked into the kitchen from the second to last step.

"Look at this. Someone from upstairs, why Mrs. Gebhart, you're a *lying* whore too."

Travis tried stepping in front of her again. "Let's just go, dude. Me and you, I'll do whatever you want."

The back door burst open and Reese charged in. He read the room in less than a second.

Wendham pointed his gun directly at Reese. Erica's lungs froze. The two men were only eight feet apart. Wendham would have to be a crappy shot to miss. He snickered. "Welcome to the party, Asshole."

Reese was still wearing his Kevlar vest, but he'd taken his gun off at the hospital earlier in the day and locked it in the trunk of his cruiser. "Lower your weapon, Officer Wendham."

"I'd rather not." Contempt and sarcasm laced his voice.

The look on Reese's face shifted to something she had never seen before. His persona went lethal. It surged from him, threatening Wendham without saying a word. The barrel of the pistol wobbled. Reese took a single step directly toward the gun pointed at his chest.

Erica had never experienced fear like this.

"Uh, uh, uh." The handgun swung back toward her and Travis. "Not so fast. I'll be able to squeeze one off before you ever get close enough."

Reese lowered his chin. His body flexed, ready to pounce. "You do that, and it will be the last thing you ever do, motherfucker."

The crazed look in Wendham's eyes widened. *He's going to squeeze the trigger.*

The seconds that followed splintered into tiny little sequences of events playing in some weird slow-motion realm inside her head. Oddly, Erica was able to distinguish every detail.

Her gaze aligned perfectly down the barrel. She gasped, broadening her chest for a better target. Reese sprung like a mountain lion, diving for the gun. Travis yanked on her shoulder and hurled himself around her like a shield. A shot rang out as a crash echoed from the other side of the kitchen.

Erica landed hard on the floor in a thudded heap underneath Travis. Another shot fired, and wood splintered off the door frame right beside Kara. A third shot rang out before the room fell silent, and time was restored.

Erica labored for breath and struggled to get upright. Something warm and sticky had splattered down the front of her shirt. Blood, only it wasn't hers. Travis rolled away, gripping his shoulder.

"Travis!"

Reese rose to his feet over Wendham's motionless body.

"Daddy!" Kara yelled.

Reese raced across the room and grabbed his daughter for a visual inspection. "Kara, are you hurt?"

"No, Daddy, I'm fine."

"Erica?" He said in a rush. "Jesus, you're bleeding."

"It's not my blood." Erica scrambled for a towel from the counter. "Kara, call 911."

"I already did from upstairs."

"Good girl." Then Erica turned to Reese. "Wendham?"

"He's alive. Cuffed and unconscious." Reese knelt over Travis and grabbed the towel from her hands. "Hold the towel here with pressure. I'll take these cuffs off."

Travis winced when she pressed on the wound.

"I'm sorry Travis, but I have to push hard."

"Mrs. G." He hissed through gritted teeth.

"Yes, Travis? I'm here."

"I wasn't going to let him hurt you. No matter what."

Erica swallowed her emotions. She had far too many things to take care of, and breaking down wasn't one of them. "I know."

The cuffs landed on the floor with a clang. Reese swayed to the side from his knees, colliding with the chairs by the table. One fell over.

Erica's gaze skirted toward him. Reese looked pale. Her eyes widened, seeing a bright red mark on his torso. "Oh my God, Reese is...is that your blood. Have *you* been shot?"

Reese glanced at the crimson red mark. "Shit." He touched his side as if it belonged to someone else. "I guess it missed the vest." The brilliance of his blue eyes dulled as the spot on his side continued to grow.

"What do you mean?" Erica was temporarily dumbfounded as the slow-motion realm took over again. She watched as Reese slumped to the floor next to Travis, and a death-curdling scream filled the room.

It came from her.

# J. ALISON COLE

## Chapter Forty

The medivac landed in the field behind the barn. The deafening roar stung her ears, and all the flashing lights only added to the chaos churning inside her guts. Precious minutes slipped away as the paramedics labored to wheel Reese through the tall grass. Loading him into the helicopter robbed even more. *Why is it taking so long?* Less urgency only meant one thing.

Just then, the blades sped up. Leaves and debris swiped across her face from the fierce uproar. Standing alone in the middle of the field, Erica held her blood-covered hands like a surgeon midway through an operation.

Steve Koontz approached cautiously. "It'll be alright, Erica." His poker face needed more work than hers.

The lights blinking from the tail of the helicopter grew small as it flew away into the night sky. A suffocating chill crept over her. *What just happened?*

Steve's hand landed on her elbow as he shuffled her toward the house.

Four officers hauled Scott Wendham from the door off of the kitchen. "It was an accident, all of it. You believe me, don't you, Chief?"

Chief Snyder made brief eye contact with her before shaking his head. "No, Wendham. I don't. Take him to the Somerset precinct. We're doing everything by the book." The chief met her on the patio. His jaw twitched when his gaze dropped to the blood on her hands. "He's got a lot to answer for."

Another shiver coursed through Erica's body.

"They bused Mr. Baker to Westmoreland. His

injuries aren't life-threatening like...." His voice momentarily disappeared. "Erica, I know you probably want to head to the hospital, but I'd like to get a statement first."

Tremors shook her fingers. Blood from Travis and Reese covered her hands. It was all smeared together, too sticky, too dark, and too much. "May I get cleaned up first?"

****

Janine drove. First, they dropped Kara off at her friend's house and then headed to Westmoreland Hospital to check on Travis. It was two-thirty in the morning when Erica marched inside. Regular people would've had to wait until visiting hours, but she was the former reigning duchess of the hospital and the town celebrity. No one even tried to stop her. As if she'd have let them.

The light in Travis's room was on, and low, muffled voices came from within. She tapped on the door twice before taking a quick peek inside. Travis spotted her right away and scooted higher in the bed. A man stood from the chair in the corner. He had mussed-up hair, a wrinkled shirt, and flannel lounge pants that told the story of someone who'd dressed in a hurry.

"Hello, I'm Erica Gebhart." He ignored her outstretched hand and wrapped his burly arms around her.

"Mrs. G, this is my uncle, Dylan Rosario." The man's arms tightened briefly before releasing her.

"Your nephew saved two lives today, Mr. Rosario."

His face scrunched, trying to hold in tears. "And you saved him. You're the reason he asked to live with me. I'm so proud of him and can't thank you enough." He looked at Travis. "Isn't that right, kid?"

Travis gave her a battered smile. "Yup."

Erica approached the side of the bed. She brushed a few dark strands away from Travis's forehead and placed a kiss above his brow. "After everything we've been through, I think you're allowed to call me Erica."

He sniffed from the heartfelt moment. "Okay. I can do that." His eyes darted down. "How is Mr. Mailing?"

A sob threatened the back of Erica's throat. "We came here first. The trauma center is on the other side of Pittsburgh. I'm headed there next."

"Oh." His chin lowered. No one needed to say what they all knew. Reese's condition was critical. "It will work out, Mrs. G. I mean, Erica. It has to."

She straightened before speaking to his uncle. "Take good care of him. I'll be in touch."

Erica left his room and headed for the elevators. Once she made it to the lobby, Janine rose from her chair. "How's Travis?"

"He's going to be fine."

"All right, let's go." Janine's voice was so forlorn. "Hey, are you okay?"

Until now, Erica had managed to find strength from somewhere. She couldn't fall to pieces. "I have to be. Let's go."

The car ran quiet, the motor barely more than a hum. The lights along the highway blurred together, but focusing on them was the only way to keep the image of Reese lying in a puddle of blood from her mind. She'd pressed so hard against his side, but the warm red liquid kept coming. It was so much, and it was everywhere.

Erica didn't need to be a doctor to know that getting shot at such a close range could cause a great deal of damage, destroying kidneys, spleen, and intestines. If the bullet hit his liver, Reese would've bled out in the helicopter.

None of this felt real. How could this happen in her small, little town? How could this happen to her? After all, she was Erica Gebhart. A scoff echoed in her mind. What an arrogant thought. Circumstance and destiny didn't give a shit who she was.

"Pull over." Erica grabbed for the car door handle as Janine jammed on the brakes and swerved to the side of the road. The car was still moving when Erica threw the door open and vomited.

## Chapter Forty-One

"What's his name?" The woman behind the desk had bright orange dagger-like fingernails. She clicked on a keyboard.

"Mailing. Reese Mailing."

The woman gave her a visual inspection before digging into a drawer for two tags. "He's still in surgery. Follow the blue line, but go through there first." She pointed to a metal detector archway flanked by two armed guards. "The surgical waiting area is three doors down on the left. I'll notify them that he has someone waiting." The woman managed a feigned smile before looking beyond her. "Next."

Erica and Janine passed through a metal detector and then stepped up to a set of steel doors. One of the guards pressed a button. The loud buzz made her jump even though she was expecting it. Her nerves were paper thin.

Once through the doors, the quiet was immediate, like an eerie sense of doom. The lights in the hallway had been set to economy saver, with only one out of three illuminated. Then the smell hit her—a mixture of a bleach-like disinfectant and some kind of artificial floral concoction. Erica always hated that smell.

The inlaid squares of blue tiles ended in front of the doors to the surgical waiting area. The lights were much brighter here, and the room was designed to look homey, perhaps to put people at ease. Despite the hour, the room was half-full of people slumped and half-asleep on the worn, lackluster furniture. The old saying *I'll sleep when I'm dead* entered Erica's mind. It was an unwelcome and untimely morbid thought that filled her empty stomach with bile. Janine picked a set of two wing-backed chairs. All they could do was wait.

An hour passed, and the world news was on its second loop of repeating when a telephone on a counter started ringing. The man sitting closest leaped from a sound sleep to answer it. A few other people in the room rousted, eager to hear if the news was about their loved ones.

"Billingslea." The man lifted the phone and waited for the family to claim the call.

Erica eased back into her seat, now more awake than before.

"I'm going to get some coffee. Do you want anything, Erica?"

Before she could answer, a man dressed in sunny yellow scrubs entered the room. The color was a beautiful contrast against his dark, ebony skin. He came right toward them.

"Excuse me, ma'am…ma'am. Are you Erica?"

Her mind blanked instead of replying. How could he have known who she was from everyone else in the room? He repeated the question.

"Yes, she's Erica." Janine grabbed her hand.

The young black man didn't look much older than Travis. "Come with me." His voice hinted at the Caribbean or some other exotic place.

Erica followed him like a mindless zombie. *Why didn't they call? They don't give bad news over the phone. They'll send someone.*

In the hallway, the man gave her a timid smile before pressing a button on the elevator. Still, he said nothing, and at this point, she was too afraid to ask. So, for the next five floors, they listened to a homogeneous, modern-day version of a Beethoven sonata.

The elevator dinged just as the song ended. It was all so serendipitous. But when the doors opened, the calm ended.

Bright fluorescent lights mask the hour of the night. On either side of the busy corridor, orderlies were pushing carts, and nurses were checking monitors. Although, they all moved out of the way for the man in the sunny yellow scrubs. A blue light above a doorway lit up at the far end of the hall, and a dinging noise blared. Erica pressed her back against the wall, giving five nurses ample space to run by. No one else seemed to be affected by the frantic events.

The young man stopped at the next doorway and turned to face her. "The surgery went well. I removed the bullet, repaired his spleen, and stopped the bleeding. He was fortunate that more damage wasn't done. He lost a great deal of blood, but I think he's out of danger for now. He's not fully awake, but he's been persistent in asking for you." The doctor pushed on a door and directed her inside the room. "He'll rest for now, but when he wakes, I think it will be good medicine for him to see you." Glowing white teeth filled his gentle smile.

"Thank you, Doctor. Thank you."

"Yes, thank you, doctor." Janine pushed her from behind.

Erica stepped beyond the end of the curtain surrounding the bed. Her gaze landed on Reese with the moon's gravitational pull on the ocean. The bed looked too small for his long legs. *He's so tall.* Monitors keeping track of his heart rhythm and blood pressure blipped silently beside him. A sheet was folded down to his waist, revealing bright orange betadine stains around the pressure bandage covering his midsection, and a single light above his head cast a warm glow on his resting form.

Erica leaned over and brushed her lips over his. His eyes didn't open, but the softest moan let her know that he was going to be okay. Her world was restored.

## Chapter Forty-Two

After two weeks in the hospital and one week of strict bed rest, Reese was all but climbing the freshly painted walls of his new home. Erica had rallied forces to have everything ready by the time he was released.

The kitchen, in all of its glorious greenness, looked like a different room than he remembered. She'd painted three of the walls an off-white color. The sink and the stove were in the same place, but the refrigerator had been moved to the other side of the room, somehow making the space more open to accentuate the plum-colored wall behind the breakfast nook. Even his shitty little kitchen table looked as if it belonged here. Shabby-chic had nothing on her.

Today was the first morning Reese was allowed to venture out of his room.

Erica was at the sink washing the morning dishes. He moseyed across the room and placed his hands around her waist. Her head tilted back, and he placed a soft kiss on the side of her neck. "Ah, you're finally awake."

"I'm more than awake. Where are the kids?" Reese snuggled closer.

"Lauren and Janine volunteered to take Kara and Sawyer school shopping. Can you believe that school starts in another two weeks? Where has the summer gone?"

His hands slid under her shirt, brazing the bare skin along her ribs. "Time flies, but what you're really saying is that we're here all alone right now?"

Erica lifted her hands from the soapy dishwater and dried them on a cotton tea towel. She spun around to face him. "Just what do you think you're doing?"

He'd managed to put on a pair of dark green

lounge pants by himself, but sometimes lifting his arms still hurt, so he forwent the shirt. His torso was bare, all but a small bandage over his incision. His eyebrows wiggled. "It's been really hard spending so much time with you and not being able to…spend time with you." He breathed on her lips before starting a trail of tiny kisses along her jawline. "In fact, it's really hard right now."

"This hasn't been easy for me, either, Reese."

"No, I mean, it's hard, now." His hips eased forward, rubbing a rock-hard erection against her.

"Mmmm." Her eyes widened, and an arousing sigh escaped. "Reese, we can't." Her argument didn't sound very convincing. His thumbs circled over her breasts for another sigh, and he squeezed her nipples between his fingers. He was gaining ground quickly.

"Actually, we can. I spoke with Dr. Jahavah yesterday, and he said I would know when I was ready but that you might have to do some of the work for a bit." His lips brushed over hers again.

"You talked to him about when we could have sex?" Her hand brushed against the bandage on his side.

"If you must know, he's the one that brought it up. I think you impressed the good doctor."

"It's only been three weeks." Her voice was breathless against his lips.

Keeping her in his arms, Reese walked backward toward the table. He sat in a chair and persuaded her to straddle his lap. "I don't think I can wait any longer."

Reese's hardened shaft tented the front of his pants against her belly, and he slid a hand between her legs and brushed his thumb against the center seam of her jeans.

Her mouth fell open. "Maybe we should wait." Those words may have come out of her mouth, but the torment of how good it felt was written all over her face.

He leaned forward to inhale her scent. God, how he'd missed it. He pressed harder against her core. When her eyelids lowered, he knew he had her.

Erica slid forward with a slow grind against him. Then she stopped. "Did you hear that? It's a truck coming down the driveway." She placed her hands on his shoulders and partially stood to see out of the kitchen window.

"No, no, no. So help me, god, if it's Steve, he's just going to have to watch again."

"It sounds like Paul's truck." She searched out the window again. "It is Paul."

Reese tugged on her waist, pulling her back down. "Tell him to go away."

"I can't do that." She climbed off him.

"Then I'll tell him."

"Be nice to Paul. He helped to get all your stuff moved in." She caressed the side of his face and gazed into his eyes. "I'll make it up to you later. I promise." Her eyes dropped to his erection, and she licked her lips suggestively.

His head rocked backward. "Jesus, woman."

Ten seconds later, Paul gave the kitchen door a cheerful knock, a perfect example of his personality.

Erica greeted him at the screen door while Reese sat at the table and felt like pouting. "Come in, Paul."

"Good morning, folks. I thought I'd come over and see how you're making out."

"Well, I *was* making out just fine," Reese said in a cryptic tone that only she would truly understand.

Erica mouthed, "*Be Nice*," and shot him a disciplinary warning.

"Oh, is this a bad time? I can come back later if you want."

He and Erica answered at the same time. Only Erica said, "No," and Reese said, "Yes." Confused, Paul exchanged looks between them.

Erica quickly interjected. "Don't be silly, Paul. You're fine. Reese is just suffering from a little bit of cabin fever. Why don't you guys have a seat on the front porch, and I'll bring you something to drink?"

"That sounds wonderful. Thank you, Erica." Paul hesitated at the doorway. "You need any help or you got this?"

"I can walk just fine." Reese followed Paul and glanced over his shoulder.

Erica mouthed *I love you* to him.

"I love you too."

## Chapter Forty-Three

A pang of guilt washed over Reese. His irritation with Paul was entirely unfair. He *was* grateful to everyone who helped. They were more than neighbors, more than friends. He truly was blessed, but given the choice of spending some alone time with Erica or getting a visit from Paul, he'd choose Erica in a heartbeat. Just ask his dick.

*God, I'm so horny.*

Erica came onto the porch carrying two tall glasses of iced strawberry tea. As she walked back into the house, Paul took an extra gander at her backside.

"You look pretty healthy to me. So, are you back to hitting that again." Paul made a gesture with his hand and an imaginary dick.

Reese half-laughed and scoffed. "You're killing me, Paul. What the hell do you want?"

Paul took a hefty swig of Erica's signature tea. "Aaaaaaaaaugh, she should bottle this stuff. You know, like that guy who did half tea and half lemonade. She'd make a killin'." He set his glass down on the freshly painted floor of the porch. "By the way, she's a ten."

Reese recalled Paul's scaling method, and his eyes narrowed critically. "You want to clarify."

"Oh shit, not Erica, although I think that's just a given. It's a given, isn't it?" Paul shook his head, trying to coax an answer, before waving him off. "Nay, I'm talking about her sister. That's why I'm here, oh, and to check on your sorry ass."

"Janine?" Reese questioned, raising his brows.

Paul gave him a sleazy grin. "Uuh, huh. You remember movie night, right? Well, I laid the groundwork then and bumped into her a few times here, helping Erica with the house. She gave me a call the other night." Paul grinned. "Funny thing, I didn't really think she'd be into me, but it just kind of happened." Paul glanced around the porch before leaning closer to him. "Let me just say, that woman did things to me…. Well, hell, she made me blush like a schoolgirl, and I'm not making that shit up. I actually blushed." Paul twisted his shoulders sideways and raised his arms, trying to recreate a pose. "She bent her leg—"

Reese held up his hands. "Stop! I don't want to hear this."

"I gotta tell somebody, I swear, I…mean I've done a lot of stuff, but she did this thing with her little finger and my a—"

The screen door flew open, and Erica joined them on the front porch with a tray of cookies.

"Oh, thank God," Reese sighed in relief.

"Care if I join you." Erica cast him one of her beautiful smiles.

"Yes, yes, yes. Come join us, Erica. Please!" She may never know how she saved him from Paul's overzealous sexcapade story that involved her sister. He might keep that to himself. Some things just aren't meant to be shared.

She sat on the footstool between his legs. "Hey Paul, I was wondering if you're attending the town's dedication ceremony for the clock and fountain project? It's in a couple of weeks."

Paul shook his head. "Oh yeah. I heard about that, and they're renaming the park or something?"

"That's right."

"Sure, I might go. Do you think your sister is going to be there?" Paul asked Erica before winking at Reese.

"I'm not sure, but you can ask her yourself." Erica

glanced up the lane. Reese followed her gaze. "Looks like they're back early." She glanced over her shoulder and mouthed, *"Sorry."*

Reese locked eyes with Erica. Guess now he had something to look forward to later tonight.

Heck, with her in his life, he had a lot of things to look forward to.

And yeah, his woman was a ten.

## Chapter Forty-Four

There wasn't a cloud in the sky. It was the perfect shade of blue. Erica surveyed the makeshift stage the town had set up at the park. Shade was at a premium. Herb Jackson and the rest of the cronies from the hardware store found some nearby under a string of red maples that ran adjacent to the sidewalk.

Juanita Fleagle and the ladies from the fountain committee chirped near the front. The mayor, city council, and even the local news channel were milling around, waiting for everything to begin. In the center of all the chaos, a big white sheet shaped like a ghost on Halloween covered the new clock and most of the fountain.

Chief Snyder called them just as they were about to sit down. "Reese! Erica! So glad you guys could make it."

"Glad to be here, in more ways than one." Reese shook the chief's hand.

"Looks like you're in pretty good hands." The Chief shook her hand next.

"Well, Chief, I must say you have quite a crowd." Erica indicated the swarm of people with a quick twist of her head.

"Yeah, I think the whole town is here. The Mayor wanted to make this a big deal to alleviate any negative attention from the whole mess with Wendham."

"How's the case going?" Reese questioned.

"Oh, he'll get the book. We have him on assault, kidnapping, and attempted murder, along with a shitload of other things that we uncovered. He's pleaded guilty to everything. And believe it or not, we've managed to keep a lot of the details out of the local papers because of the minors involved, but the one problem with that is people come up with their own stories." He glanced at the group of old gossiping men. "Sorry to tell you this, Reese, but most of them think some crazy ex-lover came down from Michigan and shot you."

Erica laughed.

Reese didn't. "Dammit."

She squeezed his hand. "Who cares what they think?"

Feedback screeched from the test of a microphone. Everyone cringed. The Chief hollered at one of his deputies near the side of the stage. Apparently, Chief Snyder was doubling as technical support for the sound equipment. "Let me see what these dingdongs don't have set right."

Twenty minutes later, the Mayor of Kensington started by thanking Millie and the others who worked on the clock and fountain project. "This park has been here for quite some time. While doing research, we learned that before it was given to the town, it belonged to a farmer who was a prominent member of this community. I think it's only fitting that we honor his generosity by renaming the park after him.

Chief Snyder walked onto the stage with a framed certificate and stood beside the Mayor. "Travis Baker, would you please join us on stage?"

Three rows in front of her, Travis rose from his seat.

Reese leaned over and spoke softly in her ear. "He's a good kid. You know that?"

"Yeah, I do."

Travis strolled onto the stage, and the Mayor continued. "The revitalization committee determined that it was your great-grandfather who farmed this ground before donating it to the town. So, if everyone could please stand and give a round of applause as we welcome you to Baker Park."

Travis accepted the framed certificate from Chief Synder and shook the Mayor's hand. Then, several committee members loosened the tarp and pulled it away. The fountain sputtered twice, but the circular ring eventually sent out a number of uniform arches of water. At the base of the clock was a temporary sign that read "Welcome to Baker Park." Eventually, it would be replaced with a cast bronze plaque once the committee raised enough funds to cover the cost.

Erica already decided to help with that, so it won't take another two years.

Refreshments followed the ceremony, and Erica had the chance to congratulate Travis. He practically leaped into her arms.

"Looks like I'm not the town's only celebrity anymore." Erica hugged him gently. He was healing, too.

"Can you believe it? How crazy is this shit? They called two weeks ago and talked to my uncle to make sure we would be here."

"It's wonderful. And congratulations."

"Thanks."

A man from the paper came up beside them. "Mr. Baker, we'd like to get a few photos of you over here."

"You go ahead, Travis. I'll see you later." She combed the crowd, looking for Reese and the kids. Lauren came toward her instead.

"Hey, Mom."

"Hi, honey." She hugged her daughter.

"Wow. He looks…different than I remember." Lauren tilted her head in Travis's direction.

"He is different."

"How old is he again?"

347

"His birthday is at the end of this month. He'll be eighteen. Why?"

"Huh, just wondering."

"Yes, he's also applied to The Naval Academy." Erica smiled. Lauren's feigned curiosity practically screamed with interest.

"Really? I don't remember him being that tall."

"That was three years ago. Travis is at least six-one now, but I think he may get taller. He's a handsome young man, don't you think?"

Lauren *pooh-hooed,* trying to act nonchalant. "Sure, I mean, yeah, he's cute for his age." Lauren could tell that she wasn't fooling her mother. "I just want to talk to him, that's all. You know, offer my thanks," she leaned closer, "for what he did for you and congratulate him on his heritage."

"And you should."

\*\*\*\*

After the celebration at Baker Park, Dylan Rosario invited them to dinner at Nicco's. Travis personally asked Lauren, which upset Kara, who'd developed a slight crush. Reese, on the other hand, was more than happy when Lauren came along for that sole reason.

Paul, Janine, Marcus, and Philip met them at the restaurant. Even Steve and Robin showed up. They were like, "One big happy family."

That's what Erica thought about throughout the meal. She cared for all these people, a kaleidoscope of personalities, backgrounds, careers, and beliefs. Society had labeled them all, but this group refused to fit into those roles.

On the ride home, she glanced at Reese behind the wheel of her Jeep. It was the vehicle they used the most because they all fit.

They all fit perfectly.

J. ALISON COLE

## Epilogue

*Five months later. January of the New Year.*

The headlights from Reese's squad car beamed against the plum-colored wall in the kitchen as he came down the driveway. Erica checked the timer on the stove just as it buzzed. The chocolate chip cookies were ready. She used the oven mitts that Sawyer got her for Christmas. They were covered in cute baby chicks. Reese told her that Sawyer had picked them out all by himself.

Reese entered the side door and tossed his coat over the back of a chair. "Yum, something smells good." He kissed the side of her neck from behind. "The cookies don't smell bad either." He snagged one from the tray.

"Watch it. They're very hot."

He tossed the cookies back and forth between his hands until it cooled enough for a bite.

"Are these for the high school?"

"I promised two dozen for the snack shack, but I made extras."

"I don't want to make us late. I only need a minute to get changed."

"No, we've got time. You should've seen Kara today. She's so excited about being on the cheer squad."

"At least now, the wild colors in her hair make sense. Go Mustangs."

"Oh, and Sawyer is still at Joey's finishing his science project. Steve and Robin are going to meet us there. I think I should probably warn you that Kara likes this boy on the Varsity team. His name is John. He's a senior and a good kid. You'd like him."

Reese grabbed another cookie from the tray and snickered. "I doubt it." He gave her another fleeting kiss and headed out of the kitchen.

Erica had another tray of cookies to prepare, but watching him walk away with that long-legged, commendable swagger, wearing his new black Kensington Police Department uniform, was highly distracting. After a minute, the spatula landed on the counter, and she headed upstairs.

Reese looked up when she entered their bedroom. He'd just finished locking his gun in a drawer. His shirt was already unbuttoned and hanging open. Erica sashayed closer to help him remove it the rest of the way.

He grinned shyly. "I know that look."

"You do?" She feigned innocence.

"Yes, Ma'am."

"Ma'am? Is that how you charm the women in town when you pull them over? Or do you just flash that killer smile? You know, the talk of the town is that most of them speed on purpose, just hoping that you will be the one that catches them."

His strong hands settled on her waist, and his barely-there smile tugged on one corner of his luscious lips. "Well, the talk I heard is that there is only one unbelievably sexy, sophisticated, famous lady that I stop for." She pulled him closer by the pockets of his trousers. "I would have thought that after this morning, you'd be all...." His words trailed off.

"Rested. Ready to go again?" she asked cheekily.

"I was about to say *tired of me*. I woke you up pretty early."

"I'll never get tired of you." Erica ran her hands over his hips, heading for his zipper—when her hand bumped against something protruding in one of the pockets. "Well, now I know it's big, but that's bigger than usual." She leaned back in his arms to get a better look at the bulge near his hip.

Reese looked toward the ceiling and took a deep breath before reaching into his pocket to pull out a small black box.

Her mind didn't have to wonder or speculate. It was that calmness of knowing what was in her heart. His other arm tightened around her waist, and his sky-blue eyes sparkled.

"Your sister is going to kill me for doing it this way. She wanted me to wait until spring and do something that involved a hot air balloon and lots of roses, but you know me, Erica. I'm just a regular guy."

Erica went to speak, but he stopped her.

"Erica, I once believed I'd never get married again, but then, I've never loved anyone like the way I love you. Do you think you could spend your life with an ex-womanizing, former marine with a sketchy past and ties to the law?" He opened the small box and presented her with a sapphire ring surrounded by tiny opals set upon a band of white gold. "I want to spend every moment that I have on this earth with you."

"It's beautiful, Reese, and yes."

Reese plucked the ring from the box and slid it onto her finger. "I know it's not a diamond or anything."

"No, Reese, it's perfect. It's you. It's what I see when I look into your eyes."

He picked her up and carried her across the room. Sharing a kiss, he laid her on the bed and shimmied on top of her.

Her body ignited, tingling with energy. She held his face, latched onto his intense gaze. It reminded her of the first time she saw it alongside the road.

"You feeling all right?"

"Never better."

## The End

**J. ALISON COLE**

**EVERNIGHT PUBLISHING ®**

www.evernightpublishing.com